In Circling Flight

In Circling Flight

A Novel

Jane Harrington

BRIGHT
HORSE
BOOKS

ISBN: 978-1-944467-25-8

Cover Art © Emma Shapiro
Author Photo: Patty LaHair

"Dear John, I've Fallen For a Dog" was short-listed for the Fish Publishing 2013/14 Short Story Prize in Ireland and was published in *Chautauqua, Vol 11* (University of North Carolina UP, 2014), under the title "Sirius" and reprinted in *The Journal of the Virginia Writers Club*, Spring 2021; "All God's Children Gonna Take A Ride" was recommended on a short list for the 2014 Sean O'Faolain International Short Story Prize, Ireland, was published in the *Anthology of Appalachian Writers, Vol 7* (Shepherd UP, 2015), and was nominated for the 2017 Pushcart Prize; "Strangers on the Road" was published in *Circa: A Journal of Historical Fiction*, April 2016 and reprinted in *New Square*, vol. 3, Issue 1, Fall 2020; "Way Out Farm" received an honorable mention for the 2016 Leap Frog Press Fiction Contest for the Novella; "Settling" was short-listed for the 2016 Colm Tóibín International Short Story Award, Ireland, and was published in *Mountains Piled Upon Mountains: Appalachian Nature Writing in the Anthropocene* (West Virginia UP, 2019).

For permission to reproduce selections from this book, contact the editors at contact@brighthorsebooks.com. For information about Brighthorse Books, visit us on the web at brighthorsebooks.com.

To the swallows who build in the eaves of houses

BOOK ONE
Way Out Farm

First Part

Dear John, I've Fallen for a Dog

It's Sirius. That's what I named him. I got him on the midsummer morning when that star first rises up in the pitch dark before dawn, marking the time of the dog days. Always thought that idiom was about heat so pervasive that it made dogs lie around for days, but when we came out here to the Blue Ridge I learned that it was really about the year's first sighting of Sirius the dog star—the brightest in Canis Major, the brightest next to the sun. It seems you just find out the reasons for things in the country. I don't know why.

Set on seeing the rising, I got up at five o'clock that day. Hadn't missed it in the nine years since we moved here, always spying it just when the *Farmers' Almanac* said I would, a pinpoint of a thing, sort of orange at first and pushing itself out of one of those mountains like a tiny spark from a volcano. Easy to pick out, that dog star, following as it does the hunter Orion, in a straight line with the three stars of his belt—all I could ever see of that constellation growing up, the rooftops and streetlights in the way. But there's more of that hunting god up there, and a weapon or two, all so clear in the night sky hanging over these hills. Remember when we were still camping, the house not yet under roof? The shadow from the tent was so crisp, a black box on the field. I shook you awake, said, "Johnny, is there an athletic complex or parking lot next to us?" And you shot right up, worried, I guess, that that might be true, that the city lights had followed us somehow and were glaring at us as we slept. But then you laughed—that laugh that used to find a bit of humor in just about anything, that had a way of skipping around inside me—and you pointed to the full moon, shining like the sun, only in grayscale. "I can see the berries on the autumn olive," I whispered. "At *night*."

Not so for Sirius's emergence this year. The mist was so thick I couldn't see anything in the sky, or a persimmon tree in the field, or even the lights on that cell tower put up on Chestnut Hill last year. So I went out to the SPCA shelter, later when they opened, and got my *own* dog star. He's big, with silky fur, all black but for a fine blaze down his neck like a stream of milk, pure and white, forever dripping from his mouth. He's a good boy. Well, in dog years, older than a boy. Maybe in his thirties. Which makes him the perfect replacement for you, so there's no need for you to be here anymore.

When I was asked by the man at the shelter, I told him that, yes, I had a fence. You'd say, *That's a lie, Leda*, and I'd say, *No, I'm just being precise. We have a fence around the goat yard, don't we?* I said that to Sirius on the way home, in fact, his taking your part of the conversation in my mind. "If he'd asked if I had a fence around the property that could keep a dog from running off, I would have told him no." Sirius was sitting in the passenger seat, freed from that cage where I'd first seen him with his head between his paws and a faraway look in his caramel-colored eyes. He'd lived in the shelter for some months and was probably getting near to the day he'd be euthanized. But he didn't know that, and I sure wasn't going to tell him. I kept up talking about other things, because I think it calmed him to hear my voice. "If he'd just made himself clear from the start so I could understand what he was all about," I said to Sirius, "I'd have told him where that fence was." From the time I pulled out of the parking lot, he'd been yipping in a forlorn way, and I didn't like the sound of that. It was terrible, familiar. I knew he was missing someone. Maybe someone from the shelter, but more likely that old person who'd given him up when she moved away to live with her daughter. You see, I asked about his background. I didn't want a dog that seemed perfectly fine now but was holding some form of trauma inside him that was waiting to spring out when it was too late. After I was already in love.

He's not going to run off. I knew that from the first night I had him, when I was out on the porch, sipping my iced coffee. Not sure why I do that, because it keeps me up and working things out in my head half the night. But the taste is good. Never really enjoyed that wine you were making in the spring, just drank it with you because it was nice to do that, to talk on the porch and watch the sun set. "To the perfect red," you would say, toasting whatever you'd concocted at the time. "This isn't it yet, but I'm going to make the perfect red." That cabernet from those grapes you bought up along the CCC road built during the Great Depression had come the closest, you thought. It tasted okay, I guess, but it was kind of thick. The word *viscous* came to mind, but I didn't say that because I figured it might seem an insulting choice of an adjective and then you would stop talking for the rest of the evening. The word stuck in my head, I suppose, because it popped right out that afternoon I was clipping hooves in the goat yard. There's still a bloodstain on the pine slat from where I grabbed the top rail and leapt over. I'd nicked my fingertip with the clipper when I heard the sound. You'd think the hard rains would have washed that away by now.

Sirius, though—I was telling you about that first evening he was here. He was sitting tall and pretty at the edge of the porch, looking out to the tree line, and he spotted a buck and shot out after him, his hackles raised. I jumped up, scared and blaming myself for not keeping him on a leash so soon after bringing him home, and I have to admit I yelled out, "Come back, John!" It was his first night, remember, and I wasn't yet used to calling him by name. I don't make that mistake anymore. I want you to know that. Anyway, I didn't even need to give him chase because once that deer had disappeared into the neighbor's woods, Sirius came prancing back, all proud-like, and he sat again at his post at the corner of the porch, looking out, scanning. Protecting me, protecting this place. You see, he's not running off.

I don't think there's any hunting dog in him. He used to be scared of the shooting that goes on out in those woods. First time he heard one of those rifle blasts he scurried into a corner of the living room, tail between his legs. So I brought him up next to me on the couch, our Target special that arrived here by UPS on the very day we moved into the house, and I hugged him to make him feel better. He licked my face for a long time. He likes the taste of salt. Now every time we hear those gunshots he comes to find me and sit with me wherever I am. Could just be all about the salty treat at this point, but it still feels like a loyal act on Sirius's part.

He looks after the goats, too, patrolling the fence lines. I don't let him inside their yard, because I'm afraid he'd just try to chase the poor things off, and, well, there's really nowhere for them to go. He used to bark incessantly at them, but I'm training him not to, using the command "Leave it!" that I read about in Cesar Millan's dog-whispering book. It works pretty well most of the time, like when I want to shoo him away from the step in front of your workshop, but out at the goat yard I have to practically yell it if I want him to calm down. Most of the time, that is. A couple of months ago there was a turn of the weather, and big yellow poplar leaves, speckled with brown, were drifting down from the little copse of trees inside the fence. They were watching the leaves, the goats, then eating them where they landed. I expected Sirius to get all worked up, figuring he'd want to get in there to see what those things falling from the sky were, to try to catch them before they hit the earth. But he was as mesmerized by the scene as I was, as the goats were, like we were all witnessing a miracle. Manna from heaven, for the Israelites left out in the wilderness.

Sirius goes on long walks around the farms and fields with me, always staying near enough to turn and see me from wherever he gets to exploring. And it's uncanny, but no matter what kind of convoluted circuit I come up with to hike, he always knows when we're starting to head back home. I can tell, because he picks up the very next stick he can find and bounces along with it, head high. He wants me to throw it once we get up to the house, and then he runs after it as fast as any dog I've seen. Every few days or so, I gather up what he collects. I won't be needing to search for much kindling this year. See what a help he is? I've already made a pile over there by your workshop, next to that enormous stack of wood you split last spring.

Seemed like you'd never stop hacking away at those logs, getting another truckload each time you'd finish up with one batch. "Shoot, Johnny, how much wood do we need for one winter?" I'd asked you. But you just shrugged, so I passed it off as maybe a bodybuilding thing or a release of anxiety, because I didn't know then that you were set on leaving, that you would be gone from here before summer's first fireflies resurrected themselves from their grassy tombs. You wouldn't be aware of this, but your woodpile is now adorned with a piece of that metal sculpture you put on the roof of your workshop. The top of it blew off in a freak windstorm in July that tore across the fields, snapped tall trees in its path right in half—a "derecho," that weatherman who wears a bow tie called it, some kind of weather system that had never ventured up from the southern hemisphere before. The clattering on the workshop roof was so loud and sudden that my heart almost stopped. I think that's when I first got the idea to go to the SPCA.

Doesn't look like a phoenix to me anymore, that sculpture. Not even one with its head blown off. Just looks like a welded-together scrap pile from the dismantling of an old still, which, of course, it is. I really did think your moonshine-making was impressive, as if we were stepping back into a time when those squiggly tubes and burping liquids were common contraband in the hollows around here. Had a few good field parties, didn't we? Invited those fiddlers, and we started learning to play that old-time music ourselves, to be a part of keeping that Appalachian tradition from dying out. But maybe that whole direction of looking—to the past—was part of the problem, got your head wrenched the wrong way. And no amount of log-splitting or metal welding or woodcrafts or any of your other pursuits were going to yank it back where it needed to be. Especially not the search for "the perfect red," one of your last quests in that workshop of tools and benches and drawers still filled up with the many ways you tried to get things right.

"You're projecting, Leda," you said when I insisted that sculpture was a phoenix. And I asked you if you'd ever heard of a thing called artistic genius, because regardless of your intention it looked incredibly like one, its bird head pointing straight up into the blue. I needed it to be a phoenix, John. That's the thing. You were just so distraught that day you took the still apart, repeating over and over how you were sure you were turning into him. "Did he make moonshine?"

I asked you, and you thought I was trying to be funny at an inappropriate moment, but I wasn't. It just took some time to understand what you were telling me, those things that happened there and happened there in that apartment where you grew up. Took a while to sink in, is all, to make sense of it. Then a lot of things made sense: like why you didn't want us to have children, like why you wanted us to live somewhere and somehow so completely the opposite of what you'd ever known. "Let's call it Way Out Farm," you'd suggested, "a double entendre, because it's way out of the city and this land is our way out of the grind." I had pointed out that it was actually a triple entendre, because weren't we "way out" people? In time, you proved a fourth meaning to be true.

As I kept telling you when you were taking your hammer to the still, you were merely a bit erratic that night before. "Loved ones lie about it," you insisted, this seeming to be an area of particular expertise for you. Which put us in a box, it did. "Just because a person gets drunk once in a while, even blacks out, doesn't mean he's hurt anyone," I said to you. "And just because the face you are seeing in the mirror is getting more like his, well, that's simply the way physical traits are over time, that's heredity." And I suggested we be the undead and throw away the mirrors. But you accused me again of not taking things seriously. I surely was, John. I surely was. And I told you and told you that you were beautiful and you didn't have a violent bone in your body. But even if you wanted to believe that, I imagine those little ones had already started twitching in your index finger.

Sirius likes to stand at the door of the house, looking out through the glass. He can see your wood stack from that spot. He doesn't seem interested in the fallen pieces of metal splayed over top of it, but keeps his eyes on the field mice darting in and out of the crevices between the logs. When he whines, I let him out to chase them. He gets one every once in a while, and if he's hungry he eats it. One time I glimpsed him cracking a skull in his jaw, and it had such an effect on me that I'm real careful to look away now. But I figure it's good having a mouser around a farm, seeing as he ran off all the feral cats, thinking them a danger to me, I guess. He digs for gophers and groundhogs, too, with little success. If I took him out regularly at night when they were more active, he'd probably fare a whole lot better, but I've been jittery about walking in the dark since you've been gone.

Had to be outside late last night, though. Sirius was pacing in front of the door and just wouldn't stop, like he needed to go. I was up anyway, full of coffee and trying to work things out in my head, so I figured I'd take him out, just in front. Didn't need a flashlight because it was one of those full moon nights, or near so. While I waited for him to poke around, I scanned the sky for the dog star. The whole constellation of Canis Major had climbed up over the mountains by the time we were out, so I connected the dots in my mind to make up the triangular head and stick body and tail of the big dog. "See there, Sirius, your star is just about where his rabies tag should be hanging," I said. And then I saw the big bear. And I don't mean Ursa Major. I mean a real bear. It was on all fours, sniffing around the step of your workshop, and Sirius was looking right at it, his muscles as taut and ready as I'd ever seen them.

"A bear is set on destroying you. It's useless trying to chase it off, and screaming or running away won't work either," you'd said on a walk we took in the woods one night. "You have to play dead in order to survive." Frightening, that. Rang in my head every time we took a night walk from then on, and rang in my head last night with Sirius, and even rang in my head that afternoon I'd been clipping the goats' hooves. I knew, of course, that there hadn't been any bear in your workshop that day, and that you weren't playing anything. But I suppose you hold tight to any little scrap of what you so desperately don't want to lose. I'd already deluded myself into thinking that that skinny stream that had seeped from floor to step in the time it took me to race over was from a broken bottle of the viscous cabernet. Even while I knew it wasn't. Even while I knew it was your perfect red. Still a fine dark blaze, forever dripping on the pale granite. About all that's left of you.

Caffeine and adrenaline must be one potent combination, because, lightning fast, I grabbed Sirius by the collar just before he sprang. Keeping my eyes steady on the bear, who was rising up on his back legs by then, I yelled "Leave it! Leave it! Leave it!" and I managed to pull Sirius against his will, all eighty-some pounds of him, and we fell through the door and into the house before the bear got heading in our direction. I lay there on the floor, my heart thumping as hard as it had that day you left me, the pain so strong I thought my sternum would break. I held Sirius as close as I could for a long time. He was making the funniest sounds, his mouth moving in an odd sort of way, like he was trying to talk to me. Trying to calm me. To stop my awful yipping.

No, I didn't follow any of your advice regarding the bear. You have to admit, survival did not exactly turn out to be one of your areas of expertise. If I hadn't done what I did, my companion would be gone for trying to keep me safe. I didn't want that, John. I never wanted that. Don't worry yourself, though. I will be keeping to the house at night. I've started making wood fires already, even though the solstice— your usual date for toasting the first fire—is just now here.

The bursts of sparks from the logs, not fully seasoned yet, made Sirius anxious initially. His eyes would dart here then there, as if tracking meteors. But now he just stretches out and sleeps, or watches lazily, his head between his paws. He doesn't much get that sad, faraway look in his caramel-colored eyes anymore. Perhaps he's forgotten about the one who left him behind at the SPCA. Or maybe he's just forgiven her. I kneel next to him sometimes on the hearth, his shadow pooled strangely around him from the bright flames lapping the sooty walls of the firebox. I rest my cheek against his side for as long as it takes to feel a pulse or a dream shudder, any sign that he is alive. Then I drop a new log on the fire before the lights of dying embers go out.

The *Farmers' Almanac* is predicting a mild winter. And while that is good news from a practical standpoint, Sirius not likely much with a shovel, I find myself wishing for snow. The kind that comes quietly in the night, filling you up in your sleep so you know it's out there before you even open your eyes. The kind that washes out everything, the way the sun erases the stars at dawn. "Silent snow, secret snow," you'd whisper when we'd wake to that world, alluding to your favorite short story while we kept each other warm and gazed through the pane to the persimmon and autumn olive covered in white, like ghosts caught in mid-dance in the field.

On the 274th Day

I've TAKEN UP WITH the born-agains. It was the morning the goat almost knocked me out that I had my revelation.

I was in the barn, leaning down to fill that old galvanized bucket with some fresh water, and the youngest one—Violet, you may remember I named her—hit me square in the forehead. I leaned an arm on the barn wall for a minute, trying to steady myself and to figure out what exactly had happened. Violet was looking up at me, sort of startled, too. It seemed she'd gotten me with that hard ridge at the top of her triangular head, just below her horns, which at her young age have not yet begun to curve so they are as straight and sharp as spear points. This was something I took special note of, seeing as the spot that had sustained the blow and was already beginning to swell was not an inch from my eye. If the geometry of the situation had been even slightly adjusted, if my angle or hers had been just a little this way or that—well, you can see what I'm getting at. I was struck by the sheer luck of my sight being spared, as if some kind of providential occurrence had taken place. And at that point of awareness, as if on cue, the morning sun eclipsed Rocky Ridge, shooting a ray of light through that broken slat on the side of the barn and turning the straw at my feet a golden yellow. But that was not exactly the moment of my awakening.

I wanted to reach out and stroke Violet's fluffy coat—she makes the most divine cashmere, that little thing—to tell her it was okay, that I was okay. But she's so skittish that I know better than to try to pet her, the way I do the other goats. She is having a real hard time settling into the herd. Gretel has seemed to forget that Violet's her offspring, and the two bucks are out-and-out mean to her, pushing her from the water, pushing her from the mineral block, pushing her from the cedars, which was the only source of green food on their hill those months ago. So, that morning I could see how one of the other goats could have frightened her, causing her to lurch into me. Both of those bucks were hanging around, poking their noses into my pockets. When one lowered his head and took a step toward her, I pushed him away and was set on giving him a good yelling-at, but a pain shot through my neck, like I might've sustained whiplash from the impact with Violet. I figured I should concentrate my attention on getting some ice on my aches, so I headed out of the barn. Gretel was in the pasture, off a ways, alone, and I had to stop in my tracks to make sure I was seeing right. She was going round and round in tight circles, stopping every once in a while and staggering around like she was drunk. Then she'd resume her circling same as before. It was obvious I would have to call on a professional to sort out this problem. Veterinarian, goat mystic, I was going to need someone. *That* was when I thought of the born-agains.

And money. You see, I was worrying that the meager funds in the checking account might disappear entirely if Gretel's ailment turned out to be a goat epidemic. Your name was still on the bank account, but unless all those remaining particles of you could pull themselves out of the plastic box they were in and form themselves back into an income-producing body, I was the only one apt to be making deposits. Without your arts and crafts to sell, my tutoring income and the occasional sale of a ball of yarn at the fiber shop were not covering much else except food for me and the dog. And Sirius had developed a skin irritation, so he was on a natural grain-free canine concoction that may well cost more per bowl than my own dinner, at least when I'm eating kale and turtle beans, which is often. He's not scratching anymore, I'm glad to report, and his coat has regained its luster and softness, which is very important to me, as I spend a lot of time petting that dog. Better than any therapies I have tried to engage in during these past months, and I mean by a lot.

I had already sold the car, in early winter. I'd been wavering between which vehicle I could do without—the car, though old, being better when it comes to gas mileage, but the truck being clearly more useful around the farm—when I had to come to a quick decision due to the pipes freezing in your workshop. It was obvious that some plumbing-related trouble was going on in there when my shower was at a trickle one morning and then Sirius, never giving up hope that I might one day let him in there, tried to climb the steps to the workshop door and slid right down on an ice floe that had formed from water pouring out from under the door before it froze in place. The nighttime temperature had hit an unexpected low, brought on by something the 24-hour news media called a "polar vortex," which got a lot of attention for a day or two, including its own musical introduction, much like the Olympics. The plumber said the whole floor was thick with ice that morning and that she had to slip and slide to get to the pipe in question and then use a blow torch to get to the part she had to replace. She suggested I go in and turn the water off to the workshop on nights when a freeze was expected, but I told her that she could go ahead and leave it off, that I wasn't in need of water in there.

"Is your husband that guy who does the woodworking?" she asked me, waving a slow and easy finger toward the open door of the workshop. "I've seen those boxes of his downtown," she added, obviously not needing an answer from me. "I always go in for the art fairs. I remember one with inlaid snakes curling around it, or some other reptilian things. Interesting. That one in there, though," and she jabbed a thumb toward the door this time, "that's beautiful. He could get a lot for that."

"If he were alive," I said, as matter-of-factly as that, which is a skill I had been cultivating, tired of feeling uncomfortable and unable to articulate the truth of my life as it had become. I'd first practiced with Sirius, sitting on the bed cross-legged (me, not the dog), pretending he was a human I might face out in the world. "I lost John in June," I'd say to him, eye-to-eye as we were, thanks to his large size and good posture, or, "I miss him desperately, but I am forging ahead." And he would lick my cheeks all the while, one or two times actually getting my eyeball with his tongue, which is not a very pleasant feeling, in case you never experienced that in your time on earth. Soon I advanced to standing in front of the mirror, and when I reached the point where I was speaking to my actual face and not a version of it swimming in a blur, I deemed myself ready. I can't say the same for the plumber, however, who was the first recipient of my newly honed bluntness and was rendered speechless. I considered giving her the wood box on your workbench to make amends, but I know that is not what you wanted me to do with it.

She was nice about waiting for her payment until I got the car sold, although it might just have been a case of her being afraid of me. I'd gotten a lot of calls right away from the notice I put up at the co-op, but most of those people lost interest when, it seemed to me, they put two and two together and figured out it had been yours. "He didn't die in the car," I'd said to one or another of the callers, thinking that this information would be enough to alleviate any qualms, but of course they all knew what had happened to you. Word sweeps through these hills like those field fires on red flag days. Finally, the couple who own the pear orchard up the road bought it for their teenage son. Now I wish I'd advertised it in places not so close to here, because I regularly have to watch it speeding up or down Route 11. Judging by the bumper stickers on its fenders, I'd say the new driver is a video gamer or anarchist, or both. The only remaining evidence of our particular brand of social activism is a fragment of that sticker we got at the rally against the coal companies up at the state capital, just two faded words of it clinging eerily to the far left edge of the bumper: *Leave Me*. The rest of that sentence (*My Mountaintops*) is lost forever behind *End The Fed! Use Bitcoin!* As you can imagine, these sightings are disconcerting at best, and full-on depressing at worst. When I spot the car in the distance, a feeling of hope revs up inside me before my sensibilities can put up a stop sign. It's you, I think, heading home from the junkyard or the Food Lion, and not a teenage boy set on convincing the world to use virtual currency instead of dollars and cents.

But the born-agains. There had been another ad in the *Gazette* for adjunct professors over at the evangelicals' college, and, what with Gretel needing to be straightened out, I got to contemplating the idea of doing a little teaching there. *But you're an atheist, Leda,* you'd say, something you always insisted, even though—and it looks like I get the last word on this—I have always claimed agnosticism. I just can't settle on any one thing when there are too many choices in front of me. Anyway, the head of the English Department didn't even ask what my spiritual affiliation is, because I suppose it is irrelevant to the pedagogy of college composition. I was put right to work teaching a class, a venture that has been taking up all of my free time, and—mercifully, as this has been the nadir of each day—I even find myself falling sound asleep at night over the grading. My students do look at me strangely when I return essays in the state of crumple and scribble that results from this habit, but they are kind people. As are the faculty members, who don't know me from Eve and thus offer smiles refreshingly lacking of the pity I have become accustomed to in my usual public encounters: stingingly sad looks that seem to be reserved for young widows. Adjunct pay is as bad as it's reputed to be, but it has surely helped with the animal care.

"She's got the circling disease," the veterinarian said after we'd stood together at the fence watching Gretel that day I was clonked on the head. This didn't sound terribly scientific to me, and I glanced over to the driveway to see if his truck was in fact from the animal hospital and not, say, a delivery van that I mistook for the arrival of the vet. But then he went on to explain that Gretel's behavior was typical of neurological problems with goats, and his best guess was that she had nutritional imbalances, this being a common occurrence in winter when the forage is poor. "Add some minerals and alfalfa to their diet until the spring growth starts," he recommended, and then he shot her up with anti-inflammatories, which seemed to stop the circling for good, although she has still remained prone to disorientation. She sometimes stops cold, her head still and pushed up, like she is having an epiphany out there in the field. "We call that 'star-gazing,'" the vet told me, offering more of his sophisticated medical terminology.

One of my students, El, has shown an interest in my animals. I have pictures of Sirius and the goats that scroll across the screen of my computer, and she likes looking at those. She told me she's from the Great Plains, worked for years at farms in the reservations to save up to come east for college. She's descended from indigenous peoples, she says, but she can't find any records, doesn't know whose blood moves through her veins, as she put it. When she asked me about my own lineage, she was surprised to learn that I don't take an interest. "Long roots in the south," I told her. "Might be some stories I don't want to dig up." "Denying something doesn't change the truth about it," she replied. But that's something I don't need to be reminded of.

El's good about coming to class, unlike the others, who seem to be constantly in the throes of violent stomach flus and other debilitating but surprisingly brief ailments. After a couple of months of observing this behavior, I announced to the class that I was thinking of calling the National Institutes of Health to come in and investigate such an unusual cluster of recurring illness, to which I received mostly horrified stares. Either I'm rusty in matters of humor or else the average eighteen-year-old has not yet developed a strong sense of irony. El laughed, but, then, she's s bit older.

She was on a perfect attendance streak that I thought would bring her through the rest of March and into April and our exams, but then she missed two days running last week. When she showed up she had a bandage on her lower arm. She had come in early, as she often does, so there were no other students in the classroom yet. "Did you hurt yourself?" I asked her. And she said, "I tried suicide." She said it just like that—"I tried suicide," like it was a food she hadn't tasted before that turned out to be poison. I honestly can't remember if I offered any immediate verbal response to that. I think I just stared into space, like I was having one of Gretel's star-gazing moments.

Yes, John, this was quite a shock to me. I wanted to run screaming, to put great distance between myself and this matter, immediately and forever. But I didn't do that, and for more reasons than that I need this teaching job. I've gotten to like El, something that started to take hold before I knew of her hauntings. Sure, I'd seen the scarring, those slits and dots on her inner arms when she wore short sleeves, some faint ones at her neckline when she wore something low-cut: a phase, I wrote it off as, maybe something left behind with her teen years. But, no, she told me she's been dealing with depression since childhood, the darkness coming on unexpectedly and enclosing her like a cocoon, as she described the situation. "And then one day I just feel better. Like I've become a butterfly."

Instead of correcting her on the matter of butterflies coming from chrysalises and not cocoons, I heard myself inviting her out to the farm to help with animal chores. She'd been asking if I needed help, and I did, specifically with brushing out Violet's coat. I'd been chasing that goat around the yard and the barn, with little success at catching her, having to gather what I could of her cashmere from the fences and the multiflora rose that snagged it as it shed off on its own. "You could come this weekend. For the spring equinox," I said. "I'd like the company." Which is true, too. You and I always celebrated this turning of the season in some way, this point at which daylight starts to gain on night. We'd be up for the sunrise, then maybe hike in the mountains or browse antiques markets—something, just the two of us.

So I went in and got her, earlier today. With both at the task, we were able to capture Violet, and El held her while I brushed first one side and then the other. "Never felt anything like this," she said, rubbing the reddish-brown strands of that cashmere between her fingers, whispering so as not to arouse the little goat from the calm it'd found there in her lap. It was amazing, really, to see that creature so at peace for once, but it is the way with farm animals, confinement making them feel safe even when they're not. Violet, though, did appear changed in some way, because she didn't run off scared when we finished and let her go; she stayed and ate corn treats from our palms. Wasn't till the bucks caught on and pushed her away that Violet got back to her unsure ways. But this was progress, as I told El when we were making our way to the house for something to drink.

She looked around curiously while I squeezed lemons for lemonade, cracked ice and shook the Mason jar hard until all the golden droplets of honey dissolved. I told her about Gretel's past troubles with circling and how she still stands like a statue once or twice a day. She told me about a cow that she'd seen with a round white blaze on its forehead that looked like a third eye, a small black mark in the middle of it, even, like a pupil. We both thought that was funny, and the air in the house, devoid of laughter for so long, seemed a little more breathable. She looked closely at the pictures on the walls—the one of us up along the Appalachian Trail, where we posed on that breezy day; the one of us standing in front of your booth at the arts festival; the one of us up on the music trail, playing a song. *That* song.

"Your partner?" she asked. I nodded, setting sweaty glasses on the table. "Where is he today?" was the next thing she wanted to know, and so I aimed an index finger at the black plastic box, which was still in the corner of the room on the floor. El gave me a surprised look. Sad, but not stinging, somehow. And we drank our lemonade in that slow and awkward way that comes from not knowing what to say.

After we were done, I suggested she take Sirius out so he could chase the field mice that dart in and out of the log pile outside the workshop, even though he does not need anyone watching him do that. "I'll just clean up," I said, but I used the time to sit and gaze out at the pastures. At the turkey vultures lazily sailing on wind currents, their naked heads cocked, looking for the carcasses of no longer livestock to return them to the elements in their unceremonious ways.

When I did go out, resolved to act more normal and give my guest a tour of my just-awakening herb garden (there is a nice crop of thyme coming in and a perfect mound of St. John's wort, that stuff I planted last year for purposes of trying to cure your low moods with tinctures and tea), I didn't see her anywhere. Sirius was on the porch of the workshop, looking at me nervously. The door was open, and I give him a lot of credit, that dog, for not having followed El in, for not stepping over that forbidden threshold that had been teasing and tempting him since he first came to live with me. I nodded that it was okay, and he perked right up. Still, he waited till I climbed onto the stoop before he raced through the doorway, tail wagging. I followed him in.

El was admiring your wooden box. "They're constellations, aren't they?" she said, moving herself around the bench and leaning in to see the sides.

"It's okay to touch it," I told her, though I never had, not once.

"Is that Orion?" she asked, tapping a fingertip on those stars you made, little inlaid dots of white pine in walnut.

"It's for you," you'd said that June day I watched you crafting the box. But that was our little joke, wasn't it, when we'd spent a lot of time or money on something we wanted just for ourselves. "It's for you," I'd said when I used up the whole season's cashmere to knit myself a long winter shawl instead of selling the yarn at the fiber shop. But you hadn't been in a joking mood for a long while. "There's Orion," you'd said, touching those same pine stars El was, "your favorite."

It's not, and it wasn't even then. It's merely an easy constellation to find, a marker by which to locate other stars and planets. You were the one who liked picking that hunter out of the sky. If anyone's favorite, it was yours. But I didn't say that to you. I was being careful with my word choices. You had been especially distant in those weeks you were making the box, the always unsettling drone of your saws and the raspy repetition of the sanding block seeming to create a nearly impenetrable fog around you.

"And here's Canis Major," you'd pointed out. "I made Sirius, your dog star, out of maple. I know how much you like to see its first rise each summer." It was still some weeks off at the time, but, yes, the rising of Sirius was already on my mind. A signpost, if arbitrary, a herald in the distance: You would be well by then, I told myself. Well gone is what you were.

When you asked me to pick the other two constellations for the box, it was Virgo that first came to mind. But I decided to be nice and pick ones that weren't so involved. Which, in retrospect, was exactly the wrong decision. I should have asked for the hardest possible constellations for you to represent in your inlays. I should have pointed out the minor errors you'd made in the position of the stars of your Canis Major, or that Orion was not my favorite so you might have replaced that side or started over from scratch. I should have been like Odysseus's Penelope, unraveling the work to buy time. But I asked for Capricornus, that simple triangle of a sea-goat, and Lyra's uncomplicated harp, so you were done in no time at all.

"What happened in here?" El was saying, pushing with the toe of her shoe some rusted pliers that were on the floor. The oxidation from them left an orangey print on the concrete. The flooding from the pipe break had swept a lot of your hand tools around the room, those screwdrivers and wrenches and things that you kept in the bin on the floor. Mold had started creeping up the legs of power tool benches, up the sides of the walls. I had not opened the door since the plumber had been there those months back. The musty smell was awful.

"He shot himself," I said, even though I knew she had meant the water damage. "In the temple."

El made a low cross with her arms. Then she glanced around the room as if looking for something.

"It's pretty much all been cleaned up," I told her. "There are people who do that, it turns out. Scrub it and paint it away."

You would say, John, that I did not need to be so blunt. But my response to that is that maybe if I'd been more blunt with you, if I'd stopped tiptoeing through eggshells and been honest, then maybe things would have turned out differently. Maybe, to paraphrase the Bible (I think), the truth would have set us free. Maybe.

"I found him," I said to El. And I wanted to add, *No amount of scrubbing or painting can make* that *go away,* but I figured I'd practiced my candor enough for one afternoon.

Sirius jumped into the truck with us when it was time to go, resting his head in El's lap. She stroked his soft coat up and down, same way I do, as we wound around Chestnut Hill and to the college. We talked about the final essay coming up in class real soon. El said she was thinking of writing on the health benefits of having dogs on campus. She bent her head down and whispered into Sirius's silky ear, "What do you think of that idea I just had?" Then she answered herself (in the voice of dog, you could say): "It is good."

When I arrived back home, I noticed that I'd left the workshop door open. I was set to pull it closed, but Sirius bounded in, so happy about his newly perceived right to romp in there. I figured I should let the place air out, anyway, before it becomes some kind of vector of fungal disease. I stood on the stoop and looked in at the box again. The plumber was right. It is exceptionally pretty. I bet I could get several hundred dollars at the artists' collective. So I picked it up—it's heavier than I expected—and I carried it out of there.

But, no, don't worry, I'm not selling it. I did what you wanted me to do. I took it out to the deck, set it down, and lifted the lid. I looked hard inside the box, and all around it, hoping, or maybe not hoping, there was some message you'd left, some secret inlay or note. But, no, you just made me a box to keep your ashes in. I opened, for the first time too, the black plastic container with your remains. They were grittier than I expected. I thought they would be more like wood ash. I poured them into their new home, and they made a sound like tiny rocks, like river sand. A puff of dust hovered over the transfer, and at first I held my breath, but then I didn't.

After, I lay down and stared up into the just darkening vault of sky. "Moon-bathing," you called this, sometimes lying with me as I watched the lights come on. Jupiter was the first, right up by the zenith. And then the dog star popped on, and soon enough Meissa, the star marking the Adam's apple of Orion. The rest of the hunter came into view—his boxy torso, his belt, his weaponry—but no matter how I connected the dots, he was, as always, missing his head. So I closed my eyes and listened to the jangling of the tree frogs. The night birds joined in. Soon Sirius found me and licked my eyes open. He barked and then barked again at his echo, which came from the west, where a slender moon beamed through the stratosphere, a face in the deep, pushing into the treetops.

All God's Children Gonna Take a Ride

I WAS SURPRISED TO find her there, flat on her side. I know I shouldn't have been, her being off since winter, and what with the warnings I'd had that she might go south at any time. But there'd been days recently when she'd eaten just fine or seemed even to protect her offspring again, like she was getting back to her old self. Same illusion I had on your good days. I guess some people never learn.

"You were a good goat, Gretel," I said to the side of her face pointing up to the sky, eye wide open, no sign of struggle or awkwardness in her pose. It was as if she'd merely fallen over there on the green grass. No blood either, I'm very glad to report, so if she appears in my dreams she should not be, as you often are, tinged in red.

"I'd go with an air burial," Tillie said when I called her to ask what a person does with a dead farm animal, never having had one before. To fill the pause that ensued, she added, "Seems awful, I know, Leda, but it's really the most natural way." And she came over without my even asking her and helped lay Gretel out on the far field, because farmers just seem to help each other that way.

I know we would have sparred over this decision. *Leda,* you might have said, *it's just not right to let carrion birds tear apart a goat we've cared for together since her birth.* But you aren't here, so we don't have to debate the merits of flesh consumption by avian versus insect larval means. I'm sure we would agree on one point, though, that neither is something to watch. So I see it as a good thing that I had, anyway, been planning on being away.

Before packing up the truck with a couple days' worth

of clothes and a ziplock bag of food for Sirius, I filled a half-barrel of water to the brim for the three remaining goats. I set another bucketful in the barn, where maybe Violet could drink in peace if the bucks pushed her away from the barrel. Fortunately, the hill in their yard is lush with all their favorite vines and volunteers from the poplars and hickories. Wild strawberry and sweet clover carpet the ground around the cedars now, and the grasses are tall, so Violet can easily find a place free of the greedy bucks to eat her fill. She's had a growth spurt these past couple of months, isn't a kid anymore. Surely doesn't need a mama goat, but I expect she'll be lonely without Gretel.

Some weeks ago, when I decided I'd make this trip, I spun the first batch of Violet's cashmere into a nice thin yarn and then crocheted a tiny lace pouch with a drawstring for the top, braided from the same yarn. I lined it with silk fabric, which, of course, I didn't make, but I do plan to try growing silk. This spring I planted mulberry saplings from the Forestry Department so I can raise silkworms with the leaves once the trees are established; hopefully, next spring I can start making thread. "Got to have a plan," you used to say, always sketching out things you'd be crafting later, like new cabinet designs or that banjo you made yourself from a gourd and then taught yourself to play. Should have been a sign when you didn't have anything out there on your horizon. Should have been.

On our way out, I paused briefly in the driveway where I could just see Gretel, a tiny inkblot on the rise of the hill. Tinier still were some flecks in the sky, drifting over the pasture. Beautiful, really, wings flashing silver from a noon sun nearly straight up and center. Sirius pushed himself between me and the steering wheel, sniffing, excited at first, like he'd smelled a deer. But then he looked at me kind of funny and stepped lightly away from the window, as if he could tell it was one of us out there.

By the time I hit the Blue Ridge Parkway, he was stretched out on the bench seat next to me and doing this new thing: when he's asleep he makes suckling sounds, like he's got memories of being a puppy. I must hear him at night in my sleep, because I wake sometimes from dreams about babies. Maybe this is his birth month and he gets some kind of message from the angle of the moon or something, an ebb bringing him back to his starting point then pushing him the rest of the year toward old age.

It was near dark by the time I pulled up to your mother's place. I'd forgotten all about traffic patterns in the city, so I hit the outer bands at exactly the wrong time. Then I didn't recognize the exit at all, a construction project seemingly having pushed it up into the sky. The interchange awakened a memory of a page in a picture book from my childhood, one by Chris Van Allsburg, which is to say that there was something decidedly surreal about looping and looping up and then down to the street where that old apartment building is, where you grew up. It's nicely painted and a few bushes and benches have been arranged adjacent to it in what the city is probably calling a "pocket park," some kind of concession, I imagine, for burying the place under a freeway ramp. I let Sirius take a pee in there before I hoisted my pack on my back, took a deep breath, and headed in.

Since you and I were last there, gravity seems to have increased its force in the apartment, sort of pulling your mother nearer to the floorboards. Hunched in the doorway, her gray-tufted pale head poking out of a dark bathrobe, she reminded me of a vulture, but I guess those were just on my mind. We sat and had tea and she opened a can of soup for me, and it wasn't long before we ran out of polite conversation and she asked, as she does in her voice mail messages, "So, Leda, when will you be having a memorial service for my John?"

This irritated me, as it always does, this idea that she would somehow manage to get out to our place for the occasion of your death, though always claimed to be too infirm to visit when you were alive.

"How will you ever find closure if you don't have a service?" was the next thing she asked, and that irritated me even more, that word *closure*.

"What is it I'm supposed to be closing?" I asked her, just as I had the counselor I saw after your demise. I mean, you're not on the other side of a door, John. And if you were, I expect I'd want to leave it propped open. One day I might wake up and decide to tell you something, who knows? Something that never got said face-to-face.

At some point, your mother stood up and rattled the dishes a little louder than they needed to be rattled, and she told me that she'd put fresh sheets on that bed in your old room, the bed we used to sleep in together when we'd go visit your parents. "Hold tight!" you'd say, sure that one of us would fall off that little mattress if we didn't sleep the whole night with our arms around each other. Though I didn't think this back then—you still keeping things under wraps as you were—I suspect that a fear of one of us ending up in a heap on the floor was not the real reason you were holding me so close in that bed where you had been a little boy.

"Sirius and I will be fine on the couch," I told her.

"I'm not so keen on dogs being on the furniture," she said to that. "We never did have a dog here."

"Well, he's special, helping me through my grief. And it's nice to have a guard dog."

"I suppose you need that out in the country, with all those wild animals. Protection," she said, sounding eerily like you at that moment. *Protection*. That's what you said on the day you bought the handgun.

Sirius seemed to feel my agitation at that point; he sat up real nice and put his head on my leg so I could scratch him behind the ears, something that may relax me more than it relaxes him. And I said to your mother, "There are wild animals in the city, too. And maybe if you'd had a dog, it would have taken a good bite out of the one that was preying on you and your son. And then maybe *my* John wouldn't have been so troubled, wouldn't have—" I could feel those eyes on me, black beads in rings of pale blue, beseeching. Those eyes you and your mother shared, proof that not all of your traits came from your father.

"Oh, he wouldn't do that," she said, though I do not know which person or what acts she was referring to. "The lord forgives," she added, which had a way of covering all bases.

Before I could open my mouth to say anything else, she abruptly changed the subject, pointing out that it was time for *Pawn Stars*, which, in that deep-south debutante lilt she has managed to hang onto all these years, sounded like "porn stars." The thought of her letting words like that escape her lips amused me enough to follow her to the living room, where, by the second commercial her eyelids were drooping shut. I told her she should go to bed, and she pulled her creaky self up, saying, "You are probably eager to have the couch," and I nodded even though I had already decided I was leaving in the night.

I gave her a careful hug—bird, again, came to mind, her bones seeming nearly hollow—and when I could hear her soft snoring coming from down the hall, I pulled out the cashmere pouch I'd brought along with me, and I set it on the kitchen table. I knew it would be necessary to leave a note with it, but I couldn't think of any way to say what I needed to say in such a way that she would hear me. So even though the pouch was the whole reason I was there in that apartment, I picked it up again and put it in my jeans pocket. Simply couldn't risk her spreading your ashes, even just the handful that it was, over the family grave. I'd have nightmares about them mixing with the bones in there.

Back on the road, I loaded up on coffee and pointed the truck to the northwest and home, zipping by the exits for the suburb where I grew up, and the exurb where we met at that field party where the air was thick with sweet smoke and the scent of honeysuckle. Then I left the highway and snaked my way through the mountains till I crossed the state line. By then, my eyes were not staying open, so I pulled over in the parking lot of a darkened diner and conked out right there in the truck, Sirius half off and half on the seat, making his suckling sounds.

At dawn I noticed a wayside sign marking the Crooked Road music trail, and I realized that you and I had been in that very parking lot before, that there was a venue directly across the street from where Sirius and I were looking through the windshield. We'd driven the whole length of that route that summer—one of those plans you had mapped out for us—going to jam sessions at hardware stores and barbershops and country markets like the one I was looking at across the way, doors shut tight in that early morning hour. As I was reminded by the sign, there were 333 miles of that driving loop all told, a number that, whenever I saw it touted along the way, made me quiet for a time, sitting there in the car with you. Trimesters of a pregnancy—that's what those numbers made me think of, because that summer I had started regretting badly that we had decided not to have children, you being so adamantly against it. "Little monsters," you once called them, but all the while it was really that you worried a monster was growing inside you.

It wasn't until I saw the turnoff to the Appalachian Trail that I got the idea to make one last stop before going home. Sirius, having been cooped up in either the truck or the apartment for close to twenty-four hours by then, seemed glad for the break. I had only ever been on that stretch of trail with you, so I found myself pointing out to the dog the things we used to stop and make up stories about along the way: that old poplar that looked to you like the legs of a giant that'd been stuck upside-down in the earth; the tree of heaven I named Octopus-in-love, its limbs so strangely, desperately wrapped around the broad trunk of that old oak next to it. When Sirius and I got up to the knob, we found a place on the flat of the rock that juts out over the valley. We caught our breath and I waited for a gap in time when there were no other hikers around. I held tightly to his collar with one hand—it is a long way down—and with the other hand I pulled the little pouch from my pocket and fiddled with the drawstring until I had it open. Then I stepped right up to the very edge of the rock and I pushed those bits of you into the air, watched as they picked up a gust of wind and were gone. Seems the currents were taking you northward. Sirius and I descended the trail to do the same.

The light of late afternoon was shooting across the fields when I drove back up the driveway, and here I am now, just where I'd carefully planned to *not* be on this day, one year exactly since I lost you on the summer solstice. I'm even standing at the same fence in the goat yard, where I was clipping hooves until I heard the shot—startling, more echoey than the sound of a deer hunter in the woods. And I'm looking right at your workshop, where I ran to that day, as fast as I ever have and as slow as I ever have all at the same time.

A goat pokes a nose into my pocket, and I push it away, thinking it's one of the bucks, but it's Violet. Surprising, given the way she usually is with people. "Sorry, Vi, don't go," I say, but she is already following the bucks to the cedars, is pulling branches down and chomping away. I wait for a buck to lower his head and start charging at her, but it doesn't happen. They just eat, side by side. I guess, in a post-Gretel world, they are finding a new equilibrium.

Sirius runs up alongside me when I let myself out of the fence. His jaws grip a branch that is so thick and long I have to smile at his optimism. He drops it at my feet, so I toss the unwieldy thing, and he runs after it. As I walk, a warm, southerly breeze pushes through the Rose of Sharon, and swallows conduct flying lessons between the bird houses you built in the field and the eaves of the house we both built here behind the Blue Ridge. Into a sky streaked with pinks and blues of sunset, two vultures rise from the far field and its shrinking inkblot. They spread their wings wide, seemingly aloft on a song—that bluegrass hymn we liked up on the Crooked Road, "All God's Children Gonna Take a Ride." I put my hands up and let the notes go through my fingers.

Second Part

Saviors

"WHAT'S THAT ONE ABOUT?" El asks me from her corner of the office, where she's taken to doing her work during my office hours. Ever since returning for the fall semester a few weeks ago, she's been claiming that assignments make her "fidgety." Fearing this to be a euphemism for taking sharp things to the insides of her arms, I have offered to share my space as long as it isn't a distraction.

"You're distracting me," I say to her.

"Well, stop sighing so loudly," she says. "Is it another paper on legalization of marijuana? Or abortion, with those descriptions of bloody, dismembered fetuses and dying mothers?"

This sort of grisly utterance is new, a quirk that she seemed to acquire over the summer (like the dark clothing she's taken to wearing, all long-sleeved). Hoping this habit will pass, I've been choosing not to react. Or at least not that she can see, my wincing in this instance directed to my desk. I reach an arm down to where Sirius is sleeping at my feet, stroke his velvety ears, gently pull into my hand a bit of that soft scruff of neck. He opens an eye, then shuts it again, and I return to my work.

"No, it's about guns," I say to El. "This young woman thinks we need to arm everyone and wear holsters, like we're all extras in a cowboy movie."

"What counterarguments has she posed?"

I would ignore her but for the fact that I like the question. Though I expend a lot of effort on teaching about counterarguments, most of my composition students remain clueless on the point. "None," I say, and I begin scribbling in the margin *What might critics of your thesis think about*

those with mental health problems having easy access to guns?
And then I slide that one off to the side and pick up a new
essay draft, this one arguing that college athletes should get a
paycheck. The issue couldn't be less relevant to my life, which
makes it nearly a delight to read.

"Maybe you should give your students a topic," El says,
"rather than let them write on anything they want."

I glance at the time and begin packing up. "I have to go
do my shift at the food bank, so you need to leave." Hearing
a level of testiness in my own voice (her moodiness has
definitely been wearing on me), I add, trying to sound more
pleasant, "Want to go with me?"

"Just like my *mother*," she says, pulling her own things
together. "You think that introducing me to pathetic people
will jolt me into appreciating my own life."

This hasn't even crossed my mind, at least regarding
her. As for me, my starting the volunteer work was certainly
about putting my own woes in perspective, getting away from
feeling sorry for myself. Getting away from always thinking
about you, John. But all I say to her is "I'm not your mother."

"I didn't say you *were*," she says, then gives a sardonic
laugh and follows me out of the door. "That would mean you
giving birth at, what, age *ten*? How does that work?"

Afraid she'll answer herself, and in graphic detail, I fill
the air space as best I can. "Maybe there's a carrel free in the
library you can use to study. Or one of those couches behind
the stacks. Unless you've decided to come with me."

"Thank you, no. But I would really like to see the goats.
Do you need some help with Violet?" She sounds, now, more
like the El I knew in the spring semester.

Truth is, I don't need help, it not being the season to
harvest cashmere. And with Violet more relaxed these days,

I can take care of her other needs without a second person helping me tackle her. All the same, I tell El that's fine, and we make a plan for the weekend before I head to the parking lot and she heads across the quad.

At the food bank, I check in with the manager to get the addresses of the places I will be going. I have, up till now, been a sorter and a packer of the boxes, handing them off to the people who will be eating the food or the people who will be driving it to outposts. Today, I will, for the first time, be among the latter.

"Rockbridge Forge, hm," he says, pulling a sheet of paper from his stack, a map, and poking at it. "See the firehouse, here? That's the hub, so leave the boxes there, except the one that goes…" and he winds a finger along a snaking waterway "…here. You'll find a house. Sullivan family's been in it since the 1800s."

"They must be pretty old," I say.

He laughs at that, I am real glad to see, my joke-making attempts with people in the community still newly awakened. I think of that as an important part of getting into a rhythm of being okay again, so I'm trying to be light when the opportunity presents itself.

"They came with the railroad," he says, "and stayed put when the tracks moved on. We used to call that place Sullivan's Holler when I was a kid." He looks off to the window, seeming in reverie, some secret hidden in his wrinkled face. "Most all gone away now. Little Shannon holds on, though," and he lets that hang there for a second, as if he wants to add something but isn't sure if he should. He pushes the map my way. "If you have a low-to-the-ground car, it might be a tough one to get to."

I assure him my truck will be fine, and I thank him and move along to the sorting and boxing tables, enjoying the new side I am standing on. Feels like I've been promoted.

"Rockbridge Forge, hm," the woman there says. I have seen her at the food bank and around town several times though haven't exactly met her before. I do, however, know that she is from New England, her husband, a retired professor of some importance, having taken a prestigious visiting post up at the state university, because this information is something she shares with just about every person she encounters. "I had that particular run last week," she tells me, pushing some boxes along in my direction. "But I am too old to navigate *that* kind of situation."

"Low-to-the-ground car problem?" I ask her.

"Only partly," she says, then lowers her voice and her head in a collusive manner. "It's *Deliverance* country out there. And the way they speak? It's as if there are marbles in their mouths. I couldn't understand a *word*."

"Huh," I say, nodding. "Kind of like the folk who come down here from Haavuhd Yaad."

I immediately regret my rudeness (call it a humor attempt gone too far), but she doesn't seem to be listening to what I'm saying, anyway. She keeps low-talking, her eyes darting to the side now and then. "And that Sullivan woman out there is im*pos*sible. Probably on drugs. She went on and on about something—wanted us to pack more desserts, I think. God knows she doesn't need them." Then, thankfully for me, she turns her attention to a food bank client who has come for his weekly box and proceeds to explain to him why she and her prestigious husband are spending the year in this backwater.

For the entire ride out to the far reach of the county, Sirius rests his neck on the half-open window, obviously glad for the breeze. Summer has seemed to ignore the arrival of the fall equinox today, the sun seeming stronger than it did even in July. So when I arrive at the firehouse I rush the boxes in and get the truck on the move again, creeping around gravelly bends and down into woods, where the air is noticeably cooler.

I'm reminded, John, of the disagreement you and I had over where to site the house, with me on the side of putting it in the low part of the property amidst trees, and you wanting it up on the ridge. "A lookout," you said, and I asked you what the heck we needed to be looking out for. So you did some rebranding: "A view, then. That's what everyone wants." Wasn't always that way, I argued, even while those three peaks that would become our daily vista were luring me in, a slaty blur on that day, as if behind a scrim. People used to settle in hollows, where the winds are less harsh, where cool water bubbles over rocks, I said to you.

I shift into a lower gear, hug the inside of the rutted road, now zigzagging alongside a gulch with roots poking from its sides like elbows from orange clay. The quick glimpses down that I get at switchbacks reveal a stream bed with spines of dry rock jutting up, barely a trickle of water. Strikes me as odd, given that we've had the wettest summer I can remember. Torrents of rain. My own woods are swampy, a seasonal branch running strong.

Things are similarly amiss at the house—part log cabin, part clapboard bungalow—which is caked nearly a quarter-way up its sides in dried mud. A seesaw and a wagon in the yard are also covered with the stuff, like sculptures made from river silt. So is a barrel of some kind, toppled over and striking me as hog-like, though I can't make out what it really is. Dirt from the door dusts my shoes when I knock. I have an eery sense of deja vu but can't place it.

"I've got Granddad's pokestock aimed at the door, damn you!" a voice from inside calls out.

I am glad Sirius is at my side, but also suddenly worried that he might consider biting someone he perceives as threatening to me, and, well, that would not be such a good thing for the food bank's public image. So I wrap a hand around his collar and say in a more pleasant tone than I've been met with, "I've got a box of food for you out in my truck."

The door opens then, and a woman is there, a baby on her hip. "I'm sorry," she says, "I thought you were my cousin pulling up. Your pickup is near identical to his, you know that?" She squints off at it, then adds, "But yours doesn't have the extended cab. I see that now."

She puts out her hand and introduces herself as Shannon, her baby as Muriel, and her son as Mitch, though there is no son I can see in the immediate scene. I am hoping it is that he is off somewhere playing and not imaginary.

"I'm Leda," I tell her, trying to seem inconspicuous as I peer around to size up whether or not there's a weapon within reach. "I've never heard that term, uh, 'pokestock'?"

"Shotgun, single shot," she says. "The old people call it a pokestock. But I don't have it here. I keep it on a high shelf on account of the kids."

Sirius's tail is wagging, so I release my grip on his collar and he begins sniffing the baby's feet, cautiously, as if he's never smelled baby before. Perhaps he hasn't.

"Not so fond of your cousin, huh?" I say, making small talk.

"It's not that. He's like a brother to me. He's just not himself lately," she says, an agitation coming into her voice. "He started into some kind of therapy, and it's made him bat-shit crazy. He had his share of haints before, no question, but what do you expect, really, with someone who keeps memories locked in his head so vividly like he does?"

I nod, as if this were a normal kind of conversation to have on a stranger's porch. "Afghanistan?" I ask.

"Iraq—two tours. Saw a lot of awful stuff. Not that I know what it was, because he doesn't like to talk about it. Which is *why* I think this therapy is turning him into a nutcase, this *PE*."

"PE?" I ask her now.

"Prolonged Exposure," she says, over-enunciating the term. "Some stupid-ass theory on how if you keep describing, in great and gory detail, the thing that's spooking you, it will go away. My cousin has a bad habit of trusting people, so he keeps going in and doing it and coming out with more and more demons following after him like he's leading a marching band."

"I'm sorry," I say.

She sighs now, forces a smile. "No, *I'm* sorry. I've just been having a hard time about some things, and no one to talk to. Or no grown-ups, anyway." She shrugs and then moves Muriel to her other hip, as if to say, *But don't get me started.* Sirius, still fixated on the baby, also moves to Shannon's other side.

We stand there for an awkward beat, during which time I am startled by a bang and a thud from off somewhere. I'm not sure what direction it's coming from or how far away it is, noises in the mountains so often hard to track in that way. It strikes me as out of place, though, in this kind of spot where you expect to be hearing nothing but soft trills and trickles and twitterings, none of which I am detecting at all. Shannon doesn't react to the bang and thud, so I take it as her normal, whatever it is, and figure this to be as good a time as any to go get the box.

"Come on, Sirius," I say, patting my leg so he will come

along. But he is 100% focused on the baby and doesn't even turn an ear in my direction as I gather up the food and carry it in.

The inside of Shannon's house, though dusted lightly with the same tawny dirt that covers everything outside, is cared-for, kind of creative. There are colorful scarves, the sort you find in bins at vintage shops, decorating the windows. Tacked to the walls are children's drawings and paintings, lots of them, some obviously very old. Some are of birds—all in the same pose, standing on stick legs, wings out—but most are of frogs leaping into or out of a pond. From a ceiling fan hangs a pull made of broken bits of jewelry and small prisms that send rainbows of afternoon light darting around the room. There's a heavy table of oak in what looks to be the most historic part of the house, the walls around it all darkened timbers and pitted mortar. I put the box on the table and pull out a brown paper bag.

"There were apples today, from that orchard in Bedford," I say, but I can see now that, aside from some potatoes and onions, that is really the only highlight.

Shannon sits at the table and shifts the baby to her lap, which puts the little thing more at Sirius's level. He sets about sniffing her arms and neck, and this seems to tickle her, judging by the giggly sounds she makes, which trigger in me an aching inside that I work to suppress. I sit in a chair that obscures my view of them somewhat and watch as Shannon lifts some cans out of the box and studies each before setting it on the table. One is filled with beets and two with green beans.

"I hope you don't take this the wrong way and think we aren't appreciative of your effort," she says, finally, "but I'm new to this taking-handouts routine, and I'm not exactly making sense of it. Beets and green beans, for instance—aren't they in season right now? And don't we live in farm country?"

I have been thinking the exact thing, in fact, as I watch her, now pulling four boxes of macaroni and cheese out and setting them next to the cans like she's building a miniature dystopian food village. It occurs to me that the things we tend to pack for this area are often more skewed in favor of processed foods over the fresh produce the farmers bring in.

"I tried to tell the last lady who came," Shannon says, "that we don't have a grocery store out here, meaning that those of us with no reliable transportation are stuck with the Dollar General, where the mac and cheese is plentiful and cheap. Same with Spaghetti-os," a can of which now joins the community of other shelf goods on the table. "I asked her if the county understands the health problems related to *food deserts*—childhood obesity, diabetes, hardening of the arteries—but she appeared clueless about an issue that anyone who has a television should know at least something about. I tried to fill her, describing in detail what a food desert is, at the end of which she suggested I take a walk up to the gas station and get a package of Twinkies. Does it make even a bit of sense that she would say something like that?"

Actually, yes, is my thought, but I shake my head.

"These blow-ins act like they are so smart, but that's just plain ignorant." She pauses in her remonstrations, looking more closely at me. "Sorry, are you a blow-in?"

"I moved here from somewhere else, so I guess I am," I say. But then, hoping maybe there is a statute of limitations on this social category, I add, "It's been almost ten years."

"Well, you do know about food deserts, right?" she asks.

I assure her I do, and I offer to pack her box myself next week. "There should be some Brussels sprouts, sunchokes, sweet potatoes, and maybe, if we get a few days of cooler weather, the greens won't be as bitter as they are right now."

"If there's radicchio, will you get me some? I would just *kill* for radicchio," she says. "And eggplant? I had such a good patch of eggplant growing, and squash, maders, oregano, garlic, tarragon—it was a ratatouille garden, like I saw on Rachael Ray. I was setting to make batches in my slow-cooker and freeze them up. But then the mud came and buried my garden."

I'm glad she's gotten to mentioning the mud, because I've been very curious about that but wasn't sure how to broach the topic. "So, where did it come from?"

She runs a finger along the thin coating of dust on the table, draws a face with a big O for a mouth. "God," she answers. "If you listen to the coal company. Those people aren't so big on taking responsibility for plugging up the headwaters when they turn the mountains to rubble. Water stops running from where it should and spits all angry from where it shouldn't."

"Are you talking about mountaintop removal mining?" I am surprised, never having heard of it so close. Come to think of it, I never really knew where *any* of the sites were, the rallies we'd gone to being at the Statehouse. "I've never heard news of that going on in the county."

"It isn't technically in the county," she says, "but watersheds don't abide by municipal boundaries." She gets up then and sets Muriel in a playpen, the baby suddenly all floppy and sleepy. Sirius posts himself like a sentry next to the sleeping child. "It's like the earth's having a giant mastectomy," Shannon goes on, picking up a tea kettle now and setting it on the stovetop. "And that's an appropriate simile, with all the cancer around here. Comes from heavy metals in the water, a

Virginia Tech study said." She turns on the burner under the kettle. "Want some tea?"

There is obviously something going on in my expression that does not exactly agree with the nod I am giving her, because she laughs—an impish laugh that almost makes me laugh, too—and then she tells me not to worry, that she gets deliveries of purified water to use for drinking.

Embarrassed for thinking she might unwittingly poison me, I change the subject by offering to bring her some cuttings of my plants when I come next week, to help rejuvenate her garden.

"That's nice of you," she says, "but it's probably useless, seeing as it appears to be anyone's guess where water will shoot from next rainstorm."

From what I've read about the impacts of mountaintop removal mining, I have to agree with her pessimism. But I figure that in my role as a purveyor of charity I should be promoting the bright side. "What is it the poet said? Hope springs eternal?"

"Never heard of anyone fishing in hope," she says, setting down saucers and teacups. They're old, mismatched, all floral patterns, just the kind I tend to look for. "Flowerdy," the woman who runs the Goodwill calls them. The saucer Shannon has set in front of me matches a cup I have at home, I realize. Morning glories, my favorite one. I run a finger around the thin edge. Not a chip in it.

"So, what brought you all to Appalachia?" she asks, pronouncing it as you did—Appa*latch*a. Uncanny how the vernacular soaked into you almost instantly when we arrived in these mountains, like you wanted to fill up with so much of the new that there would be no room for any of the old.

"My husband and I wanted to get out of the city," I say.

But then I correct myself. "He did, actually. I just came along because I loved him."

"Does he still like it here?" she asks.

Somehow it does not seem right for me to share my own personal misfortune with her. On the other hand, given even the small connection we have made as human beings, it seems wrong to be evasive or dishonest. That is the interior struggle I am having when the screen door to the backyard flies open and visions of a post-traumatized and possibly armed cousin pop into my head. Luckily, that is not who actually enters but a small boy with a bullfrog in his hands. The screen door slams closed behind him, causing the baby to startle awake and begin shrieking. Sirius scuttles over to me and sits close, pushing all his weight against my leg, either out of fear of or a need to protect me from this alarming noise the baby is now making.

"*Good lord*, get that thing *out* of here, Mitchy," Shannon says, picking up Muriel and holding her against her neck to calm her down.

"I found it at the edge of the hopper pond, Mama," he says, holding it up. It's noticeably limp, but a long leg gives a kick. "Told you they weren't all dead."

"And I *told* you to stay away from there," Shannon says. "Go on up to the woods and let the frog go in the leaf litter."

"Papa let me bring them in, when he lived here."

"He still *lives* here," she says.

"He left us," the boy says now, looking straight at me, in a peculiar, wide-eyed sort of way. A stripe of a rainbow from the prisms jiggles across his forehead. "He took the car and he left us." Then he goes back through the door and is gone again with his frog.

Shannon sighs loudly, and looks off into the void of the

dusty screen. "Ever since those machines came and replaced the workers in the mines, well, lots of people have been going off. For a long time."

The Grapes of Wrath. That is what I'd been deja vu-ing about. It is as if I have stepped into a Steinbeck novel.

"Almost lost him in the mud," Shannon says, nodding in the boy's direction. "Might have, but for the compost pig."

My face conveys bewilderment, I am sure, though I have a sense that she is referring to that unidentified object in the front yard.

"Our composter—it's in the shape of a pig? You turn the drum with its tail, which, fortunately, is well attached, as my Mitch discovered. And the belly of the thing was full with food scraps and grass clippings, so it was heavy enough to stay put till the flood subsided."

I cannot think of a thing to say that would be appropriate, so I just get up and stand next to her there. We aren't familiar enough for me to feel comfortable putting a hand on her arm, so I just stroke the baby's head, there on her shoulder. It is warm, her downy hair so soft.

"If his father had been here," she continues, "Mitch would've listened to him calling from the porch when the gush started. I yelled and yelled his name, but I might as well've been a mute for all that was worth."

I could tell her that I know all about yelling and yelling someone's name who isn't responding, but I sure don't want to get back on the subject of you. I feign needing to go, promise to be back in a week.

I spend the next day working in my garden, seeing what might be hardy enough to survive dividing and transplanting. I round up as many planting containers as I can find around the yard—most tend to get shredded because they are Sirius's very favorite things to play with—and I pot up some cabbage, kale, spinach and broccoli. I still have carrots (always puny, but tasty) and cauliflower left to work on when I realize I need to go pick up El. Maybe, I think, she'll help me finish up with the gardening. But she does prefer the animals, always opted to help with them when she came out in the spring, taking Sirius on long walks in the woods, mucking out the goat barn. I'm behind on hoof trimming, so she could do that.

When I pull up to our meeting place at the library steps, though, she isn't there. I wait alone in the truck, students appearing now and then under the enormous oaks that pepper the campus, but none of them emerge from the shade as El. I check my phone every few minutes, though I know fully well that I would hear a chirp if she sent a text message, which is her preferred method of communication. I power the phone down and then up to be sure I'm picking up the nearest tower. I scroll through the most recent messages from her: *How's Violet?* from July, when she was at a lake with her family, and a few more from that trip—*I'm allergic to everything here* and *I don't like boats* and *Just saw some roadkill*, which she went on to describe in more detail than seemed necessary, I remember thinking. Then no other texts till the fall semester started: *Are you bringing Sirius today?* There were a couple of those. Another *How's Violet?* And *Where are you?* when I was running late for office hours earlier in the week. "People are just late sometimes," I'd said to her when I got there.

After a half hour, I turn the truck back on and tell myself to go home. I even say it out loud: "Go home, Leda." And I remind myself of a conversation El and I had last spring, after her suicide attempt. I had told her that I would not come looking for her if she went missing, that that would be asking too much of me. And she had understood, had said I should not have to go through that twice in one lifetime. "I wouldn't want that," she said, and I believed her. "Anyway," she added, "living in a dorm means someone will find me pretty fast." She's not one to hide the truth, you'd have to say, no matter how frightening. I'm not sure which is worse, openness or secretiveness—that dropping of hints, like pebbles that only pick up the light of too-late. The buying of a handgun, for instance. *Protection.*

"What are you protecting yourself from?" I'd asked you.

"It's you I want to protect," you said.

And I should have known what that meant, but I let another pebble drop unnoticed, your lack of an answer to my "Protect me from what?"

I steer the car away from the library steps and past Main Hall and around to the gate. And all I need to do next is make a left and I'll be heading in the direction of home. That's all I need to do. But I turn right and climb the hill behind campus to the women's dorm complex.

I have never been there, though I assume there will be mailboxes or a guard or something, but I am met by a locked door with nothing but a keycard slot next to it. I knock, but no one comes down the hall. I walk around the building and eventually come to some windows that open into a room where a television is on, and I can see backs of heads sticking up from the couch, and a side view of someone's face in a rocking chair.

"Hey," I call through the window, obviously louder than I need to, because a few of the young women shoot up in their seats like an alarm has gone off. I tell them I'm sorry to have disturbed them, that I'm looking for El.

One turns to a part of the room that is obscured from my

view by the couch, and says, "El, someone's at the window for you," which makes the others laugh.

I don't wait for her to see me there. I just head off to the parking lot, working out in my mind how I'm going to tell her not to come to my office anymore, that I won't be having her at my place, either. That I can't take the scares. I'll do it by text message, so I won't have to face her. Given my part-time schedule, I could probably get through the semester without even running into her. That's what I'm hoping for as I round the corner of the building and set eyes on my truck, El leaning up against it.

"How'd you do that?" I ask her.

"I'm dead," she says. "Ghosts do amazing things."

"That isn't funny," I say.

"I walked through the building. It's shorter than going around the outside."

"Why are you wearing long sleeves when it's 85 degrees outside?" I ask, although that is the absolute last thing I want explained to me.

"I didn't hurt myself. Violet stops me."

"What are you talking about? Are you having some kind of break with reality?"

"I'm not *mental*, if that's what you mean," she says.

"Well, technically, you are. People who hurt themselves are 'mental' by definition."

"Then that proves I'm not mental, because I'm not doing that anymore."

"Why?" I ask. Then thinking that is kind of a weird response, I say, "I mean, when did you decide this?"

"In the summer. I made a promise to myself that every time I pick up a piece of broken glass or a needle or a blade from an Exacto knife or—"

"You don't need to be that specific," I say, stopping her before she gets going.

"That's what you always say, though, 'be specific, don't be vague,'" she says, parroting the writing advice I give my students.

"This time, be vague," I say. "Be *very* vague."

"Whenever I pick up *blank* and get the idea to do *blank*, Violet appears in my head."

"A goat is keeping you from hurting yourself?"

She nods.

"Don't you think that's odd?" I ask.

"Doesn't Sirius stop things from hurting you? Didn't you get him to keep you from thinking about your husband, about finding him all blown—"

"*El*," I say, my hand up and blocking her from my view, as if she were shooting infrared light from her pores. "What *is* it with your mouth these days?"

"Sorry," she says. "I've been thinking about that, actually. Since I stopped, uh, doing what I was doing, I think the pent-up gore comes through my lips."

Now I am making a conscious effort not to look at her mouth, I realize, but I don't know what I expect to be happening there.

"I'm thinking of it as a channel change for my macabre tendencies," she adds.

I nod. "Nice adjective."

"I know. I looked up 'deathly' in a thesaurus, and found a lot of good ones. I haven't told anyone yet, but I've started writing short stories—vampire fiction, set on the Trail of Tears. Do you teach creative writing, by any chance?"

I shake my head. *Thankfully* is what I'm thinking. "So why the long sleeves?" I ask her.

"I know it's immature, but that is about the attention.

The mysteriousness. I really like that part." And she lifts her sleeves to show me there are no fresh wounds, just the many scars of various lengths and shapes that she's etched into herself over the years. Deep space, that's what her arms are like, those Hubble pictures, only hard to look at. "And if you're wondering," she goes on, "why I didn't meet you today, it's because I lost track of time." She opens the passenger door and climbs in. "People are just late sometimes."

We ride along, mostly quiet, the wind washing through the cab, until we've wound our way over Chestnut Hill and can see the driveway up ahead in the distance, your "Way Out Farm" sign pointing down into the woods. The "m" is a little askew from the last windstorm. I should probably nail it down before it blows off. It would be real hard to find in the leaves and I don't know how to carve letters out of wood the way you did.

"You're there, too," El is saying as I make the turn. "In those images I get, of Violet, that save me from—you know. You're there, too."

I am trying to work out my response. A thank-you wouldn't get at what I am thinking, but, then, I don't know what I am thinking.

"You're thinking that you really wish you could have saved *him*," she says, filling the void. "But I don't think we get to choose who we save, any more than we get to choose who saves us."

I let the sound of crunching gravel fill the cab, the trilling of toads in the woods, until we pop out into the open space of the lower field. Up in the house, I know that Sirius is hearing our approach. He's filling up with anticipation so entirely that he will be wiggling and whining by the time we open the door to let him out. He'll probably run in a wide circle and then fall over from happiness in the front yard, and we will rub his belly. Maybe grab onto his tail.

"You ever hear of a compost pig?" I ask El.

Lesser Dog

It's a holiday miracle: the boy is smiling.

"Hi, Mitch!" I call out, and I flip on the porch light and wave at him and this man of their family I haven't met. When Shannon let me know they wouldn't need a ride over, I had hoped this was the reason. "Is this your papa?" I say, even though I think I know the answer.

I don't, as it turns out, something that's obvious when Shannon—who has come around from the driver's side to extract Muriel from her carseat—gives me the *cut* sign. But it is too late: the boy is not smiling anymore.

Sirius's tail is going full speed, whacking against Shannon's cowboy boots while he waits for the emergence of the baby, as patiently as is possible. But then his tail stops suddenly and a white retriever squeezes itself past Shannon and out of the vehicle that I now notice to be a truck very like my own. It seems a lot of bodies coming out of it, even though it has an extended cab, bringing to mind a clown car. Especially so, as the dog is wearing a bright red vest.

The two dogs make introductions, which is to say that they sniff each other's rears and then circle around, ears twitching. Sirius seems particularly interested in the clothing the dog is wearing, which has stenciled on it the words *Working Dog*.

The man I have mistaken for Mitch's father steps up onto the porch. He has a cadaverous physique, and he holds out a hand with a visible tremor. "I'm Sean," he says, his voice as shaky as the rest of him. "It wa-was nice of you to invite me."

I didn't technically invite him, of course, but I don't say that. I just take him up on his handshake. The skin of his palm is softer than I expect. I know from his name that he is Shannon's war veteran cousin, but why I have equated this fact with calloused or otherwise hard hand skin is anyone's guess.

"This is B-Barney," he says, nodding toward the dog who has taken up residence at his side, seemingly reporting for duty. Sean pats him on the head, a gesture that comes across as unnatural.

"That's not a dog name, Uncle Seanie," Mitch informs him. "That's a dinosaur name."

"I d-d-don't like it, either," Sean says.

"Is he a PTSD dog?" I ask, though it occurs to me, too late, that that might not be in good taste, that he may not have wanted Shannon telling people about his personal problems. I know he was recently hospitalized, the details surrounding the event unclear to me. But judging by how uptight, and tight-lipped, Shannon was about it last I saw her, it must have been a bad scene.

"For you, Leda!" she cries, handing me a jar with a yellow chiffon scarf attractively made into a bow around its lip. "You said no presents, but it's nothing big, just some kimchi I fermented from those cabbages you brought me. A thank-you for all your help, especially with my garden. Not your fault it flooded out again."

"Why no presents?" Mitch asks. "It's Christmastime."

"It's the winter solstice we're celebrating today," I say, and then add, in response to his blank stare, "the shortest day of the year." This does little to alter his expression.

"Leda wants to show us her sky," Shannon says, which brings a polite rumbling from the porch inhabitants.

"Is-is that a b-b-bird sculpture?" Sean asks. He's got his eyes on the roof of the workshop.

"What are you *talking* about, Sean?" Shannon says, looking

up at the roof, too. The pique in her voice is noticeable, seems carried over from some prior argument. "There's obviously nothing the least bit birdlike in *that*." And she takes the children into the house.

I have been thinking the same thing lately, John—since a hailstorm that sent more of those metal parts plunging noisily to the earth—that the bird I once saw up there is no more. And that maybe, as you said, it never was there to begin with. But what I say to my guest is this: "Yes, it's a phoenix." And I lead him inside and show them all where to hang their coats.

I pull some beers from the fridge. It's a new ale from that brewery that you may remember was slated to open a year ago summer, right around the time you made your departure. Reviews say it's something special, but I can't say for sure, being no great fan of beer. Turns out that Shannon isn't either, what with breastfeeding the baby still, and Sean passes, too.

"I learned the hard way that alcohol and m-my medications are a dangerous du-du-duo," he says. "I sure miss beer. I've been wanting to tr-tr-try that one."

"Probably nothing special," I say, and I slide the six-pack, intact, back into the fridge, pushing it behind the milk and a large glass jug of cider. "I'll make coffee and hot chocolate, how about that? It'll warm us when we go outside."

"*Beer* was never the trouble, Sean," Shannon says. "It was that *PE*. That's what started those delusions about the soldiers. And all that never sleeping, never eating. Not *beer*."

"I know, I sh-sh-should've listened."

"Yes you should've," she says, wagging her head at him. "Should've listened to me back in high school, too, when I told you not to join that army. *Shit*, Sean, you didn't even like hunting, and there you were signing up to be in a *war*."

"Uncle Seanie! Uncle Seanie!" Mitch pipes in, leaping

up and trying to grab onto the bill of the baseball cap Sean's wearing. "Granddad says it's rude for boys to wear hats inside." Mitch leaps again, Sean lurching clumsily away from him.

It is visceral, the urge I am having to save this poor man from his family, but Shannon steps in before I can work out a plan. "Leave Seanie alone, now," she says to Mitch. Her tone has gone tender, seemingly in reaction to the look of terror that has come across her cousin's face. "Granddad would want him to keep it on today."

"Why?" Mitch asks.

"Never mind," Shannon says. "He'll take it off when his hair grows back."

"Ohhh," the boy says, "it's a special hair-growing hat! I think I saw that on TV for $19.95."

"No you didn't," his mother says to him.

There is something decidedly strange about all this, but it doesn't seem my place to pry. I can't help but notice now that there is a tattoo of some kind on Sean's scalp, though the subject matter is impossible to glean from the bit of it that shows below the edge of the cap. I don't want it to appear that I'm staring (I kind of am) so I turn to the cabinet and wiggle the big coffeemaker from out of the back. It's been a long time since I've had people over, so spiders have taken up residence in it. I disassemble the thing and run the pieces under the tap.

Shannon looks around and says, "Nice place, Leda. Fire makes it real cozy, even with the room being so open. Kitchen, dining and living all in one, I like that." She settles into a chair at the table. "My house is such a jumble, built in parts over the years as it was."

Sean sits at the table, too, and Mitch tries to get the dogs to play with a half-shredded squirrel toy he has found in the corner. Barney, though, has parked himself next to Sean and seems in a trance, like a guard outside Buckingham Palace, and Sirius is, as usual, all about the baby.

"Would you like to help me, Mitch?" I ask, pulling a stool up to the counter for him. "You can mix up the hot chocolate." I pour milk in a glass bowl and slide the sugar and the cocoa powder across the counter to where he is climbing up. "Add one scoop each," I say.

"Smells dreamy," Shannon says. "Is that veggie soup on the stove?"

"Uh-huh. With chicken. I'll add some egg noodles when we're ready to eat."

"Leda is a locavore," Shannon says to her cousin.

He nods agreeably, then after a pause, asks, "Wh-what's that?"

"It's someone who believes in eating local foods," Shannon says. "And she can magically find summer pickings even in the dead of winter. Leda, where'd you find that arugula a few weeks back?"

"Organic market at the edge of town," I say. "They've got a greenhouse up."

Mitch, I notice out of the corner of my eye, is scooping copious quantities of sugar into the bowl of milk, which has somehow also turned the color of pitch, so I slide the bag of sugar and the carton of cocoa powder out of his reach. "I think you can start stirring now," I tell him, handing him a wooden spoon.

"I've-I've been here before," Sean says, looking out the window.

"Is that right?" I say, though I am quite sure it's not, and also concerned that he may next be reporting that the Taliban is moving across our field out front.

"You had s-some musicians out there," he says, pointing a shaky finger toward the deck. "Someone was playing a banjo made from a g-g-g-gourd."

I stop in my coffee making, unsure how many spoonfuls of beans I have put in. I dump them all back in the canister and begin again.

"A *gourd*?" Shannon says. "That can't be right, Sean."

"No, it is," he says. "The first b-b-banjos around here were made from gourds. They were brought to the m-m-mountains by, um…" he rubs his forehead, looks troubled. "I used to know this."

"Slaves," I say. "It was an African instrument."

He nods now. "Nice sound. Your party was, what, t-t-two, three years ago, Leda?"

(And I can hear it, it's eery, you plucking on those strings.)

"Something like that," I tell him. "We had a few. Lots of people came."

"Done," Mitch says lackadaisically, slipping off the stool. The spoon is practically sticking straight up in the sludge he has created.

"Do you mind if I breastfeed right here?" Shannon asks, and I tell her that of course it is fine, that she does not need to ask. But I am glad she has warned me all the same. Makes me feel strange inside when I see her feeding the baby. Like a heart string is being plucked.

I get the coffee going and pour the cocoa into a saucepan. Before I add a few more cups of milk to it, I look around to make sure Mitch isn't watching, as this might insult his efforts. But he is busily looking at (meaning: touching) things in the room, particularly fascinated with a geranium that has snail-like leaves, two of which he has picked from the stem and is studying in the palms of his hands.

"Want to give the dogs some treats, Mitch?" I suggest, in part for the survival of my geranium and in part to lure Sirius away from Shannon. The way he stares at the nursing baby has got to be annoying to her, especially when he gets to drooling. I pull the bag of Sirius's jerky sticks from the pantry and hold it out to Mitch, but then think better of that approach and give him only two.

He calls out the dogs' names, but they don't budge, so he runs back and forth between the dining room table and this part of the room and that, waving the sticks in the air. The dogs seem mildly tempted, at best. They don't leave their posts.

"Must b-be a challenge, that gourd banjo, having no frets," Sean is saying, his features seeming to relax now, maybe the talk of music doing that to him. "Who w-w-was that playing it, Leda?"

I turn just enough to catch sight of Shannon kicking his leg with the tip of her boot. She knows you played music, John, and I'm touched that she is trying to steer the conversation away from something that might be stressful to me. She, who is from a hollow devastated by the coal companies and whose boyfriend, and the father of her children, seems to have moved on. "'Way Out Far,'" she says, obviously to change the subject. "I like that, the name of your place."

"It's actually Way Out *Farm*, but the 'm' blew off of the sign," I tell her.

"I should get a sign for my place," Shannon says. "'Collateral Damage,' it could say. That's how they refer to the hollow now."

"Not a b-bad idea, Shannon," Sean says. "We could send pictures of it around to the n-newspapers and that faceboy thing, to raise aware-awareness. It could be carved wood, like the one here. Leda, who m-m-made your—"

"It was at the town hall last week that they used that term, 'collateral damage,'" Shannon says a little too loudly, talking over him. She knows, too, that you were the woodworker.

I want to tell her that she doesn't need to avoid the topic of you like this, but I guess she figures I'm fragile on that point, given that I don't talk about it. It just has never seemed the right time to drift into the topic in our weekly conversations. We mostly talk about food, about flora and fauna, and it just seems wrong to add the details of your death to that peaceful mix. I have gotten the impression that she's filled in some blanks with a narrative involving a terminal illness. A bit of truth there, if you get creative about it, but not enough to feel honest on my part. She's starting to be a friend, after all.

"There was an environmental lawyer there, sitting in the back the whole time," she goes on. "She stayed and talked a while about legal options."

The coffeemaker starts groaning, and I pull cups from the shelf and set them, and spoons and sugar and cream, out on the table. I pour the hot chocolate into a teapot and set that out, too.

"Look at that," Shannon says, picking up the teacup in front of her. "I have the saucer for this at home."

"I know," I say, because I have put it in front of her for this very reason. "I love that pattern, the morning glories."

"Me too," she says. "It's antique, from the 1940s."

"Maybe we should g-get those two together, then," Sean says with a little smile. It's Shannon's smile, I see now. Mitch's too, the one I got a quick glimpse of when they pulled up.

Shannon has finished feeding the baby—who has, as usual, been rendered nearly unconscious by the stuff—and she gets up now, holds Muriel out like a rag doll, in no particular direction. "Can someone take her? I need to use the bathroom," she says. Sean and I lock eyes for just long enough for me to see his smile replaced by his look of terror. But then his expression softens, goes a little curious, because he has to have noticed my reaction, too, my trepidation. I've never held that baby in my arms, Shannon in a routine at her house of putting Muriel in a playpen when she's not holding her. I've never volunteered, something that she's had to have noticed, perhaps has applied her own narrative to, as well. Now, though, after the awkward beat, I go to her and take the baby.

"Thanks," Shannon says, heading off to where I've pointed down the hall. "And *Sean*," she calls over her shoulder, "you have to *stop* being afraid of children one of these days. It's stupid."

I stand and sway with the infant for some minutes. Sirius sidles up, looks at me, head cocked. He's not sure what to make of this, either.

"I'm afraid I'll dr-dr-drop her," Sean finally says.

"I'm afraid I'll kidnap her," I say back.

"*Mitch*! Get those *out* of your ears!" Shannon cries, announcing her return. The jerky sticks are projecting from the sides of her son's head, something Sean and I have failed to notice. Shannon pulls them out, only to have him grab them back and slide them up his nose. Sean and I both have the same knee-jerk reaction and laugh at this, until we see Shannon's expression, which seems to be reminding us that we are adults. Mitch, I suppose realizing he is in danger of losing these objects of his enjoyment, takes them from his nostrils and tucks them benignly atop his ears. They have the look of antennae.

"You are gross," Shannon says to him, taking the baby from me and settling back in her chair.

"Thank you," Mitch says, seeming to take this as a genuine compliment.

I pick up the coffee pot and offer some to Sean, who takes a half cup only, an embarrassed look on his face. I'm thinking it's concern over medicine interaction again, but when he lifts it to his mouth I realize it's probably about the shaking, not wanting to spill. I pour my own and then leave the pot near him in case he wants a refill.

Shannon helps herself to hot chocolate (caffeinated breast milk makes babies "scary," she claims, a tidbit I put in the memory bank in case I wake up living someone else's life one day), and she pours some for her son, who is on all fours now, his head turned so one of the jerky sticks is in front of Barney. He still doesn't take it.

"You can eat it," Sean says to the dog, then adds some kind of hand movement, as if he's just remembered a command, an *at ease*, it appears. The dog takes the treat and inhales it, then flops on the floor, apparently released from his shift.

Mitch approaches Sirius now, who looks at me, but I really don't know why he would ask permission. I suppose he is just confused, having never seen one of his treats behind anyone's ear before. I nod, and he does pretty much what Barney has done. Then Mitch, his work apparently done, stands at the table and takes a slosh of his hot chocolate, oblivious to the drips that run down his shirtfront.

"So, where did you get Barney?" I ask Sean.

"There's a program at th-th-the hospital. We're in training t-t-together. I'm not sure it's right for me, though."

"Change his name," Mitch says. "That might help."

"Can you d-do that?" Sean asks.

"I did, when I got Sirius," I say. "He didn't seem to care that he had a new name."

"What was his name before?" Shannon asks.

I have to think about this. "Kenny?" I say, but that doesn't sound right

"Can we go outside?" Mitch asks, loudly slurping his cocoa.

"In a minute," Shannon says.

"*Kirby,*" I say now, the memory coming through a fog that, more and more, envelopes that period of time, muting the edges, the colors. I look to see if there is any recognition in Sirius's demeanor having heard his original name. His head lifts a little, an ear perks up. But I can't see his eyes from where I stand, his focus back on the baby, so I don't know if that old faraway look has come into them.

"Can we go outside *now*?" Mitch asks, holding the mug upside down and watching cross-eyed as the last drops go into his mouth.

"See those blankets stacked up?" I tell him, pointing to the door to the deck. "Why don't you put them outside and set up a camp. We'll be right there."

He races off and we finish our drinks and put our dishes up, then make our way outside. The cosmos has cooperated with my entertainment plan: the night is clear. When everyone is settled in a place, wrapped up and warm enough, I turn all the lamps off, inside and out. The moon has already set, so it is just the stars and planets that light the night but for a soft glow on the northeast horizon where town is.

"It's too dark!" Mitch cries. "Where are you Uncle Seanie? I want to be next to you."

"Wh-wh-what about your m-m-mom?" Sean warbles.

"That's *not* who he wants to be with," Shannon responds. "It won't *kill* you."

Sean takes some discernible breaths, and then there's a rustling sound like a big wing is enclosing the boy.

"Give it a minute, Mitch," I say from the blanket where I have settled. "Your eyes have to adjust, and then it won't seem like night at all."

"Are y-you an astronomer?" Sean asks.

"No, I just like to look at stars."

They start popping, and soon Shannon is pointing to the notch between Rocky Ridge and Chestnut Hill. "What is that thing? Looks like a UFO."

Before I can answer, Sean says, "Dog star," and I know he's spent some time with the night sky.

"That's what my dog's named after, Sirius." Hearing his name, he lumbers over and stretches against my side. Maybe it is just that he has lost track of the baby in the folds of Shannon's blanket, but I am glad to have him next to me, whatever the reason.

"I see Sirius from the hollow, but I guess I never see it rising from that vantage point," Shannon says. "Why does it bounce around like that? And change colors?"

"It's an illusion," I say, "because it's low and we're seeing it through layers of atmosphere."

"They c-c-call it the rainmaker in the Middle East," Sean says. "The sky is so clear in those d-deserts."

"I want to go there, Uncle Seanie," Mitch says.

"No, you don't," he tells him. "We h-have our own deserts here in this c-country."

"Will you take me to one?"

He says, "Maybe. S-s-someday."

"When Papa says 'someday,' it means 'never.'"

"Well, when Sean says 'someday,' he means what he says," Shannon tells her son. "Someday he will take you to the desert."

"Wh-what happened to the 'maybe' part?" Sean asks.

"Leda," Shannon says, ignoring her cousin, "what is that other really bright star, up above Sirius?"

"That's Betelgeuse."

"Beetle juice?" Mitch repeats. "Is that like beetle spit? Or guts? Or pee? Or poop?"

"Lovely," Shannon says.

"Let's name Barney like that star," Mitch says. "Come on, Uncle Seanie! Come on!"

Sean calls out, "Come, B-b-betelgeuse," and the dog, who has been curled up by the door since we came out, still in off-duty mode, bounds across the deck and takes an alert pose next to his master.

"Beetle Juice, Beetle Juice, Beeeeetle Juice," Mitch has made a chant out of this, sort of high-pitched and grating. "Tell me more stars, Leda. What is *that* one called?"

I don't know which he is pointing at, the sky pretty much riddled, now that our eyes have adjusted. I make the assumption that it is the other one I've come out to see this evening.

"Procyon," I say. "And that's the whole of the Winter Triangle there—Betelgeuse, Sirius and Procyon. Sirius is part of Canis Major, the big dog constellation. And Procyon kind of follows behind. Means something like 'lesser dog.'"

Sirius's muscles get tight, and he jerks his head in the direction of the driveway. Soon we are hearing it, too, the tires over the gravel, and headlights shoot through the trees and light up the field. "I'll go let El in," I say, and Sirius follows along.

"I've got a present for you in the back!" she calls out to me when she gets out of the car, which she has borrowed from students she is staying with over the holiday.

"I didn't want any presents," I remind her.

"Okay, I'll give it to Sirius, then," and she opens the back door and lifts out a puppy.

"Is this for *real?*" I ask. "People usually like to be warned when they're getting a new pet. So they can get ready for it."

Sirius makes a beeline to El when he realizes there is something alive in her hands, and he jumps up on her, which he knows better than to do. But he is so excited he can't contain himself.

"He seems ready for it," she says, holding the puppy in front of Sirius. He is yelping and yelping, in a happy way I've never heard from him before.

"Just look at this little thing," El is saying, in a talking-to-a-baby voice that I haven't, either, heard from her before. "She's just like Sirius, a mini-me." And it is true—the pup is all black, every bit of her except a white blaze down her neck. "I didn't have to pay the puppy fee, since I'm working there. Not even a charge for the shots. I *had* to get her. How could I not?"

"You know I start teaching again soon, so how can I possibly take care of a *puppy?*" I say, but I find myself lifting her out of El's hands. I hold the furry bundle against my chest, the way I held Muriel. I can feel her nervous little heartbeat.

Sirius bounds ahead of us out to the deck, my normally quiet dog barking away, a clarion for this news of his incredible expanding family. I introduce El over the din, and Mitch starts bouncing in front of me, trying to get the attention of the puppy.

El points to Sean's dog, who no one has introduced her to. "Who's this in the red suit? Santa's Little Helper?"

"No, Beetle Juice," Mitch says.

"Beetle juice?" she repeats. "You named your dog for insect guts?"

And we are revisited by the solstice miracle: the boy is smiling.

"Or maybe you were thinking snot?" she asks. "Like, smeared all over the place, slimy and putrid?"

"Or *poo*?" he adds to her list, "or *pee*?" and he's giggling full on.

The puppy, as if on cue, pees down the front of me, and Sirius takes a break from his yelping and jumping so he can sniff that for a while. Mitch, at this point, is in hysterics.

"*You're* going to pee yourself," Shannon says to him, and he shakes his head no, because that's what little kids seem to do when confronted with that possibility, or so my limited experience tells me.

I hand the little dog to El and head inside for a wardrobe change, and when I return, she and Mitch are playing with the puppy on the deck and are still discussing bodily excretions in graphic detail. They have just started in on pus.

"Are you going home for Christmas?" Shannon asks El, perhaps trying to shift the subject to something that doesn't encourage her son's tendencies toward the disgusting.

"No, I was home for Thanksgiving," she says. "It's too expensive to do both. So, I'm sleeping on the couch of some grad students' apartment until the dorms open back up. They're recently married, so it's a little, uh, uncomfortable."

"Do you want to sleep on my couch, instead?" I ask her. "You can wake up with the puppy."

"Yes! If you can drive me to work."

"I think we can manage that," I tell her.

"You should-should name her Procyon," Sean says. "Then w-w-we'll have a Winter Triangle of dogs."

"What do you think of that, Sirius?" I ask him, but it seems likely he may never hear another word I say, so intent is he on his new little charge.

"I'm starved," El says. "I didn't miss dinner, did I?"

"No, you didn't. It's still early. Just seems late, it being dark already."

"Tell my stomach that."

"I'll get it going," I say to her, and noticing that Sirius has started zealously licking the puppy, who is no bigger than his head, I add, "if you'll make sure he doesn't accidentally ingest that thing."

"I'm all over it," she says. "I'll make sure his saliva doesn't encase the puppy in slime."

"Or throw-up!" Mitch adds, and they're off again.

Sean gets up and stretches, and from where I am standing it's as if the stars are emanating from his quivering fingertips. "The d-days have already started getting longer, technically. The solstice was at n-noon," he says. And he follows me into the house, though I have not asked for help. Maybe just seeking a kid-free zone.

I dump a package of noodles into the simmering pot and leave the top off. I root around for bowls, count them out.

Sean is looking at the pictures on the wall, points at one. "Is that the hardware store jam on the Cr-cr-crooked Road?"

"It is," I say. "You've been?"

"Sure," he says. "I know that f-fiddler there in the p-picture. It's...." He bangs his head with the palm of his hand a few times.

"George," I say. "Friend of my John's. Taught him music and moonshining."

"*George*," he sighs, leaning his head against the wall. "This is-is *so* frustrating. I've known him my whole life. These m-meds I'm taking are k-killing my powers of recall." He looks at the picture again. "George is from a l-l-long line of moonshiners. They used to make it up in the m-mountain above my homeplace. My grandfather, too—he used t-t-to take me up to the stills when I was a kid. Until something happened with my father." And he stops, then corrects himself.

"No, it was my uncle." He sighs again. "That's the w-worst of it. Forgetting f-family, home. G-good stuff f-fading out with the bad." He lets out a grim laugh. "Collateral damage."

"It'll get better," I say.

(But how many times did I say that to you?)

"So, w-were you doing that song there?" he asks, his finger dancing in the air in front of the glass of the frame. "Th-the one I heard you singing at the party? It was, um, I know...."

"Nobody's Darlin'," I say. "That was the song. John liked it."

He looks over my way, and our eyes meet. There's something in his that seems to say *Now, that isn't fair.*

I turn back to the job of finding bowls. "That's the gourd banjo in the picture, too."

"Oh, yes, l-look at that. What a f-f-fine thing. He played it clawhammer style."

"You remember *that* right," I say, encouragingly.

"I can tell from the p-picture," he says.

"Yeah, John considered that the most authentic way to play. And he called it his 'banjer.' He liked the sound of the Appalachian dialect as much as he liked the music. When he started going out and jamming, even those old-timey guys were surprised to learn he was really just a southern city boy."

"Some people are-are like that. They meld right in," Sean says.

I check the soup and turn the flame up a little. "What about your accent, Sean? You sound like you could be from anywhere. DC or California. But you grew up in the hollow with Shannon, right?"

"You're treated b-better in the s-service when you don't sound like a hick. I lost m-m-my mountain-speak along the way." He's moved from the picture, is studying my bookshelf. "Lots of Barbara Kingsolver h-here."

"Yeah, I read *Pigs in Heaven* a long time ago and was hooked."

"What's it about?"

I pick up a long wooden spoon and give the soup a stir, separating the clumps of noodles as best I can, thinking of how to answer that question. "Motherhood" is what I decide to say.

"*Books*—n-nothing like them. My house, when I was a kid, had so many books. I used to be able to call up our shelves in my mind's eye, see the titles, even. My brain worked like that."

It is noticeable how much calmer his voice suddenly seems. I look at his back, there, as he peers at the bindings.

"When I was overseas," he goes on, "I'd ch-challenge myself to remember every one of those books back home, in order. Now I can't even p-picture that living room sometimes." He runs a finger across the spines there. "Which is your favorite of these?" he asks.

"*Poisonwood Bible*," I tell him.

"What's that about?"

And I turn back to the stirring, try to think of a different answer. But there is only the one, really. "Motherhood," I say.

"Look at this," he's saying now, and I hear a book slide off the shelf. "A first edition of *The Grapes of Wrath*."

"You've read it?"

"Not a f-first edition. You should see my p-p-paperback copy, though. I took it with me when I was traveling on my motorcycle. The c-cover blew off somewhere, it got rained on in the pack, got f-filled with sand on a beach in Monterey. I finished the last page in Salinas, where Steinbeck lived."

"You still have a motorcycle?"

"No, lost that along the w-way, too. Loved that thing, made me f-feel whole," he says. He is working his way closer to the corner of the room, to where I am at the stove, but he stops at the mantel, is looking at the box with your ashes. "Is that, uh-uh…. Is he in there?"

"Yep," I say, leaning against the counter, arms crossed over my chest. "He's a jack-in-the-box. I open it and he pops out and kisses me."

He turns and looks my way again, seemingly amused and confused at the same time. "I guess that's one w-w-way of staring down the dead. How long has it been?"

"Year and a half."

"You must still b-be in the 'anger phase,'" he says. "Or is it d-d-denial?"

"Oh, no, I slid right by denial. Lingered in 'bargaining' for a while. Asked myself a lot of questions. Till I got the dog. Then I asked him instead. The deep dark stage, though, that hung around. Those nights that just won't ever end. Ever."

"*Ever.* Headless d-dead tramping around the r-room." Then, sort of shaking something off, he says, "Sorry."

"Don't be. I've had plenty of nightmares about headless dead. How long have you been back, Sean?" I ask.

"From Iraq? Nine years now."

"And it's always been, um, hard?"

"You c-could call it that. At first it was anxiety. I couldn't g-get through a day without a deluge of p-panic attacks. The world would shrink to a b-b-bead, then just black out. I started 'self-medicating,' as they say, and that m-made me really unproductive, which m-made me really depressed. I'd get sick of it every once in a while and go-go-go to the doctors. That's how I ended up in that therapy last s-summer. It must work for some people, that reliving things, but for me it just d-dug up corpses. I felt like I was living in a movie, some cross between *Apocalypse Now* and a z-zombie film."

I smile, because I think he means me to. "Hopefully, the credits are rolling."

"I don't know," he says, holding a bony hand out flat and watching it quake. "I n-n-never had *this* before. I might need a m-mainline for the s-soup."

"You'll be fine," I say, and I turn back to the pot and watch the bubbles come up through the broth.

"That looks g-good," he says, next to me now, watching the pot, too. "Want help s-setting the table?"

"Sure," I say, and I can see up close that small part of his hidden tattoo—droplets, maybe tears, in black. But I still can't visualize the rest of it.

"Where d-d-do you keep the spoons?" he asks.

I point to the drawer and he starts rattling through it. Together, we set everything out on the table and pull chairs and stools from here and there.

"I'll g-go get everyone," he says, heading off toward the deck.

I lift a noodle out and test it, and then I give the soup a final stir: chicken, sweet potatoes, parsnips, kale, chard, carrots, Jerusalem artichoke, garlic, turmeric, tarragon. I'm wondering now if maybe it's too odd a combination, too many different textures and flavors. Reminding myself that these are all things farmers grow for us here, indigenous or not, I dip a spoon in, blow on it, and take a taste.

Hollow Sounds

"That's right, 'essentials,'" I say.

"Like my cellphone?" one student asks. It's Nick. He's from a state faraway, one with taller mountains and people who don't buy their clothes at Walmart. Or so I'm to conclude from listening to his daily pattering of college town criticisms. His was the first name I committed to memory this semester.

A harder task than I expected, trying to keep all these students' names straight. I thought it would get easier, that the exercise would make me sharper. But my brain doesn't seem to shoo away the old faces, just opens the door to the new ones. Three semesters of this teaching, now, to chink the income gap. Three semesters of students crowding into my head. And you, still, John.

"If you consider it 'essential,' then, yes," I tell him. "Write about where it came from."

"It came from Best Buy."

"Before that," I say.

He takes the thing out of his pocket and looks at it. "Motorola."

"Before that," I say, and he looks stumped. "That's the research part. It's an essay to practice research and reporting methods. Find out what some of the component parts are, where they came from and who made them. Then explain what you've found to your reader, citing sources in MLA style."

The radiator sighs loudly, an audio track for those students who see this as an enormous pressure, writing an essay that can't be easily lifted from the internet like a literary analysis of *Frankenstein*.

"Maybe food would be easier," a young woman suggests.

"Okay," I say. "Where might your food come from?"

"The food court here," and in response to my *before that* hand gesture, she adds, "some kind of institutional food provider, and then…I have no idea."

"You've made the thesis too general. Pick one food, or one meal—steak salad, for instance. Figure out where each ingredient comes from. Talk to people, get on the internet. The lettuce grew somewhere. So did the tomatoes. The cow was slaughtered somewhere."

There are some facial expressions that let on who will be staying away from subjects involving meat.

"Do you consider a t-shirt essential?" a voice from a corner asks, and that makes a few students giggle, which is obviously the aim.

"Haven't ever before," I say, playing as if this were a legitimate question. "But if you have, that's fine. If it's made of cotton, that grew somewhere. Polyester? Made out of something. Where is the manufacturing done? Who does it? Local people? Children? Find out where the shirt comes from."

"Everything comes from God," a normally silent student says. Maybe her name is Marissa.

"Let's concentrate on what happens after the point of God's role, how about that?" I say, and I tap one of the tables that make up the semicircle we sit in, workshop style, which is how I like to run my classes. Many freshmen hate this, not being able to hide in a back row and tap-tap text messages to friends. "This table is made of oak, and let's just say, hypothetically, that it was made by a local woodworker who buys his supplies at a lumberyard at the edge of town, and that lumber comes from those mountains," and I point out the window to the Blue Ridge.

"Only that wouldn't happen," Nick of the essential cell phone says. "The government protects those *hills*." He never misses an opportunity to call the mountains *hills*, obviously finding some pleasure in insulting land forms. "It's a national forest. I went there with the Outing Club, for a little walk," he adds with a smirk.

I fight the urge to roll my eyes but am not as successful ignoring a passive aggressive itch. "That's wonderful, Nick, that you took a hike in the mountains. Then I guess you saw the sign at the entrance to the national forest, the one that says 'Land of Many Uses.'"

"Including *logging*? That's not okay," a young woman pipes up, clearly angered by the prospect. "We can reclaim wood. We don't need to cut down trees in an old growth forest. They give us oxygen. Animals live in them."

I could tell her about some of the other "uses," about how hydraulic fracturing is on the way, but I shy from any topics that could go political. I learned my lesson one day, early on, when I made the mistaken assumption that all teenagers learn the science of climate change in high school. I take a moment to glance at my computer screen, open the class list, and find this student's picture. I can at least use her name. "Good arguments, Lucy," I say. "I hope you bring that into your writing. A counterargument you may want to consider is the need for the government to have income. They may believe their methods show respect for nature."

"But what about respect for God?" It's maybe-Marissa again.

"Right," I say, and I give the table another pat rather than try to address that directly. "If you were writing about this, you would skip up to the act of man and machine going into the forest and cutting down the oak tree, and describe the processes and resources used to turn it into a piece of furniture—driving it down the mountain, milling the wood, crafting the table, getting it to a store. Include as much information as you reasonably can, within the confines of the assignment. Does that make sense?"

The rustling begins that indicates we are down to the last few minutes of class. It's like a breeze moving through the room—one person starts pushing things into a backpack and then the rest follow.

"Have your choice made for next class. Let me know if you want to bounce some ideas around. I won't be on email today, so text if you have a question." My voice has had to escalate to be heard over the noise of chairs moving, conversations already begun, the stampede to the door. But I let the pitch drop now, and my signature "See ya' on the other side" comes out in a more deflated way than I usually allow it to.

One of my students, Gabriel, has hung around, a football player who is always concerned about maintaining his grade point average so he is eligible to play. "I can't think of a topic," he says. He is of the belief that he's not smart, but the maturity it takes to communicate his concerns to me shows a kind of intelligence that matters a lot more than SAT scores. I have told him this.

"What do you consider essential to your life?" I ask.

"My brother," he says.

"Let's stick to the non-human, okay?" I make a mental note to be explicit on this point in future. Frightening thought, these students writing on where babies come from.

"Heat?" he offers now. He's from Florida, and our winter was tough on him.

"Okay," I say (*Bingo* is what I'm thinking) and I point to the radiator, which is gurgling in a threatening sort of way.

It is old and inefficient, sometimes stone cold but at this moment forcing out way too much heat for the first day of spring. "Do you know how that works?"

"Furnace?"

"A boiler, to be specific," I tell him. "Hot water goes through the coils and then the heat radiates out into the air. So, you might figure out how the water is heated, to begin with. The maintenance crew can tell you, and you can see where that leads."

Students have started streaming in for the next class, so Gabriel and I retreat into the hall and out of the building, and I point him in the direction of the physical plant before I climb into my truck and leave campus.

When I get home, I sense that the dogs are a little too quiet. Sirius is skulking guiltily. It takes me a few minutes, but then I find the source of the shame, a tattered corner of the couch. I know it is the younger dog and not Sirius who did this, but he seems to be taking the blame, if just for not successfully reining in his charge. I get down on the floor and pet my big dog. "It isn't your fault," I say, scratching him behind his ears. I try to pull Procyon into our embrace, but she doesn't understand the gesture and scurries off, going corner to corner in the room, never a good sign with a still-not-entirely-housebroken dog. I open the door and send them outside, and they race to the goat yard and start barking at Violet and the bucks, one activity they do come together on.

I peel off the "professional dress" I am required to wear at work (a makeshift ensemble today, involving a wraparound skirt and a shawl, as I have nothing I would call "professional" and buying a suit is out of the question on an adjunct salary), and I change into the uniform of my real life: jeans and a sweatshirt. I toss some things in the cooler in the back of the truck and call the dogs, who don't listen to me until I yell, "We're going to see Muriel and Mitch! *Mitch!*" Then they race over and hop in. Okay, another thing they agree on—a fondness for those kids.

At the food bank, I leave the dogs in the truck while I get the day's boxes and return to find Sirius barking at Procyon, whose jaws are around the gearshift knob. I have caught her in the act so can give her a correction for this. "Leave it!" I say, giving her collar a yank, and she looks up at me and then at Sirius, who actually seems to nod at her in my support, but that's likely my imagination. In any case, she stops the chewing and turns her energy to digging at the seat, as if it were a gopher hole. Threadbare already, I know the upholstery will not long survive this. "Leave it!" I say, and yank at her collar again. This is something I spend a lot of time doing these days.

The long drive out to west county calms her, and after a bit of wobbling she curls up on the seat and closes her eyes. The winding mountain roads make her carsick, so I have learned not to take her out on a full stomach. The truck still smells from the first time I discovered this problem, and I've been trying to mask the odor with bundles of lavender I gather from my cold frame and pile onto the dash every day. At first she kept eating the sprigs, which worked against the point of the effort in more ways than one, but she seems to have gotten the message on that infraction now. So there is hope that she can learn to behave and that Sirius will be able to relax one of these days. I look over at him, the poor exhausted dog, his neck resting limply out the open window.

When I have dropped off all the boxes but the one, I steer us to Shannon's house.

"This is weird," I say to her when she answers her door. "Muriel is not attached to your side."

"I know, right? Two days ago she up and decided to walk, and she has not hardly stopped since."

"Sounds like Procyon," I say, and the little dog pushes by, Sirius on her heels, and we follow, the prospect of them and a toddler on the loose a little frightening.

Muriel, who is indeed standing on her own, cries out with glee when she sees the dogs. It isn't long, though, before the excitement takes her legs out from under her and she plops down in the middle of the braided rug Shannon's grandmother made from clothing scraps. A rainbow from one of the room's prisms adorns the child's face, and that combined with the way she waves her arms at the dogs brings to my mind the Hindu goddess Vishnu.

"I have good news," Shannon says, moving things aside on her table to make room for what I have brought in. "I found morels! Took some hunting, but there's a little copse of trees over on the slope of that old sheep pasture, and it wasn't affected by any of the floods."

"No kidding," I say, taking the paper bag from her and peeking in at the dark, earthy-smelling chunks. Shannon is sure there are some of these growing in my own woods, but I have been unsuccessful at finding even one of these notoriously elusive fungi. "I saw some morels at the farm market last week—the price was outrageous! How do you cook them?"

"Simple. Soak them real well in water and rinse hard as you can so no dirt is left in the crevices. Then slice and sauté in butter till they're cooked through, like any old mushrooms. Chopped thyme is nice with them. Did you bring me some?"

"I did. The herbs are here in the cooler. I've also got

rosemary, sage, tarragon, and two kinds of parsley. I made you a couple of kefir sodas, too. Want one?"

"Thanks, but I think I'm in the mood for tea. You?"

I nod, and she adds a little water to her kettle from the jug on the counter.

"Where's Mitch?" I ask, realizing he has not descended on the dogs, a thing that usually takes only seconds when we come out.

"At Head Start," she says. "I decided it was time so he'll be ready for kindergarten next year. I want him to have a lot of confidence."

"He seems pretty confident to me," I say.

"But in a new environment, you know..." and her voice trails off. "You want Irish breakfast? Or would you rather chamomile-mint? It's that blend you made."

"You keep that for yourself," I say, though I'm starting to feel that a calming tea is what I should be asking for. "Irish breakfast'll be fine."

"That is some kind of good stuff, your chamomile-mint tea. You could sell that, you know, it's that kind of good. That and those kefir sodas of yours. My favorite is the one with the apple juice you got up at the orchard in Bedford. Or, *no*, that lemon one, with the ginger root you grow. You should set up a stand at the farmer's market: Leda's Concoctions. You could call it that. Coupled with your yarns, who knows, you might make enough money to quit that job you're always complaining about." She's not one for nervous chatter, but that's what this is.

She sets a couple of her pretty teacups and saucers on the table, and drops a teabag in mine and a tea ball full of mint leaves and chamomile flowers in hers. I just watch and listen to the clinking sounds, the murmur of steam building up inside the teakettle, Procyon rattling around in the toy basket in the corner of the room. Muriel, who is making chirping noises, gets up and holds onto Sirius's back. He remains stock still, his head tipped, eyes glued on her.

"I've never seen a dog so good with babies," Shannon says, pouring hot water into the cups and sitting across from me at the table. "He's like Nana in *Peter Pan*."

I decide it's better to just ask. "You're moving, aren't you?"

She sips her tea too soon out of her nervousness and sprays out the too-hot liquid. It strikes me as a spit-take, and I laugh despite myself. She laughs, too.

"That settlement for the Clean Air Act violations came through," she says, wiping her mouth and the table with a napkin. "Not a lot, but it'll get me started somewhere else."

As if a soundtrack to our conversation, there are three horn blasts, carrying on the strong westerlies of March. We wait for the explosions. Another mountain gone.

"I don't understand why our county doesn't stop this," I say.

"Yes, you do. The mining is affecting only we 'hillbillies in the hollers.'"

"It is wrong, what is going on."

"And that's why I'm getting that check from the coal company," she says.

"Oh, that just punishes them a little. And they move the toxins from the air to the water. Someone needs to stop them. They're like monsters—can't stop themselves." I let that replay in my head.

"And that's why I'm getting the hell out of here with that check. My kids are too young to be exposed to all this. In that last big rain, one of those slurry ponds overflowed and some of that gunk has found its way into the creek. Mitch came in covered with it the other day when he was out hunting tadpoles. I had *told* him to stay away, that there won't *be* any tadpoles this year. There won't be any tadpoles *ever*."

"Why don't we do something to fight this?" I say. "Let's take it on, Shannon. There are people fighting for the mountains. We can join in."

"Oh, Leda, the coal issue is so complex." She squeezes her forehead like she's nursing a migraine. "We Sullivans started working in the mines a real long time ago, and there are still a few employed by coal companies. There's an infighting that goes on, is what I'm telling you. Most people want to just let it go, stay quiet about the bad things that happen."

"Shouldn't be that way," I say. But I get it, all too well.

Procyon, I now realize, has been chewing off the head of one of Muriel's dolls, and I get up and take it out of her mouth. I don't tell Procyon it's wrong, don't have the spirit of "correction" in me at this moment. I just apologize to Shannon.

"Don't worry about it," she says. "I don't much like baby dolls, anyway. I'd rather she play with a tanker truck, or an airplane. Something with power."

I coax the dog back to where Muriel and Sirius are now curled up on the rug, her eyes closed, Sirius's open. Procyon flops over and I sit next to her on the rug and rub her soft belly, look around the room, at the walls, the children's art. There's generations of it, it seems. "How old is that, Shannon?" I ask, pointing to a piece of wood hanging by the back door. It has a bird scratched into it.

"Oh, that's gotta be a hundred and fifty years old," she says. "The drawing, anyway. My Irish ancestor, who came over as a little boy, used to go around in the woods and put that bird on everything. It was a game that Seanie and I played when we were kids, looking for them scratched into trees or painted on rocks. That one we found on the side of a fallen chestnut tree, and our granddad sawed it off of there and hung it up. It's an Irish bird."

There's always been something strangely familiar about that drawing, but I can't ever settle on what it is.

"Sometimes that's how Granddad tricked us into helping him gather creasy greens, or black walnuts, or persimmons, or ginseng, or whatever was ready to be foraged. He'd say, 'It's a-time for a bird huntin'!' and then, after we were up on the paths, he'd hand us the paper sacks." She laughs at this.

"Sean grew up in this house, too?" I ask.

"No, his family was up the hollow just a bit. Where the old pasture is."

I nod. I've driven by the house. Thought it was abandoned, on account of how dilapidated it is, but one day there was someone in a rocker on the porch. "Is that still in your family?"

She shakes her head. "Got sold a while back."

"So, what are you going to do with this house?" I ask her.

"My aunt and uncle live in a big RV upstate, and we're going to swap. They always wanted this one, it being the original Sullivan homestead. I warned them about how it is these days, but as loyal subjects of King Coal they figure I'm overreacting when I tell them it's like living near the set of *The Terminator*—gargantuan machines and explosions and smoke and all. They don't have any kids around anymore, so at least they're only risking their own bodies."

"Where will you go?"

"Heading west, far as we can get. Going in June, when the Head Start lets out. Then we'll have the summer to explore new communities, find a good school district before September, find a trailer park with some amenities."

"John and I lived in an Airstream for a year, when we were building our place. It was comfortable," I say. "Sold it, but there's still the hook-up at the end of the driveway. You can come visit any time you want, stay as long as you want."

"Thanks, Leda. You've been a good friend these months."

"*I've* sure needed a friend," I say.

"You should spend time with Sean," she says. This is a topic she's been bringing up, one I have been deflecting. "I think he might be sweet on you," she adds. A new twist.

"Why on earth would you think that? Since we met, I have never heard word one from him."

"He's just got a confidence problem in some departments," she says. "Always has."

"How's it going for him at the community college? Okay?"

"More than okay. He was afraid he had no concentration skills after all he's gone through, but he gets A's. Same as high school. He used to help me with my homework even though he was a year behind me. It's ironic that it has taken him all these years to get to college, because that's the entire reason he signed up for the military in the first place, so his education would get paid for. But the recruiters forgot to mention how you can come back with your brains so scrambled you can't read. You'd think they would've told us every little thing we needed to know, given how often they were strolling the halls of our high school and eating in the cafeteria with us post-9/11. I think they must have had Airstreams out in our parking lots."

I smile because she's meant for me to, but it's no joke that the teenagers with the fewest options end up on our battlefields. "What does he want to study?"

"How to sabotage large mining machines, I expect. But

they don't offer degrees in that. His program is alternative energies—windmills and solar, waste-to-energy, geothermal."

"That's impressive," I say. "So, how's his health?"

"He's off all those really awful meds, so he doesn't shake anymore. And that stutter only comes out when he's really anxious. Has a naturopath now, and an acupuncturist. He likes this chamomile-mint tea of yours, too, says it helps him sleep."

"So, I guess he hasn't had any more of those, uh, episodes," I say. I'm vague because I still don't what it was that went on in the fall, when Shannon was so upset with him. She's never filled me in.

"Nope," she says. "I know you may be worried about getting close to someone who has had mental health challenges, but he's doing well. And, anyhow, I'm not suggesting you get married. Just maybe have sex now and then."

"Don't be subtle, Shannon. Say what you mean."

"We're in our thirties, Leda. Sex is something we need. God knows I'm tired of gettin' it on with the image of a runaway man in my head, if you know what I'm saying."

"I know what you're saying." I flop onto my back on the rug and watch the ceiling fan blades move rhythmically against the air, making the prisms on their strings shiver.

Shannon holds a hand up, palm curved, moving it slowly till it catches one of the colorful darts at play in the room. It's something she often does, absentmindedly, and I'm always fascinated by how instinctual the act is, almost spiritual. She closes her fingers, then opens them again, seemingly letting the rainbow go free now. Then she slides her phone off the table and comes to lie next to me on the rug, scrolls through some pictures, then lets the screen hover over our faces.

"Where was that taken?" I ask, looking at the selfie-smiles of her and Mitch and Sean crammed into the frame.

"Folklife festival," she says. "Sean took us over the weekend."

"So he's more comfortable with the kids these days?"

"Getting there," she says, though there is something not so convincing in her tone. "Boy, he was fascinated with the sheep herding demonstrations. And the pie-eating contest, too. I skipped that event, but apparently there was some projectile vomiting that he can *not* stop talking about," she says, tapping the screen of her phone. This is the part when she sends me the picture.

She looks over at me. "You know I was meaning Mitch, right?"

"I was hoping," I say.

"Cute, that look Sean's got going, isn't it? His hair just got long enough for a ponytail."

It is a good look. But I don't say this. I don't encourage her. "Where was Muriel?"

"Same place she is now. In Lala Land," Shannon says, glancing at her daughter stretched between the two dogs, an arm flopped over Sirius, who still keeps an eye open, ever vigilant. Procyon, though, is snoring, out like a light. "So, will you do it? Invite Sean over or something?"

"I tell you what, Shannon," I say. "I'll think about it. But under one condition. I want to know what happened last fall, what you were hiding under his hat."

She grimaces, then exhales resignedly. "Okay. I'll tell you. You know Sean had a bad jag. I think it was a reaction to some meds he was prescribed mixed with some he wasn't prescribed, but in any case he was having what they call dissociative events. Do you know what those are?"

"Isn't it when you're out of your mind?"

"That's one way of putting it. So, he'd go off on a bicycle

or on foot, to who-knows-where and doing who-knows-what, and he had no clue what was going on. I kept telling him to get help, but he would not listen to me. Until, that is, he woke up one day on the floor of his apartment and his head was shaved and there was a fresh tattoo on his scalp. He thought he was hallucinating, so he came over here and asked if I could see what he could see, and I sure could. That's when he agreed to go to the hospital and check himself in."

"That's intense," I say. "But what is the tattoo? A swastika or something?"

"Oh, no, no," she says, "nothing antisocial. It just demonstrated his level of pain, you could say. It's a bullet hole."

I let out a laugh because I don't know how to appropriately respond to this. "Oh, Shannon, I can't go out with someone who has a bullet hole in his head."

"It isn't *real*," she says. "He can't even remember doing it, and you can't see it anymore, or not—" but she stops there, gets up on her haunches and looks down at me, because I have started crying. "I'm *sorry*, Leda." She has a look on her face that is pained, but also puzzled. Because what happened to you, John, is something I've still not filled *her* in on.

But I do now, I tell her all of it. *All*, yes, some in a whisper (the part I've never told you). And she holds me close, wipes my tears with the soft sleeve of her t-shirt. And it feels so nice, because no one has held me so tenderly since long before you left. A quiet sinks into the spaces around us, a sad quiet, full of all kinds of missing. And we hold each other there for I don't know how long, until I hear my phone pulse from across the room.

"I told students they could text me this afternoon," I say, getting up and retrieving it from my bag. "They're working on research and have a deadline." I open the message. "It's Gabriel."

"I like that boy," Shannon says, getting up, too. I've told her about him. She looks over my shoulder, reading as I do. The text may be a mess of misspellings, but his pride comes through in the details he shares. He's found that the boiler at the school runs on electricity, and he has the name of the company, is going to contact them and see how they make their power.

"He's researching where his *electricity* comes from? For most people, that's a greater mystery than God. The light just comes on—poof! Doesn't come from blowing the tops off mountains, oh no, not from filling streams with torn-up trees and toxic rubble. Not from houses taken off in floodwaters and children choking on bad air. Tell Gabriel he is a genius."

You're a genius, I say in my reply to him. "The assignment was actually El's idea," I tell Shannon. "It's all about the impact we have without realizing it."

"She's a genius, too, then," Shannon says. "Mitch just loves her."

"It was learning that he's exposed to all this bad air and water that got her thinking last spring. She realized that, at the heart of things, she's part of the problem, never paying attention to her own carbon footprint. She's even starting a conservation group on campus."

"Can you bring her with you next week? I'll keep Mitch home."

"I'll ask her," I say, calling the dogs.

Shannon takes my phone from me and begins tapping onto the screen. "Sean's number," she says, then hands it back. "In case you decide to call him one day." She gives me a hug, says softly in my ear, "He'd never hurt a fly."

"Thanks," I say, picking up the bag of morels and shaking it as I go.

Once home, the dogs race to the goats again. The bucks are waiting for them. Lately, there seems to be an escalation of tension between the caprines and the canines. Maybe, with Procyon getting bigger, the bucks find the dogs more threatening. They pound the generous flats of their curved horns against the fence, and the dogs stay right where they are, barking, nothing but 1/8 inch of steel mesh between them and the goats. I find myself wondering, worrying, that if there were no barrier between them—if a gate were left open, say— would the dogs understand that the goats, these animals they share the farm with, are actually capable of hurting them.

My phone whirs, and it is Gabriel again. He has texted that the electric cooperative runs their plant on coal, and he has the name of the supplier, Mountain Energy Systems. I tell him to research how they get the coal out of the earth, reminding him to take good notes, to document his sources. When I have sent that message off, I find myself pulling up Shannon's photograph from the folklife festival. And then I scroll through the others she's been sending over the months, some with her or Mitch or Muriel in the frame, all with Sean. The changes in him are fascinating to look at, a man's return from the Land of Nod.

I should call the dogs in for dinner, start my own. But I am drawn into your workshop. More mine now, John. My spinning wheel is in the middle, your old workbench covered with this year's cashmere harvest. Over the winter, I scrubbed the place good, and I had Emmett push your big tools into the storage closet and help me sort through everything else. You remember, he's the youngest son of Tillie's, now has a handyman business. He was interested in your wine-making kit, knew what a "carboy" was, even—you would have been impressed. So I gave him that whole bunch of stuff, and he said that was enough payment for the work. But it really wasn't, so I offered him some of your hand tools, and he picked out a few that would be useful to him. We also piled into the closet the pieces of your rooftop sculpture that have fallen. There is still a raggedy mass of that creation atop the workshop, which I considered asking Emmett to help me pull down, but in the end I didn't. I regret that now. Whenever there's a strong wind at night, the rusted pieces clanking together wake me up. Especially so when I've fallen asleep in the workshop. I keep our camping mat and sleeping bags in the corner, you see, so if I'm cleaning and carding the cashmere into the early hours, I can just curl up there instead of venturing out and worrying what harm might come to my dogs from out of the umbrage.

Your banjo, John, was the last thing I put into the storage, that day Emmett came. I didn't want it to get damaged in the jumble, so there it is in plain view every time I open the closet door. Which I do now, and I hold the instrument in my arms. It is something, really. I don't know how you did it. When you said you were going to make a banjo out of a gourd, I pictured a temporary, primitive thing. Who knew you could whittle and polish the skin of a swollen torso of a vegetable into something this fine? I hold it out to a ray of evening sun sliding over the fields and into the workshop door. It illuminates the tiny drawings you scraped around the sides: your simple suns in their yearly progress, rising up from curved lines, the outer contours of our view here, those three peaks of the Blue Ridge. I run my fingers over your summer solstice with its sun peeking out from far left; then fall equinox, its sun halfway along, dead center; then winter solstice with its rays far right; then the one I witnessed this morning, the waking of spring, the sun returned to equinox, due east. I tip the banjo just so, and the light touches the metal rivets, reflections dance on the walls. The leather you stretched over the front has darkened, seems ancient, somehow. Still, it looks as if it could've lasted your natural lifetime, this banjo, if you had given it a chance to try. I knock on its side, and the sound is hollow. I knock again.

But it's time for me to acknowledge that you can't hear me. It's time now.

Third Part

The Wickedness of Mankind

"First we do a timber harvest," the man on the television is saying.

"It's as if he's talking about bringing in the corn," the man on my couch is saying.

"And then we eliminate the overburden." The TV man is perky, proud of his work. It is apparent that no one has told him what this story is about.

My couch man knows. He says to the television, "Meaning of 'overburden': trees, rich soil, animals."

"Then," TV man explains, sweeping an arm in the direction of a worksite in the background of the shot, "we expose the coal seams." There is a cartoony crackle and he flashes for a microsecond in negative exposure, his darks where his lights should be.

"How do you 'expose the coal seams'?" This is the interviewer. Or just her voice. It is more like the camera itself is speaking to the man. Or God.

"MTR techniques. A very efficient way to get inside the mountain."

Couch man again translates: "Blast it apart."

"And after extraction is complete, we do a controlled gravity placement of excess material," TV man explains.

The faceless voice repeats that: "Controlled gravity placement of excess material." There is a pause, then: "You mean that you push all that stuff off the side, right?"

The shot zooms in for just a second on the man's hardhat, which has on its front the acronym for Mountain Energy Systems: MES. I—along with a laugh track—giggle at this.

The man hasn't heard any of this laughter, of course, but he's beginning to look suspicious all the same.

"Yes, we fill the valley with it," he says in a measured way.

"But isn't a valley a riparian zone?" the voice from the ether is asking.

"A what?" TV man asks.

"A riparian zone," the voice says. "Where waterways are. You know, those things that start in these mountains and then move east toward the Atlantic Ocean, giving life to people all along the way? Or, as in this case, giving toxic byproducts to them from your 'MTR techniques'?"

The MES man takes a step toward the camera and there is a scuffling before the picture goes black.

A moment passes, and then we are back in the same scene, and the voice, now attached to a young woman with palms flat against her cheeks and a look of Munch-esque surprise on her face, says, "I guess he had to go."

I laugh again. "You didn't tell me this was a comedy."

The camera pans out a little bit, taking in the whole woman (dressed, oddly, in bright green oversized boxer shorts), who turns to the next person she is interviewing. Excitedly, I pat the knee of my companion on the couch, and he smiles the same nervous smile he is wearing on the television screen.

"Sean Sullivan, a veteran who did two tours in Iraq after 9/11, came home to find a different kind of devastation in his own backyard in Appalachia," and she's the one sweeping a hand this time toward the view of the worksite, its tank-like machines rolling around debris piles on tarnished earth. "He is using the GI Bill to get retrained in new energy technologies. What is the project you are involved in, Mr. Sullivan?"

"We are a group," TV Sean is saying, "made up of residents of the mountains, students from the community college, and people from nonprofit organizations." He is speaking woodenly, as if he's memorized the lines. "We are petitioning the coal companies all throughout the southern Appalachian states to put windmills on summits instead of destroying the mountains."

"How is that working out for you all?" the woman asks.

"Not so well. There is resistance to change from the industry, of course, but also from the working people. They fear job loss. It takes going and talking to them in their homes and at community events. So we are doing that. We show them pictures of windmills in northern Appalachia, where they are being used successfully. I tell them that if I can learn a new skill, then anyone can."

"It is a mystery to those who study this," the interviewer is saying now, "that Appalachia is so terribly poor and has the highest unemployment rates in the United States, while there is so much highly valuable coal coming out of it all the time. What is the story with that?"

TV Sean says, "There has been a relationship of dependency and poor treatment since the first coal companies arrived in the 1800s. There were always promises of prosperity that never panned out for most Appalachians. And mountaintop removal mining takes that to a new level by not only destroying huge swaths of land but also decreasing jobs. It brings machines that do fast work and leave communities worse off than ever before."

The scene widens then to take in Sean's full height, including Betelgeuse at attention by his side, and the machines in the background speed up, sort of stop-action-like. They resemble four-wheelers racing around in a desert.

"Wow, that's high-tech," I say to real-life-Sean. "How'd they do that with you standing there? Blue screen, or something?"

"No, low-tech. There was more creativity than money put into this project, from what I could tell. The dog and I stood still for about twenty minutes while they shot that footage."

The interviewer is now saying: "Mountain Energy Systems says they reshape the land when they are done, to turn the sites into useful and attractive places for the local people. Have you ever seen any of these useful and attractive landscapes?"

TV Sean nods his head tentatively. "One was a golf course, which did bring some enjoyment, at least in terms of providing people with something to joke about when out having beers. You see, folk around here are not so keen on golf. It's not our style. And it's expensive. Most people here prefer summits and woodlands. They hunt, hike, fish and camp. We tried to tell the coal companies that."

"Did they listen?"

"Well, yes, they did start trying to make hills in their reclamation projects, covering them with pine seedlings and introducing some animals. Elk, for one."

"Did they like it there, the elk?"

"I think they did, maybe," he says. "Up until they'd finished eating all the pine seedlings."

"You're *funny*, Sean," I say, giving his arm a fake punch now. His bicep inside his t-shirt sleeve is harder than I expect it to be.

"They could've used a consultant there, someone with a wildlife background, maybe?" the woman asks TV Sean.

"Maybe. But the trees don't do well, even when the animals don't eat them," he says. "The taproots find the riprap quickly enough. It's all detritus from the explosions and not a healthy situation for plants."

"How about for humans?"

"The pollution is generally awful, in both the water and

air. There are studies now that have tracked a lot of diseases, cancer in particular, but I'm not an expert on that. You should talk to someone else."

"Good idea!" the interviewer says, and the camera zooms in to her face—all the way to her eyeball—then out again, and someone else entirely is standing next to her.

"Well," I say, "this *is* creative. Who are these production people you got hooked up with?"

"A group of students from the state university found us. They made this little film to show in schools and entered it into a contest. It was one of the winners, which is why it's on this network right now. 'Green Shorts,' I think is what they call the series."

"Ah, that explains the boxers," I say.

We watch the end of the segment, the interview with a health expert who discusses cancer clusters connected to coal-related pollution throughout southern Appalachia, and then the program advertises the episode it will be showing next week, another contest winner by students in Bejing, China, where everyone owns respiratory apparatus because of coal emissions and they often can't see three feet in front of them.

"Well, Mr. Sullivan, war-veteran-turned-windmill-expert, aren't you the cool guy," I say, flipping off the television. "Thanks for calling and asking me to watch that with you."

"Th-th-thank *you*," he says, the stutter surfacing for the first time since he arrived. I'm thinking now that maybe I shouldn't have insisted he let Betelgeuse go off and play with the other dogs outside. "I don't have cable," he adds.

"Oh, I *see*...." I nod, give him a sidewise glance.

"I don't mean that was the only reason I called. It was just a good excuse. Maybe that's not the right word, *excuse*. Wr-wrong connotation." He takes in a breath and lets it out, then another, like he is in a Lamaze class. "I think I'll start over. I've practiced this part about a hundred times so I have it down: Hi Leda, how are you?"

Though awkward, I can tell he's meant this to be humorous. "I'm fine," I say. "But does this mean we have to watch the show again? Because we can't. Unless it happens to be on YouTube. In which case, you should expect some attention from the public, because it could go viral."

"I don't like the sound of that. Social media makes me paranoid. And I mean clinically."

"But the whole point of the project is to raise awareness of the issues, right? If things change, maybe Shannon will think about turning that RV around and coming home."

"I wonder where they are right now," he says.

"If you weren't such a Luddite, you would know. She's been posting pictures on Instagram since she left."

"Luddite…. I used to know where that term came from." He bangs the heel of his hand against his forehead a few times, then says, "Something about weavers in pre-industrial Europe?"

"I always just thought it meant stuck in the past. I don't know the etymology, I admit."

"I looked that up once in the library, when I was a kid. I used to spend a lot of time there. It was a good place to de-stress after a day in school."

"What stressed you about school?"

"The usual, I guess—tough guys. And girls," he adds. He clasps and unclasps his hands, maybe a way he relaxes himself. "I could have that Luddite thing wrong."

"No, you got it, Sean," I say, because I have pulled up a definition on my phone. "Luddites were textile workers in the 1800s, 'famous for destruction of manufacturing equipment because they were upset by the reduction of jobs.'That is what you're doing, in a way, isn't it? Messing with the machinery of coal mining. Ideologically, anyway."

"Sometimes I do surprise myself," he says, and a shy smile comes over his face.

"See? Your memory got better," I say. "I guess the inner nerd is still alive and well. Still afraid of girls?"

His expression changes to one of *ouch*. "That's hard t-to answer," he says. "But my therapist says I really sh-should get out ahead of this."

I should tell him that I was just asking that to be funny, but now I'm curious about what "this" is.

"I've never had a relationship with a woman," he comes out with, in that stiff, practiced kind of way.

"Oh," I say, and I am taken by surprise at how deflated I am feeling at this moment. "You're gay."

"No," he says, "I'm heterosexual. I-I-I just haven't...*you know*."

"What?"

"I know it sounds impossible at my age. But I was too shy to ask anyone out when I was a teenager, and then I went into the service when I was eighteen, and, well, I didn't have many opportunities to meet women. And then after I got home the anxiety set in, and there was just no w-way *that* was happening. And everything pretty much got worse from there. I've missed over a d-decade of, uh, relationship exp-p-perience."

Nothing is coming out of my mouth, though I know there has to be an appropriate response.

"So wh-what is this Instagram thing all about?" he asks.

I think this nonsequitur is meant to be comedic, in a straight-man sort of way, but I am not sure enough to acknowledge it with a laugh. So I just switch my attention back to the phone. A text from Shannon is scrolling across the lockscreen: *Happy 1st date! Hope you get lucky!* I push that off, probably too frantically, and pull up the pictures she's posted.

"So...here she is in Tennessee," I tell him, and I show him a bungalow broken in half by a flood, Shannon in front with her arms around the shoulders of a couple.

"And here's one she took in...Tennessee, again." This one is of a couple standing over a bucket with black stuff in it. Shannon's caption reads: *The water from their well.*

"Now, here's the most recent one she sent," I tell him. It's of a school with several large coal silos looming over it, the air thick and gray. Caption: *Mitch will not be going here.* "That's from a few days ago, in Kentucky."

"She's been gone two weeks, and hasn't gotten out of Kentucky?" he says. "She won't get very far that way."

"Oh, now here's a picture she just loaded! It's of you, Sean, on the television screen."

"See, now, that's just what freaks me out."

"She says she got some people together and watched it," I tell him, reading her caption.

"How did she even know?" he asks.

"I told her about it," I say. "She also writes: *Sean sure looks cute on TV.* Want me to send a message back to her?"

He looks embarrassed in a little-brotherly way, and says, "Tell her she needs to drive faster and stick to the highways."

But I don't do that. Instead I type in: *Tell me you didn't know he was a virgin.* The reply shoots back immediately, all the more impressive considering the physical terrain that separates us: *Whaaaaaat?*

I turn the phone all the way off, and get up and push my feet into my muck boots. "I need to tend to the goats before it's completely dark out. Want to come?"

He nods and follows me out into the gloaming, to the narrow path I've been beating through the overgrown grasses.

"Is this Timothy hay?" he asks, in step behind me.

"Some, yeah," I say. "A nearby farmer plants it, comes and hays now and then. He leaves some bales for me, but takes most to use for his cattle. Mows all my fields when he comes—even those that aren't planted—which is nice."

"Country symbiosis," he says. "My family was like that. My grandfather had the bush hog, and my aunt had the milch cow, another aunt had chickens, we had apple trees. Each of us had a vegetable garden and enough hunters to keep the game coming. No money in our pockets, but I honestly never felt poor until someone told me I was, when I got to the county school."

"That sounds nice, not needing cash to survive. Not having to go out and take a job just for the sake of the paycheck."

"You need to teach this summer?" he asks.

"No, and *yay*," I say. "Don't get me wrong, I've been grateful for the work, and the distraction. But I've been yearning to make some things."

"What kinds of things?"

"For one, silk," I tell him. "Technically, the silkworm caterpillars make it, but I'll harvest their threads. I plan to spin it with the cashmere. I've been processing that fiber over the spring, when I can put some hours together, getting it all into runnings for the wheel. I have Violet's yet to finish. Saved the softest for last. It's still in the bag from back when I brushed her out. Well, mainly El did. Credit where credit is due."

"Is she around this summer?"

"No, she's gone home. It'll be a quiet one here."

"Just you and the animals in Elysian Fields. You've got a

great place here, Leda. Pasture, woods. What are the names of those mountains you see from here?"

"The middle one, straight east, is Rocky Ridge. In the winter, when the deciduous trees have lost their leaves, you can see why it has that name. There are boulders all along the top. And there, north of it, is Milly's Mountain." I always think of this one as breast-shaped, but I don't share this bit, especially given what I've just learned about my company. "I used to wonder who Milly was. Asked around the first few years we were here, but no one seemed to know. 'It's just its name,' the locals would say, seeming surprised that the question ever even came up. As if the mountain had parents who christened her 'Milly' and that was that."

"That doesn't surprise me. Mountains around here are definitely personified," he says. "The ones that stood over our house in the hollow were like guards. Protection."

A mist is rolling in, the way it does on a summer's eve, and it seems as if that word—protection—is sinking right into it.

"Good thing those are still standing," I say.

"Choking from valley fill, but, yes, I feel lucky that I can go back and see them there," he says. "You know, people go through actual grieving when they watch mountaintop removal in their homeplaces. I've seen it. First they're stunned. Then they get upset with themselves for not trying to stop it. Then they're depressed, then angry, and finally they just try to forget. If anyone had ever blown up one of our mountains when I was growing up, well, it would have been a lot like," and he pauses here, as if to make sure he means what he's about to say, "watching a human being turn to bits and pieces."

I don't know if his hesitation has had to do with my experience or his. I consider this as we tromp along, our boots sounding eerily soldier-like to me now. I wonder if they do to him, but I ask him something else instead. "What are those mountains' names in the hollow?"

"Whiskey Mountain—named for the moonshining that was done there—and Elephant Mountain. When I was little, I used to ask my grandfather why it was named that, and he would make up stories. One was about how elephants were living on it, too shy to ever be seen. Another story was that there was a big rock on top that was shaped like an elephant, but I never did find that. I looked awfully hard. Sometimes he'd tell one about how there was a tree that grew prolifically on that mountain—an elephant tree, taller than the rest of the trees—and how it dropped big thorny husks with delicious nuts inside, and people gathered them and roasted them and sold them. They built barns and cabins from the wood that grew thick as an elephant, the trunks over ten feet wide on some of them. But that last tale wasn't entirely made up, I eventually figured out. It was the story of the American chestnut, which was a real important tree here until maybe the 1920s or 30s, when it was lost to a blight brought over from Asia by someone who wanted to sell exotic plants for fancy gardens. The chestnut was the dominant tree on a lot of these mountains."

"Well, thank you, Sean. Now I know why *that* one got its name," I say, pointing off to the southernmost peak in the viewshed. "That's Chestnut Hill. Mostly pines up there now. You can get to a waterfall if you're willing to go through some brush." I peer over my shoulder at him. "If you want to hike up there sometime, let me know. I could show you."

"O-okay," he says.

I stop at a mulberry tree that I planted too close to the pasture fence. The leaves within the goats' reach are completely gone, as are the berries. But most of the branches they can't get to. Luckily, with the other trees I planted, I am finding that there are enough leaves for my new project. "This is what the silkworms eat, mulberry."

"Are they on there now?" Sean asks, gently touching a branch, twisting it enough to see under the leaves.

"No, they're not wild. It's a domestic insect, the only one on the planet. They've been used for textiles for so long that they have no real instincts. I have to gather these leaves to feed the caterpillars. My first batch is almost full grown, so they eat a lot. I'm out pulling leaves three times a day for their feedings. They live in shoeboxes in the workshop."

"No kidding," he says. "Can I see?"

"Sure. As soon as we're done here." I fumble with the hasp of the goat yard gate until it swings open. "After you," I say, and then snap the gate closed, give it an extra push to make sure it's secure.

We trod to the barn, and Sean helps me empty the galvanized bucket and slide it under the hydrant's tap inside. I stand over it as it slowly fills, and he leans against the barn wall, watching me. After a couple of false starts, he says, "Leda, back there in the h-house, I, uh, didn't mean to sound like, uh— I just w-want to be honest with you from the start. Not that I'm saying this is— I'm not tr-trying to be presumptuous about what you— It's just that if something happened, I mean l-later, not today, I'm not saying—"

He's flat out miserable, tying himself in knots. But I'm not sure how to rescue him.

"—I wouldn't w-want you to be surprised, or have to deal with something w-weird—" He runs a hand over his hair, then pushes it into his pocket and sighs. "I r-r-really shouldn't be bothering you."

One of the bucks, who has unfolded itself from a dark corner where all three goats have been in repose, has appeared in front of Sean. It lowers its head in a threatening way.

"Don't take your eyes off of him," I tell Sean. "I think he may be picking up an alpha vibe."

He looks at the goat squarely, says, "I don't think you'll find one of those here, Billy."

I consider the possibilities for a comeback, something to lighten up the atmosphere, but I'm actually getting worried now, as the other buck has gotten up and is moving toward Sean. I reach for a muck rake that's hanging on a hook from a ceiling beam. I used to whack the bucks with that in the days when they picked on Violet, but I'm not sure it's wise to use inside here, with Sean up against a wall as he is.

"Pretty big horns," Sean says, seeming oddly nonplussed about this. He reaches his hands out, one to each buck, and scratches the sides of their heads. I know they like that spot, just below the eye, now that I see him do it. They push their heads against his hands, like cats being petted.

"Let me get this straight," I say to Sean. "Talking to me can rattle you, but the possibility of being lanced by two one-hundred-fifty pound farm animals…not so much?"

That shy smile returns to his face.

I turn off the water now and head to the barn door, and he sidles away from the bucks and follows me. "Don't you need to feed them?" he asks.

"No. I know it's hard to see in the twilight, but there is a cornucopia of species on their acre here, so I only have to supplement in winter. That's when I use the hay. Right now they have cedar, wild grape, that invasive kudzu vine, brambleberries—it just goes on and on."

"What a paradise—a garden of eatin'."

"A subversive one," I say, letting us out of the gate and leading him back into the tall grass. "Two Adams and an Eve."

The fireflies have begun rising up in the fields, the three dogs in the distance leaping after them. In the fog, the blinking lights look downy, the dogs like cavorting spirits.

"See? Betelgeuse is on a lark," I say. "Aren't you glad you let him off work for the evening?"

"N-not exactly," he mumbles.

"He's a good dog, huh? Helps you?"

"In public, definitely. Crowds can be hard, and meeting new people. But sometimes it's he who is the stress. I have to care for him, and that's a worry."

"Why?"

"He's helpless, when it comes right down to it. He needs me to survive, and what if I don't deliver?"

"You do fine, from what I see." I could point out that he could loosen up a little, hug the dog now and then, but I don't.

"When I got back from my second tour, a niece of mine gave me a kitten, and I could not sleep a wink worrying that I might accidentally step on that thing when I was getting up out of bed in the night. Or it'd appear in my nightmares, following after me, skin and bones because I'd forgotten to feed it. I had to give the kitten back. The thing is, I had dogs and cats growing up. I never had any phobia about them. One of our hounds had puppies sometimes, and I'd be the one always with them, carrying them around, letting them sleep in my bed. I'd have to curl up in a corner for room, but I was happy like that. I was good with animals."

"I think you still are, judging by your talents at goat-whispering."

"It's different with cats and dogs. They're like children, which, of course, scare the hell out of me on a whole different scale. Something I was keenly reminded of in the past couple of months, when Shannon—for reasons known only to Shannon—kept trying to talk me into babysitting Mitch and Muriel."

I can guess at her reason. She would have bragged on that, told me all about, shared a picture of Uncle Seanie babysitting the kids. Obviously her attempts failed, but I ask anyway, "So, did you?"

"Babysit? No. It put me in a sweat just t-talking about it. Don't get me wrong. Shan's kids are great. That Mitch reminds me of myself as a kid. I just c-can't be in charge. What if something happened to them?"

What if something happened to them? I can hear John's voice saying that, his reaction whenever I revived the idea of having children. I never knew how to respond, so I'd let the subject die, every time. Never tried hard enough.

"What does your therapist say?" I ask Sean.

He hesitates, thinking maybe. "I guess we haven't spoken specifically about that. Given as bad as things got, a fear of kittens and toddlers seems minor. But, yes, I should raise it now that things aren't so out of control. I don't anticipate being asked to babysit, now that Shannon has left, but it'd be nice to get more comfortable with my dog."

I steer us onto the driveway, where we can walk side by side now.

"So, you think this therapist will, uh, lead you out of your PTSD?"

"Well, actually, he doesn't exactly *believe* in PTSD. Or not the name, anyway. He sees acronyms as stress factors in and of themselves. At first I thought that viewpoint was kind of useless, just a theory an academic might write about. But I get it now. It's like some destructive force is hiding in those big letters, crouched in the angles, ready to spring—PTSD, IED, PE, MTR. Bottom line, he thinks the focus needs to be on finding stress-reducers. Management. He tends to approach my issues as all part of 'traumatic grief.'"

"What stage does he say you're in right now?"

"I don't think it's linear with me, but more of an accrual. I saw a nature show once about the abalone, and how it builds up a shell over the years, made of calcium from the ocean floor. It doesn't shed anything. The shell just gets bigger and stronger. Does feel like I'm carrying something heavy like that."

I give his shoulder a lighthearted squeeze. "Is that why you've been working out?"

"It's one of those 'stress-reducers' the doctor ordered," he says. "The college gym is free, so it's easy to comply. I do weights every day, and then run five miles outside. Only I had to run an extra five the other day to get up the courage to call you."

"Explains the breathlessness," I say.

"Sorry about that. I was afraid the runner's high would go away and I'd have to run another five."

"Ah, endorphins," I say, nodding, "effective against anxiety *and* depression. Too bad it can't be bottled. Only then there'd be a co-pay."

"You seem to be handling your own grief well, Leda." Again, I pick up something practiced in what he's saying. I picture him in front of a mirror, making the hard words line up. Haven't done that in a while.

"I suppose," I say. "I see my grief as sort of like a trek into a ravine that's so steep I know I will never be able to get back up the way I came. I've gotten to the bottom, crossed over the water, and I'm working my way up the other side now. I don't know what's at the top, or if I even want to struggle that hard to get there. Maybe I'll stop along the way, set up camp and call it home."

"Nothing wrong with that," he says. "Assuming no poison ivy," he adds with a smirk.

"I don't react to poison ivy," I say.

"Lucky you."

We pass a patch of Queen Anne's lace, luminescent under the brightening moon, and I pluck a long stem, hold the flower between the two of us as we walk. "See this? It's the model for the crochet pattern I'm going to make when I get the spinning done," I tell him. "I love how intricate this umbel is—all the blossoms on it, each one so perfect, the creamy white petals flayed open. This is the exact color of the silk in its natural state. There's only one part of the flower head that's not white, and I'm thinking that I might use the fruits from the mulberry tree to dye some yarn for that part of the lace, to represent that teeny flower. It's in the very center, there," and I move it closer to him so he can see just how exquisite it is. "Pollinators land on this flower because they want to get to these soft red petals."

"W-wow," he says, "I always thought that w-was a weed." His voice cracks, the way a boy's might.

While Georgia O'Keefe might understand how a floral description can sound sensual without my intending it to, I worry that I have made Sean uncomfortable. So I find myself glad for something that usually just annoys me anymore, the clattering of what's left of the would-be-phoenix on the roof of the workshop. A wind gust out of the west has pushed through it, banging the metal against the roof and startling the both of us. We stand in front of the workshop, looking up together, as if at a steeple.

"Those are parts of an old still, aren't they?" Sean asks now. "I didn't notice that before."

"Yeah," I say. "That fiddler in my photograph, George, sold the still to John, showed him how to make a batch."

"Didn't turn out so good?" he asks, eyes on the weird mass of metal.

I laugh, in spite of the memory of that day he dismantled it. "No, that wasn't the reason he busted up the still. He was afraid he was becoming his father, a mean drunk. Abusive."

"Was he?"

I almost say *no*, as I did so insistently to John, never admitting. But he knew. He could see I was changing my clothes in the bathroom, wearing things that covered, instead of the strappy peasant dresses I favored on those kinds of spring days. He felt me flinch at his touch that morning after, before I willed myself to suspend disbelief. He knew. I look down at the granite stoop, the dark line of that drip gone now. I can't say for sure when it disappeared.

"Yes, actually," I say to Sean. "The night before he destroyed that thing he raped me. He had been changing for a while, something going awry in his head. But I think he could've tried to get better. Didn't have to go and destroy himself, too."

"I'm sorry," Sean says, and seems to be trying to work out what to add to that. Couldn't have practiced for this conversation.

"I'm working at it, trying to get over it all," I say, filling the gap. "To forget his violence, erase the memory of his death." I gesture to the open door. "See? Can you tell a person shot himself in there?"

Sean shakes his head, then, scuffing his boots in the gravel, says, "I hope this question doesn't bother you, but is the gun still around? Being near f-firearms is one of my phobias."

"It's gone now," I say. "Did take me a while to figure out what to do with it. I couldn't live with the idea of someone else getting shot with that thing, so I sure wasn't going to sell it. Finally I discovered an artist here in the valley who dismantles guns and makes the most interesting things with the parts. Animal sculptures, mostly. I gave it to him. Suggested he make it into a bear."

He cocks his head, says, "Why a—" but we're interrupted again by wind hitting the roof and starting another wave of clanking. A small fragment of the defunct piece of art flies off and lands near his feet. He crouches down and picks it up, looks at one side of the tarnished metal, then another. Then he holds it out for me to see.

"What is that?" I ask, but I know what it is—that bird, the one from the children's drawings, at Shannon's house in the hollow, the one that had seemed familiar. It was here I'd seen it, scratched into the side of that still.

"George sold the still to him?" Sean asks.

I nod. "He said it was an antique."

"It was," Sean says. "My grandfather sold it a long time back, to George's father. My uncle, Shannon's father, had developed a substance abuse problem, so our grandfather quit drinking and quit making the moonshine. Ballydonegan Dew, he had called his brand. He was a master at it, or so the old guys used to say. He learned the craft from his own grandfather." Sean rubs a thumb over the etched bird, says incredulously, "I haven't seen this since I was a kid and used to go up and help. I was a stirrer. I loved that hidden place in the woods."

"What a shame that the still's ruined," I say.

"It's all right," he says. "I didn't expect to see it again, in any kind of state."

A bolt topples off the roof now, lands in the grass. "I should take it down," I say.

"I'll help," he tells me. "I have classes this summer, but weekends are free," he says. "I was thinking of spending some time on the Crooked Road. Music is one of those stress-reducers."

"You planning to play?"

"No, just listen," he says. "I pawned my guitar in the wicked days. Do you ever go out there and sing, Leda?"

"But for some harmonizing now and again, I really only ever sang that one song, that one you remember from the party."

He pauses, and I wonder if he, too, is hearing that melody in his head. "You should sing some others," he says. "Your voice is like a keener's, you know. You have a way with a minor key. It made me think of Ireland, that day I heard it. Have you ever been?"

"No."

"On one of my leaves when I was overseas, I went to the Sullivan homeland, out in West Cork. They were miners there. Copper." He looks again at the shard that is still in his palm. "They came over during the Great Hunger. They lived in some poverty, worse than Appalachia. But what a place—mountains sliding off into the sea. There's good music over there in the pubs, too. Harps and mandolins, uilleann pipes." He pauses again. "You still have that gourd banjo?"

I nod. "When you come help me get that thing down, I'll pull it out so you can play."

"I'd have to teach myself. I never learned the banjo."

We're startled by another surge of wind, this one the strongest yet, that smacks the metal hard against the roof. Another bolt tumbles off and lands near the woodpile, once so towering but now a ragtag stack of logs that won't likely get me halfway through the next winter.

"Sean?"

"Yes?"

"I have something to be upfront about, too. You see, I almost called *you*. About twenty times. It's a war I've been having with myself."

"A war?"

"Yes. One side—I call it Now—wants to be with you. It fantasizes about you."

(I don't say that I'm not always sure it's exactly *him*. I stick to the broad strokes, the less complicated story.)

"Oh," he says. It is hard to read his response, but I go on anyway.

"The other side—I call it Forever—wants to have a baby."

"*Oh*," he says. This I can read.

"That's why I didn't call. May never have. Seems unfair, in a lot of ways."

Sean clears his throat. A mustering. "I never knew a war to be fair."

My eye lands on his neck, that droplet of ink I had wrongly guessed to be a tear. *Like a stigmata*, Shannon once said of the tattoo, given its strange appearance. I told her her Catholic upbringing was showing.

"But I have to admit," I say, "that I'm glad you called."

"The 'Now' is glad I called?"

I nod. "And if I had to put a wager on today's battle, I'd put it all on Now."

I take the few steps up and into the half-dark of the workshop. He follows me in, the chit-chit-chit of the room closing in around us.

"What *is* that?" he whispers.

"It's the silkworms, eating leaves." I motion to the shelves. "Children raise them in some parts of the world, keep them under their beds. The sound puts them right to sleep."

He takes in the room—the collection of small boxes, the spinning wheel, my stool, the piles of cashmere, a magazine and an empty coffee mug next to my jumble of sleeping bags and pillows on the floor.

I take his hand, so different than the one he offered me on that first day of winter. It is warm, vital. A resurrection.

Nobody's Darlin'

"'BUT THE EVIL ARE like the churning sea. It isn't quiet, and its water throws up mud and slime.' Isaiah 57:20."

"That has two! Slime *and* throw up," and he is bouncing in his seat now. "Do another one!"

"What haven't we searched yet? Mucus?" she taps that into the box. "Nope, sorry, no mucus in the Bible. What else you got?"

"I know I'm not exactly an expert on this subject, but isn't this sacrilegious?" I say from the kitchen counter, where I am drizzling olive oil over the lasagna.

"Of course not," El says. "God wouldn't have given us Biblehub if we weren't meant to have some fun with it. And Mitch is learning verses."

"Snot!" he cries. "Look up snot!"

"How about something nicer, Mitch?" I suggest.

"Yes, Mitch, let's pick something *nicer*," El says to him, "so the professor doesn't think we're blaspheming."

"Look up *dog*." He puts his feet on the sleeping Sirius's back as if he were an ottoman. The big dog is flopped on his side on the floor, Procyon curled up against his belly, where he just fits.

"Got it. Here's one, from Peter the Apostle: 'But it is happened unto them according to the true proverb, The dog has turned to his own vomit again.'"

I turn away from the cutting board and the rosemary I have just started mincing and give her my best dumbfounded look.

"I *swear* I only put in 'dog,'" she says. "God obviously wants Mitch and me to enjoy ourselves. And *you* seem to be enjoying it, too, judging by the grin on your face."

I try to wipe away my smile, but it is persistent, as it has been all day.

Mitch has his arms wrapped around her neck now. "I love you, El," he says. "I haven't seen you in a hundred billion days."

"You're choking me," she croaks, melodramatically falling over on the couch, her eyes open wide and her tongue hanging out.

"If Mama goes west again, I'm staying with you," he tells her.

"But I live out west, Mitch," she says. "That's where I was all summer. I wasn't here, either."

"Oh," he says. "Who was here?"

She cups her hands around her mouth and whispers loudly, "Leda and her boyfriend."

He giggles at this. "Where *is* Uncle Seanie?"

"He's at the library," I tell him, my attention back to the herbs.

"Is Beetle Juice allowed in the library?" Mitch asks.

"Sure," I say. "Service dogs are allowed anywhere. He just sits quietly while Sean studies. He's writing a paper."

"Betelgeuse is?" El asks. "You need to be clearer with your pronoun reference, Professor."

"I see you've been reading the style manual I gave you."

"Yes, and online resources," she says. "I did a lot of writing at home. Two short stories that are linked, both set on an Oklahoma reservation that keeps having earthquakes. It's an allegory of the Book of Revelations."

"Sounds chaotic," I say.

"Oh, *it is*. I'm going to be working on a third one in my creative writing class, once we get past the poetry unit. I'm thinking of setting this one on a mountaintop—locusts, seraphim, coal company CEOs. I need a character to represent

Isaiah. Maybe Sean would be a good model for that. When is he coming around again?"

I look out the window to the bend in the driveway that his truck so often now comes around. My heart always skips a beat when I see it emerge from the cedars. Only I'm never sure, really, if the skip is for Sean, or if it's a form of muscle memory, my heart recalling another truck, one loaded with scrap from the lumberyard or logs to split. The thought has made my smile fade, but it returns now, from the scent of the rosemary leaves I chop. So incredibly potent. So *fascinating*.

"Sean'll be here tomorrow," I finally say. "We're going to the fall festival at Fairy Stone Park. The jam starts at noon on the outdoor stage. Can you come?"

"No, I have services and then there's a picnic," she says. "It won't technically be fall yet, by the way. The equinox doesn't come in until nighttime tomorrow. I'm keeping track. See? You've had an influence on me."

"Environmentalism *and* pagan worship," I say, shaking my head. "I better work fast at getting this farm producing, because the provost is going to boot me out of that school soon enough."

"My dad made chicken tractors this summer. You should try that here. They're not at all expensive to build, and you just roll the whole pen along to a new spot when the chickens have eaten up all the bugs and grass. They leave behind a freshly composted bed to plant in, so you can grow more veggies at the same time you're getting fresh eggs and roasters."

"That's an idea," I say. "The yarn is coming nicely, though. The silk costs nothing to make, but it's time-consuming gathering the threads. I hope I can get a good price."

"Maybe with all that's going on here, you could just stay home and farm and craft. You'd pollute less, too, because you wouldn't be driving to school all the time." Then she adds, "Not that I want you to leave there. Nor would Gabriel."

"Did he join your club? *What* was it you decided to call it?"

"Canaanites. Dwellers in the land of milk and honey, and determined to keep all that flowing. We're making posters right now. You'll see them around campus."

"Let's play more Bible, El," Mitch says, putting his hands on the keyboard of the laptop. "How do you spell 'blood'?"

"I'm kind of tired of that game, Mitch," she says. "But I'll share a verse from memory, how about that? Here's my very favorite: 'Yes, though I walk through the valley of the shadow of death, I will fear no evil: for you are with me.' Psalm 23:4."

I look over at her. "Nice."

"I was just rereading Psalms, because the dean suggested I spend more of my days with the good books, as he calls them. He's been worried about my getting caught up in 'liberal causes.' I told him I just think we all should be a little more aware of how we affect others. 'Like maybe if you turn out that light on your ceiling,' I said to him, 'and open the blind to the sunlight that is right outside your window, then maybe my little friend Mitch will be able to move back home someday.' And I explained about how life is in the hollows, and how we should try to reduce our coal use, and he agreed to turn the light off if I agreed to turn to scripture."

"Sounds like a fair trade," I say. "Mitch, you do like the RV, though, don't you?"

"It's a spaceship," he says, correcting me. "We're landed on Venus right now. I like it bestest when we stay still."

"Looks like it'll be here for a while," I tell him. "Your mama went to the first PTA meeting last night and came home pleased." I open the oven door and push the pan in, set the timer. "You like the kindergarten here, don't you?"

"I guess," he says. "They have hissing cockroaches."

"What do you do with them?" El asks.

"We look in at the holes on their sides, where they squirt the air out to make hissing sounds," he says. "We study them with magnetizing glasses like we are antimologists."

"Be careful not to step on one if you drop it," El says. "I saw that happen once at a museum in Tulsa. The bug was crawling around in a kid's hand one second, and then the next it was white goo on the floor and she was crying her head off."

"I'm real careful," he says. "I love those bugs."

"More than you love me?" she asks, getting up.

"No," he says, jumping off the couch and following her as she moves around the room. The dogs get up, too, and join the parade.

"More than you love Violet?" she asks, sliding her feet into the shoes she left by the door.

"Maybe," he says. "She's gonna have a baby, you know, any day."

"I heard! I'm going out to see her now."

"Just look over the fence at her, okay?" I ask. "Sean and I set up a temporary pen in the corner, to keep the bucks out, but I'm afraid they're going to nudge their way in if too many of us are in and out of there."

"And Leda isn't letting the dogs bark at her. She sprays them with window cleaner."

"Say what?" El looks over at me.

"It's water. I just put it in an old window cleaner bottle. When I discovered the kid was on the way, I figured I should do a better job of calming the dogs so they don't keep getting the bucks all riled up." I hand her the water bottle. "Just spray them right in the face and say 'Leave it!' if they start barking."

"Yes, I know the drill. We used water pistols at the animal

shelter," El says. "It startles them and then they forget what they're doing."

"Why can't we use a water pistol?" Mitch asks.

"I'm just more comfortable with the spray bottle," I say to him.

"But why?" he asks.

"I don't like the idea of pointing guns at the dogs, even if they're plastic."

"Your dogs are plastic?" El asks, and I gather her point is more to change the subject than to call me out on another grammatical ambiguity, right though she is about that.

"*Nooo*," Mitch laughs, "the dogs aren't plastic!"

"*Ohhh*," El says, opening the door and guiding him out, Sirius and Procyon pushing past them both. "Tell me more about those hissing cockroaches, Mitchy."

"My teacher thinks one is growing babies inside it."

"A lot of that going around," El says.

"Yeah, and they make fifty hundred garillion at one time," he tells her. "My teacher says she'll give them away, but Mama says they're too gross."

"They are," El says. "That's the beauty of them." And the screen door moans and closes behind them.

Alone again, I consider a repeat performance of what I did this morning soon after I got out of bed—dance with abandon throughout the house—but I let go the urge, pull off my apron, hang it over a chair, and wander out onto the porch. I watch El and Mitch skipping to the goat yard, then I take a last look at today's sun. A Forever sun, I've been calling it all day. Not one cloud obscured it in its entire journey across the sky. It touches the horizon as I watch, begins its swift fall into the trees. And with that I get the pang of guilt I have been pushing off all day, refusing it an audience. I take a deep breath and head up to the top of the driveway, the sun now a black hole in my retina, something I have no choice but to follow until it is gone on its own. I hear Shannon's voice before I am up the steps and in the RV.

"There's a little city park, yeah, that's where they show films on the green, and *believe it or not* there's an authentic drive-in movie theater just up the valley about twenty miles, and I will check that out too—*Hey*, Leda's here. I need to talk to her, so I'll see you later on."

"Hi Leda, bye Leda!" I hear from the tablet computer, and I lean in and wave, say, "Hey, Dot!" but her face moves herkily-jerkily and she's gone in a poof. I'm getting now why Mitch thinks of this as a spacecraft.

"Go-go-go!" Muriel is yelling from the other side of the gate Shannon has rigged up to keep her a safe distance from the RV steps. "Go! Go!" She is looking at me insistently.

"She isn't telling you to leave," Shannon says. "Not that I know what she *is* telling you. She woke from her nap with this in her head and nothing else. I can't figure it out. I've gone through all her favorite foods and her toys, but none seem to be 'go-go.'"

"Go-go-go," she says, reaching her arms up to me, so I pluck her out from behind the gate and sit her on my lap at the drop-down table across from Shannon.

"She's grown so much in these few months. It's amazing," I say, stroking her hair, down to her shoulders now, cut straight across at the bottom.

"She's full of herself, too. Walks with a swagger, I swear. I blame Dot for that."

I nod toward the now-black screen of the tablet. "So what radical tree-hugging activism do you and Dot have in the works?"

"We've got a couple of showings lined up of that *Coal Country* movie. Your park system here says we can do it for cheap in the town square. We'll have some refreshment sales and put out a donation can, and that'll cover expenses. Can't charge admission. Copyright laws and all."

"Such a good idea you and Dot have," I say. "People like to go to movies. Much more so than reading up on a topic. And it's powerful seeing that footage of exploding mountains, hearing real people talk about it."

"Are you really sure it's okay for me to set up here? We're not a bother?"

"Stop asking that, Shannon. I'm glad you're here. Stay as long as you want."

"The school year, that's all we should need. After that, we'll take off and land somewhere else."

Mitch's spaceship metaphor comes to mind again.

"With all the artists around, and the organic farmers, and the people at the colleges," Shannon goes on, "Dot calls this valley 'fertile ground.'"

(I hide an uncontrollable smile by giving Muriel a nip on the neck, making her giggle.)

"Yeah, Dot is really good with the political end of things. She gets email addresses and works up petitions—*Oh*, that's what I needed to talk to you about. Dot is going up to a protest in Washington this week, at the Capitol, and she wants to slide by and pick me up on the way. Would you mind getting Mitch to and fro the bus stop for a day or two, and keeping an eye on him? I know he can be a handful. I could take him."

"No, it's fine. The dogs and goats keep him pretty amused," I say. "You want to leave Muriel? I could cancel a class and have my students email their assignments."

"Go-go," the little thing says, her cheek brushing mine as

she leans her head on my shoulder.

"No, but thanks. Muriel's a good traveler. And she is also a very good little activist. Last rally we were at she held a sign and got herself on the local news."

"Well, okay. You *are* coming to the festival tomorrow?"

"Definitely. Can't wait to see you and Sean do that song. Good sign that he wants to perform, right?"

I nod. It is.

"I got to warn you, though," she goes on, "Mitch gets nuts-nuts over bluegrass. I need to get him some proper dance lessons. And that 'Sail Away Ladies' is his *favorite*."

"Yeah, Sean said he likes it."

"That's an understatement. When we were at that folklife fest we went to with Sean, a group was playing that song, and Mitch was wild with some kind of crazy footwork he was making up as he went along. *Somersaults* and things. Sean was beside himself worried that Mitch would crack his head open."

"Huh," I say. "He didn't mention that part."

"Well, Sean is a few notches more relaxed than when I left," she says.

"The music has really helped. He took to the banjo. He's good. Wait'll you see."

"He was learning all *kinds* of new things this summer, wasn't he?" she says, her head tipped and eyebrows raised.

I set my hands over the baby's ears, anticipating where she's going with this. "Don't listen to that mama of yours," I say.

"Clawhammer, sex...what other educations-of-Sean were going on?"

"He's a fingerpicker, not a clawhammerer," I say. I was relieved that style came more naturally to him, that he wouldn't be sounding so much like John running his hands along those same strings.

"I bet he *is*," she says.

I give her a *You're obnoxious, you know that?* look, and say, "No love interest on the road for you, then?"

She looks now like a cat who has swallowed a mouse.

"*Oh*," I say. "*Tell.*"

"It's someone I've been mentioning since I got back."

"You've been telling me about a lot of people, Shannon. I'll need some clues."

"Okay. It's someone that shares my same concerns."

"That isn't helping."

"It's someone who—*shit*, I'm no good at games. It's Dot."

"Wow. That's news," I say. Then, "*Really?*"

She nods.

"Have you, uh, *always* been…."

"Bisexual? You're feeling insulted that I never made a pass at you, huh?" she gives me a faux-coy look.

"*No*," I say. Then, "Maybe. Or not so much *that*, just you not, uh, sharing that."

"It was news to me, too. Or kind of. I didn't understand the signs till I got myself out of that hollow where I'd spent every minute of my life. Something about the change—it was like that what-do-you-call-it, metamorphosis. I felt like I was turning into a more fully developed person on the road. And then I met Dot in Kentucky, and a lot of things started making sense."

"So that's why you never got out of Appalachia."

"Partly. Truth is, Leda, I belong to these mountain ranges. I tried pushing past, but a force kept pulling me off the highway. I needed to see if it was bad for others like it was for us. And I found out it was *worse*. I decided not to care anymore that I have relatives working in coal. I mean, they have little concern for the health of my children, so why should I care about their jobs? The very next day after I got my mind set on that, I met Dot."

"How'd you meet?"

"At a movie, actually. One night, I saw there was a showing of a documentary about a mountain in West Virginia and a community fighting mountaintop removal. It was being shown in the local theater, and since the kids had been having a hard time sleeping—the air conditioning in this vehicle is a joke—I decided to go to the theater to get us all cool. The kids conked out right off, which was a *good thing* because I hadn't thought to look at the rating. The movie was 'ecosexual' themed. Definitely not Disney. Afterwards, I let the kids sleep in there as long as I could, but had to rouse them up eventually, and by that time there were only a few people in the lobby. One was Dot, and she asked me to sign a petition, and we got to talking, and, well, that turned into the rest of the summer. And we worked out this whole plan to take coal documentaries on the road. Only not that one. At least not for family showings."

"So, you and Dot just plan to see each other at these movies, and rallies and things?"

She nods. "And she'll crash here in the RV sometimes. The kids make her jumpy—she's never really been with children—so I don't think she'll be around here much. Which is fine. Whatever happens happens."

"Then you don't see yourselves as a couple in the long run, is that it? You don't call it love?"

"I call it love," Shannon says. "Dot calls it love."

I look around the RV, at Shannon's colorful scarves everywhere. They make this new home of hers whimsical, corners of chiffon and silk and satin flapping from the rearview mirror, from the gearshift knob, from every drawer pull, and all along the top of the baby's gate. Muriel is reaching from my lap for one that hangs from a window latch. She can't quite get it, so she blows on it instead, then giggles as it comes alive. Then she does it again.

"I like your style, Shannon, that 'whatever happens happens,'" I say, sighing. "Wish I could adopt it."

"Is there some problem, Leda?" she asks, looking concerned now. "Seemed like you and Sean were getting on fine."

"Real fine," I say, nodding. I think of Sean's gentleness, how well our bodies fit together. "That's the problem. Mainly because of this whole matter of, well…" and I hold Muriel's perfect little hand in mine, the fingernails so small and pink.

Now Shannon sighs, only more dramatically. "Why can't you just let yourself have a good time *right now,* and worry about having a baby *later*? Who knows—Sean himself might get it together. You don't know what all will happen. There's *time.*"

"Um, actually," I start to say, but the ring of the Skype phone interrupts me.

Shannon pushes a button, revealing Dot's face again on the screen. "Is this too soon?" Dot's pixelated mouth asks.

"Yes, it is," Shannon says to her. "Take a chill pill and I'll buzz you." She signs off and turns back to me. "She has got a compulsive sort of personality, that Dot. Gets all excited about things and can't turn down the clock speed."

"A go-getter," I say.

"She is. But let's get back to what's making you sad."

"I'm not actually *sad*, that's the thing. I was bouncing off the walls happy all day, which is why I didn't come up here to see you before this. I knew reality would seep in once I put it into words."

"Put what into words?" She is looking a hole in me.

"I'm pregnant, Shannon," I say. "I took a test this morning."

"No *shit*," she says, and she scoots around the table and hugs me, Muriel squished up between us. "That's what you want!"

"But what about Sean? I feel evil, like I've set some kind of terrible trap for him."

"*Did* you?" she asks, sitting back down, her chin propped in her palms, ready for a juicy story.

"No! It was an accident. We were out hiking on Chestnut Hill, to that waterfall I like, and, well, I guess neither of us expected to be visited by Eros out there. I mean, there's no sensible place for that. Sean got a terrible case of poison ivy."

"Just *him*? she asks, eyebrows raised.

I choose to ignore that and continue on with my train of thought. "Not that it turned out to be necessary, but after that we made sure we were always prepared, no matter where we went. There's just no telling what'll happen once we touch each other. Or look at each other, for that matter. There's not much control there, between the newness of it all to him and, well, I don't know what to call it with me."

"Why can't you just call it *love*?"

"*Is* it love? Or am I just *remembering* love, projecting it onto Sean somehow? Sometimes he even *smells* like John, I swear. I feel like I'm cheating on him."

"On who—Sean or John?"

I meant Sean, but now I'm not so sure. I shrug.

"Leda. You. Think. Too. Much." Her chin has punctuated each word. "So, how far along are you?"

"About six weeks, by my count."

"What will you do?"

"Run away!"

"You're kidding," she says.

"I am. But maybe Sean should. I'm going to give him the out, convince him he doesn't need to worry about this at all, that I'll be fine taking care of a baby on my own. I would, you know. I've long had a sense that that'd be the only way I'd ever end up with one. Sean talks about going on another road trip, getting another motorcycle. Might be a good idea. Clear me out of his head."

"I don't see *that* happening even if he got the most powerful Harley on earth and then drove nonstop to Alaska at two hundred miles per hour," she says.

"Go-go-go-go!" Muriel cries, now scooting her whole body toward the open door of the RV, shifting back and forth like she is riding a rocking horse.

I take this as a cue to check on the lasagne and start a salad. "I'll bring Muriel to the house with me," I say, nodding toward the computer as I get up, "and give you some privacy with Dot."

"Oh, shut up," Shannon says. "You and I are going to *talk more later*."

I hold Muriel close and safe, and begin down the RV steps, my smile pushing up against my cheeks again, despite the forces trying to keep it down.

"You put those hot peppers I brought into the lasagne?" Shannon asks.

"When I sliced one, it about knocked me over," I say, stopping on the gravel of the driveway and looking back up through the door. "So, no I didn't."

"They aren't *that* spicy," she says. "Must be that your senses are sharpened from the pregnancy. With Mitch, I couldn't go near anything evenly remotely pungent or I was retching immediately. Kind of the opposite with Muriel. I was surrounded by a sweet smell, like a fog that clung to me. It was so familiar, but I could never identify it. Sometimes that made me retch, too."

"Thanks for all that," I say, feeling a little queasy now myself as I head back up to the house.

The next day I am especially glad to not have eaten anything spicy, because I wake with a nervous stomach, and the feeling stays with me right up to the time of the music jam.

"Never had butterflies those times John and I played," I whisper to Sean, as we wait for our turn to perform. The trio on stage is doing a rendition of "Rocky Top," a song played so often in these hills that it seems indigenous, like swallows in the morning, cicadas in the evening.

Sean whispers back, "We don't have to do it. Someone else'll jump in."

He puts his hand over mine, which rests in my lap, and he touches each knuckle, as if he is mapping my hand. The feeling of his skin is calming. "I'll be fine," I say, loudly now, the audience giving a boisterous applause to the musicians.

"Time to go! *Go!*" Mitch yells at us, his mouth open so wide it's as if he has suddenly turned into a cartoon character. He grabs his little sister's hand and starts pulling her to the boards that have been set on the grass for dancing.

"Go? Go?" she is saying, her eyes like saucers, scanning the place as she is tugged along.

"Careful, Mitch!" Shannon, cries, bolting after them.

We take our place on stage, the two of us and Betelgeuse, who stands tall next to Sean's stool. He has the gourd banjo on his lap and checks its tuning, then waits for my nod from my place at the standing microphone. He picks the opening chords with his fingertips and we begin.

Me: *I got a home in Tennessee*
Sean: *Sail away, ladies, sail away*
Me: *That's the place I wanna be*
Sean: *Sail away, ladies, sail away*

And now I am singing the chorus, and I think Mitch's voice is drowning out my own, in spite of his lack of electronic amplification: *Don't you rock, Daddy-o; Don't you rock, Daddy-o; Don't you rock, Daddy-o; Don't you rock, Daddy-o.* He lets me and Sean take over for the next verse, but keeps perfect time by stomping the boards.

Ever I get my new house done
Sail away, ladies, sail away
Give the old one to my son
Sail away, ladies, sail away.

And the *Don't you rock, Daddy-o* chorus comes again, Mitch's voice even louder this time, while he flings himself around the floor, his hand still attached to his sister's arm, Shannon somehow attached to her other side, trying to keep her upright.

Come along boys and go with me
Sail away, ladies, sail away
We'll go back to Tennessee
Sail away, ladies, sail away

And by this round of the chorus, Shannon has managed to catch up with Mitch's other hand, so they are dancing in a circle. Then we get to the verse that I anticipate, correctly, to be his favorite.

I chew my chew and spit out juice
Sail away, ladies, sail away
I love my son but it ain't no use
Sail away, ladies, sail away

The boy is in such a frenzy at this point that I wave him

onto the stage to sing the chorus with me at the microphone. After I lip-read a demonstrative *Thank-you* from Shannon, we hit the last verse and another chorus and then finish to robust applause, though I don't take that as an indication of our talent. People are just supportive at jams.

We inch our way through the row and back to our seats, Sean in the lead with the banjo held above his head with one hand, his other in mine, and Mitch holding onto the back of my cotton dress and starting in on a reprise of the chorus on his own.

"What a nice family," I hear a woman in our row say to the person next to her, and I glance at her face. She is smiling in our direction, but I don't openly acknowledge that I have heard her. I settle back onto my folding chair and watch the next group take the stage.

"Look, it's George," Sean says.

And it is him, up on the stage now. He looks a little worse for wear since the days of our parties, but you wouldn't guess at any ravages of time just listening to his dainty taps with the bow, it pressing more firmly now and bringing up that woebegone purr that only the best fiddlers can.

"Makes your heart hurt, the way he plays," Sean says.

"Yeah," I agree, the warming-up of the strings reminding me of what I have to do today, and why the butterflies, apparently not born of stage fright, remain in my gut.

Sean leans over after the opening riff and asks me if I'm okay, because he recognizes this as the song I sang with John. I tell him I'm fine, but in truth the words sting as they fill the air, cover my skin, make it hard to breathe.

Come sit by my side, little darlin'
Come lay your cool hand on my brow
Promise me that you will never

Be nobody's darlin' but mine.
Be nobody's darlin' but mine, love
Be honest, be faithful, be kind
Promise me that you will never
Be nobody's darlin' but mine.

I push myself up from my seat, tell Sean I am going to take a walk. His eyes ask if I want company, and my eyes say no. I take the nearest trail, several stemming from this stage in the woods, and I find an old oak, set my back against its rough bark and wait for the last verse to find me.

Goodbye, goodbye little darlin'
I'm leaving this cold world behind
Promise me that you will never
Be nobody's darlin' but mine.

I think of how this had become my standard work song on the farm—at first practicing to perform it, then as the involuntary soundtrack to chores, sung softly under my breath, phrases occasionally coming out in contorted bursts when it was necessary to lean into a task, like putting extra pressure on clippers when a goat hoof was especially overgrown. That day—that last time I let this verse wend past my lips—I had taken care of the bucks first, gotten them out of the way, and was holding onto Gretel's right front leg when I heard the sound. John saying goodbye, goodbye.

"A fairy stone!" It is Mitch, his voice reaching me before any sight of him on the trail. Soon he is in front of me, though, his hand outstretched. In it is a small rock, in the shape of a cross.

"It's made of a fairy's teardrops." He takes a long look at my face now, pauses, and goes on with his story. "You see, there were these fairies that lived on this mountain. Uncle Seanie says the fairies came from Eye-land, hiding in the pockets of all the people who sailed over the land-a-goshen because they ran out of taters."

"Close." It is Sean, who has come up behind him, looks at my face as Mitch did, but lets his gaze glance off. "Hey, buddy," he says, "you shouldn't run off like that. It's not good to be alone in the woods."

"I was following Leda," he says. "And I know this park good. Papa used to take me here."

Sean pokes the boy's shoulders—a gesture that strikes me as, if not natural, something trying awfully hard to be normal—and says, "Why don't we walk together a little bit, you and me? And Betelgeuse."

"But then *Leda* would be alone in the woods," Mitch says.

"She's grown up, Mitch. She can be alone if she wants to be."

"Do you want to be?" Mitch asks me now, wide-eyed, bringing to mind that first time I met him, the frog in his hands.

I am not at all sure how to answer that. So I say, instead, "How about you tell me more about the fairy stone?"

He holds it out in front of him again. "The tears turn to starlight, see?"

"Staurolite," Sean says, correcting him. "That's the kind of rock it is."

"That's what I said, starlight," Mitch says. "And when you find one, you have to hold onto it until you make a wish, and then you have to put it in someone else's pocket so the wish comes true. And that person has to keep it till he makes a wish and puts it in someone else's pocket, and that goes on and on until the rock ends up in the same pocket where a fairy lives, and then it melts back into the fairy's eyeballs, where it belongs."

Sean, whose back is up against the oak now, leans over and says to me, "He made all that up."

"Nuh-*uh*," Mitch says. And he looks down at the stone, pinches his eyes closed for a second, then opens them and looks at my dress searchingly. He pulls at the light fabric here and there.

"What do you do if there's no pocket?" Sean asks him.

The gears seem to start moving in Mitch's head, a tall tale forming, but I show him my pocket before a new plan is necessary. It is a hidden slit on the side. He drops the stone in.

"What did you wish for?" I ask.

"That I can have my own hissing cockroach," he says.

"Just one?" Sean asks.

His eyes get wide again, and he darts to the edge of the path and begins sifting through the dirt, looking for more of the stones, humming "Sail Away, Ladies" as he works.

We watch him there for a while, and then, in an uncomfortable kind of way that shows Sean has been practicing this next step in his head, he whispers in my ear, "You're somebody's darlin' now." I should tell him what I have been practicing in *my* head. I should tell him right now. But I don't.

There isn't much left of daylight by the time we pull into the driveway, but enough to see what Sean is pointing to when he stops the truck near the goat yard.

"It's the kid!" Shannon cries. And we all fall out the doors and run over to the fence.

It is an absolutely precious thing, like a stuffed animal sewn out of the softest fluff and set in the grass next to its mother. It looks like Violet has known just what to do. The kid is shiny and beautiful, leaning over now to nurse.

"Go-go," Muriel says from Shannon's arms. She is just

coming around from napping and has realized what we are looking at. Her legs start moving so fast that Shannon has to let her down. "Go-go!" she cries, her tiny voice escalating as she pushes an arm through the fence.

"*Ohhh*," Shannon says, "she's been saying 'goat.' She wanted to come out here and see the goats, is all."

"Go-go!" Muriel yells again.

"That's a great name for the kid," I say.

"How come I can't name it?" Mitch asks.

"What did you have in mind?" I ask.

"Spit Out Juice," he says.

"Sorry," I say. "Go-go wins."

Shannon looks at her phone. "It's getting late, Mitchy. We've got to go to the RV and do some stuff. School day tomorrow. You have any homework?"

"What's homework?" he asks.

"Never mind," she says. "I've got to pack, though, so come along. Don't worry—the goats aren't going anywhere."

The boy turns about face, and begins stomping off, knees high. "Don't you rock, Daddy-o, don't you rock, Daddy-o," he says over and over as he goes, this version more marching song than bluegrass tune.

"I'll let the dogs out," Shannon says to me, walking backward long enough to give me a warm but furtive look. "You two take your sweet time."

Sean pulls the vest off of Betelgeuse, and he turns dog and races to catch up with Mitch. We lean over the fence, side-by-side, watching Violet and little Go-go. The kid finishes with its mother's teat and then pulls itself up onto wobbly legs.

"Look at that," I say. "How do they do it? How do they know how to survive?"

"Instinct," he says.

A big leaf, yellow with brown spots, wafts down from the poplar that shades the two goats and lands on the grass just under the resting Violet's nose. She picks it up and eats it.

"And luck," he adds. "A little manna from heaven now and then."

Another leaf, then another flutter down, neither of these within Violet's reach. She lets them lie where they are.

"Early for the leaves to change," I say.

"It's because of the dry summer, according to the farmers at the co-op."

The dogs are bounding down the driveway and across the field toward us now, all three of them, seeming about as happy as any animals could possibly be.

"It *was* a dry summer," I say.

I reach into my pocket and feel the fairy stone, still there, and I curl my fingers around it, hold it like that for a moment. Then I slide it out and into the pocket of Sean's denim shirt.

"What's your wish?" he asks me.

I look at his face, his kind smile lighting it just so. And I tell him.

Long Night Moon

WE ARE LOOKING OUT at the fields going gray. December air pushes through the seams around the window, gaps ever widening from the settling of the house. I loop my fingers into the edges of the shawl and pull it more closely around me.

Sean rubs the lace between his fingers. "It's like building up laughter out of inadequate materials," he says.

He is paraphrasing a line we read from *The Grapes of Wrath*. It's in Chapter Eight, which we finished last night, began Chapter Nine. We've had a habit of speaking in quotes since starting the book, that first edition from my shelf.

"What do you mean?" I ask.

"I can't understand how you can make something this soft and pretty from what grows on the back of a goat and comes out of the mouth of a caterpillar."

"Inscrutable, that Gaea," I say, and I cast the shawl around the both of us now.

"It feels like I'm in a cocoon," he says. "Can I overwinter in this thing?"

"Depends on what you plan to emerge as in the spring."

And I think I can almost see the word on the tip of his tongue—maybe he is going to say it now—but the door opens with a crash and Mitch shoots through it in a burst of cold air and takes up the spot at the coffee table he had to vacate fifteen minutes ago when he was called away to supper.

"So how long does it take to get *here*, Uncle Seanie?" he asks, jabbing at the map.

I let Sean out of the swaddle, push the front door closed, then lean against the warm stone of the fireplace and watch the two of them.

"Oklahoma City? About a two-day ride," Sean says to Mitch, sitting next to him on the couch now. "The land gets real flat in the middle of the country, every direction you look. It's like you can see forever. There's not a mountain, not even a hill."

"Nooo," Mitch neighs, laughing his *You're tricking me* laugh, "there isn't any place like that." He moves his finger along the yellow highlighted route and stops at the next star. "Don't tell me, don't tell me. Um. Um. Um. Um. Um. Um. Armadillo!"

"Amarillo. Texas."

"Oh, yeah. Then…" his finger slides along and stops, and he screws up his face to try to remember. "Albaturkey?"

"Albuquerque, New Mexico."

"Oh, yeah," and he slides right over to the biggest star. "Then the hobby desert."

"Mojave," Sean says. "But I'm thinking about staying over in Arizona a little longer, seeing the Indian nations there."

"Are there real Indians there?"

"Yes, meaning real poor people. They lost their lands in the east a long time ago."

"Like us?"

"Worse. And they didn't have any RVs to get around. Maybe you'll learn that story in school one day."

"Why can't you tell me now?" he asks.

"It's long," he says. "Ask your friend El. She's got Indian blood in her."

"Okay," Mitch says. "Will you tell me about the animals in the desert again?"

"Well, there are porcupines, badgers, mountain lions, bighorn sheep—"

"Are their horns bigger than the goats'?"

"A lot bigger. And there are also roadrunners. And coyotes, though they aren't so different than the ones we have here."

"Roadrunner and Coyote—like Looney Tunes!"

"Only without the Acme Company blowing up stuff. Or so we can hope," Sean says. "And on the other side is California."

"Did you set the course exactly like the Joads's on purpose?" I ask Sean.

"Well, I do know this route," he says. "There's safety in that. It's the same one I took on my motorcycle."

"You have a *motorcycle*?" The boy is awestruck.

"Not for a long time," he says. "But maybe I'll get another one sometime."

"Will you take me on it?" Mitch asks.

"That is a definite *no*," he says, horror plain in his expression.

"You're going to like this road trip, Mitch," I say. "Or maybe we should call it a Joad trip."

"What is a joad, anyway?" Mitch asks.

"They're the family in *The Grapes of Wrath*," Sean says. "It's a book that makes you understand things better. About how people are, and how the world can be."

"Will you read it to me?" he asks.

Sean sighs, looks up at me. "Just making good on the desert promise, and he's hooking me with another big one."

"Think of it as a jerk," I say, picking up the poker on the hearth and stabbing at the smoldering logs till they show some life again. "Trip to the desert, and that's a jerk. Reading a book, and that's a jerk."

He knows what I'm referencing, quotes it properly: "Someone dies, and that's a jerk. Baby's born, and that's a jerk." Then he has a look of regret, as if he wished he'd thought through that before opening his mouth.

"It's not nice to call a baby a jerk," Mitch says.

"It's not that kind of jerk," Sean tells him. "It's a stop-and-start kind of jerk, like when my clutch was out in the truck. Ma Joad, one of the characters in the book, says men live in jerks and women are all in one flow, like a river."

"Is that true?" Mitch asks, looking from one of us to the other.

But before either of us ventures a reply, the door flies open and Shannon rushes through it, yelling, "They want the *RV* back!"

"Now?" Sean says. "We're leaving in the morning."

"I told them they would have to wait on the trip being over. But I am *so mad*!"

"What happened?" Sean asks.

"Aunt Sue had to get her gall bladder out, and a nurse at the hospital told her there'd been a spate of those surgeries, and she looked into it and said it's true, that there's hardly a gall bladder left in the hollow."

"Is that the part of you that holds the pee?" Mitch asks.

"It's an organ that filters poisons out of your body," Sean tells him. "Sometimes it can't keep up and you have to have it taken out."

"I *told* them to stay a mile from that tap water," Shannon says, "but they accused me of being dramatic."

"Why are you giving the RV back?" Sean asks. "A deal's a deal."

"We didn't sign anything. The house is still in my name and the RV is still in theirs. *Idiots*!" And now she is directing her anger at the ceiling.

"Shannon, it was kind of predictable that something was going to happen," Sean says. "I mean, that's why you left."

"I guess I thought they would solve their problems on their own, you know, being all buddy-buddy with the coal company like they are. *Were*. Aunt Sue says they gave her the 'Act of God' line about the whole of the hollow losing digestive organs, and she's talking some trash about them now. Didn't know she had such a mouth on her."

"Good," he says. "Maybe she'll join the alternative energies lobby."

"Do you have to be so *damn* optimistic, Sean?" She plops down on the couch as if all air were coming out of her at once.

"I want to move back home," Mitch says. "I don't need a gold bladder."

"Yes you do," Shannon tells him. "Dot says the kindergarten is real good where she is. You can finish up the year there, and we'll figure out the next step later."

"They have hissing cockroaches?" he asks, his eyes filling now.

"I told Dot you would ask that." She pulls him close to her. "She knows where to get them, Mitchy, says she'll get a few for you to have as pets."

"The fairy stones!" he says. "See, Uncle Seanie, it *is* true. You didn't believe me about the wishes."

"Dot works at a nature center, Mitch," she goes on. "So she knows about lots of other disgusting things, too, such as snakes. Only *do not* ask Dot for one of those. Not *ever*."

"Kentucky's not so far, Mitch," Sean says. "I'll come out when I can. Just give me a call."

"You promise?" he asks.

"Yes," he says.

"And will you read to me that grapes of rats story?"

"That, too," he says.

"What are you talking about?" Shannon asks, but she is

back to complaining to the ceiling before she waits for an answer. "I just can't *believe* this is happening!"

"Hey, Mitch," I say, "El's out showing Gabriel the goat chores. Why don't you go help them?"

"Why can't Gabe go with us on the trip?" he asks. "I counted up the seatbelts, and there's enough. Seven." And he holds his hands up and counts the six of us—himself, Shannon, Muriel, El, Sean and me—on his fingertips. "See? One leftover."

"Good math skills, buddy," Sean says.

"We're picking up Dot along the way," Shannon reminds him.

"And I need someone to stay and take care of things," I say.

"Is Sirius coming?" he asks now.

"Of course." I set my foot on the dog's back, curled there in front of the fire. The fur is so hot I can feel the warmth of it through my wool sock.

"And Procyon and Beetle Juice?" he asks, looking off to where the other two dogs are sleeping together on the far end of the room, far from the heat.

"Yep," I say.

"But don't they need seatbelts, too?" he asks.

"No," Shannon says, pushing him up from the couch and onto his feet.

"But what if we're in an accident? What will happen to the dogs?" he asks her.

"Let's not think of reasons to *worry*. You're sounding like your Uncle Seanie. Now go on, Mitch. Help El and Gabriel before it's too dark. Where's your coat?"

"In the RV."

"You go get it," she tells him, "but be quiet. Muriel's already asleep. And we need to do the same real soon. Platoon Sergeant Sean is insisting we leave before dawn tomorrow."

"It's just plain sergeant. I never made it past that rank," Sean says, pulling on his own coat. "I'll head out with you, Mitch. We need some logs in here." The door opens and closes with an icy blast.

"Want me to put on some chamomile-mint tea?" I ask Shannon. "It'll calm you."

"I don't want to be calm. I'm too angry."

"I wish you wouldn't move. We can figure out a way to squeeze some beds in here."

"No, Leda, I am not crowding you," she says. "Dot has a whole house, just her in there. We might as well see how we do together."

"You really did great this fall, Shannon. I ran into a couple at the Food Lion just the other day, some people John and I used to have dinner with a lot, and they were talking about that movie you showed in October, *The Last Mountain*, and they said they're using 100% renewable energy sources now, through those credits you told people they can ask for from the electric cooperative. And, you know, that was the first time in a long time that I'd had a conversation with them that was not awkward, that was not like talking with a dead body stretched out between us. You see? You've made a difference in lives around here."

"Won't get us back home," she says, getting up off the couch.

"Remember, I'll be real flexible, with not teaching this next semester," I say to her. "The laying hens don't come till March, so all I'm up to now is crocheting those cuffs and collars for the art collective. I can do them anywhere. I'll come out, help with Muriel while you get settled."

"Thanks, Leda," she says, and she comes over to the fireplace and looks at me tenderly—a rare sentimental gesture from her—then places a hand on the small hill that is now my middle. She rubs her palm against the tautness of the baby growing in there. It feels so nice, her firm stroke on my belly. I start to thank her, too, but before I can she is back to imploring the invisible above. "Act of *God*?" she cries, heading to the door and pulling it open. "Crazy as *shit*!"

Sean is standing there on the other side of the screen, logs in arms. "Not lately," he says.

"Sorry," she says to him, and slips out and is gone to the twilight.

"I'll get a truckload of wood when we get back," he says to me, setting a log atop the dying embers in the fireplace, and a couple in the bin on the hearth. "Your woodpile is getting low out there."

"It's nice of you to do that, Sean," I say, and then add, "but just get enough for one winter, okay?"

He looks as if he's weighing whether he should ask why or not, but then the door flies open again and El's voice carries on this gust of chilly air.

"Hey, I left my hiking sticks in the dorm. Do you have any extras, Leda?"

"Yeah, over there in the closet."

"Look, look, El," Mitch is next to the coffee table again, pointing at the map again. "We're going to your favorite skip-your-verse valley."

"Do what?" she asks, half-in-half-out of the closet.

"Death Valley," Sean says. "That's where we're going."

"Oh, right. That *is* like in my scripture verse—the shadow of the valley of death," El's muffled voice is saying. "Nice call, Mitch."

"And you will fear no eagle, because I will be with you," he tells her.

"And guess what? These things are in the verse, also: 'a rod and staff to comfort me,'" and she pulls the hiking sticks from the closet with a flourish, one catching on a picture frame on the adjacent wall. It falls to the floor, glass shooting in all directions.

Sirius startles awake, and I grab onto his collar. "Mitch, hold onto the other dogs, okay?" I say, and he races over and latches onto their collars as Sean gets the broom in motion.

It seems just a matter of seconds before the mess is cleared, the dustpan in Sean's hand and destined for the kitchen garbage, but he isn't moving, and my eyes follow his to El, who is holding a particularly long piece of glass in her hand and looking at it closely. He holds the dustpan out to her like a collection plate in church. "Here, that thing's scary."

"I know," she says, admiring the shard, holding it toward the reawakened fire now. "It's like an icicle enveloped in flames—flashes on the flat side, flickers on the broken edge," and then she seems to notice how Sean and I are looking at her. "I'm just *saying*, you know. In Creative Writing we're told to study things closely to make our descriptions compelling, and I've been writing a short story with a character who is kind of, uh, obsessed with glass."

"Oh, I see," Sean says, nodding. And I nod, too, though I did notice the look in her eyes. Faraway. Missing something, maybe.

She drops the glass atop the other broken pieces in the dustpan and says to me, "I'm sorry about breaking that picture. Can it be fixed?"

"Maybe," I say, letting Sirius go and picking up the cracked frame from the floor.

"I can fix the frame," Sean says, looking over my shoulder.

"I wouldn't know what to do about the picture, though, that tear in it."

It's the photograph from the Appalachian Trail, of John and me sitting on the wall of the overlook, a through-hiker having taken the shot for us. "You can't tell from this picture just how spectacular the view was this day," I say. "A fog had settled into the valley, but the sky was clear above it, sun shining onto the peaks, blue and seemingly suspended in air, as if the mountains had grown right out of clouds."

"It looks pretty spectacular to me," El says. "Like Heaven."

I jiggle the picture out the frame, turn it so El can see what John wrote on the back: *Heaven*.

"That's so weird," she says. "Did he mean literal 'Heaven' or the metaphor 'heaven'?"

"Which did *you* mean?" I ask.

"Both, maybe," she says. "That's what I think Heaven actually looks like. Or part of it, at least."

"I think he wanted this valley to be the metaphor, but it became, well, what it became," I say.

"We could try some of that acid-free tape," she suggests. "To save the picture."

I set it and the frame at the end of the closest bookshelf, leaning up against my copy of *Animal Dreams*. "I should put something else up."

"Like what?" Mitch asks, reaching up the wall and touching the rectangle of dark cedar the picture has left behind. It is striking how time has faded the walls around it. Something you don't notice day by day.

"Maybe a photograph of Go-go," I tell him. "And I think I'll replace all the rest of these, too, Mitch, with pictures of my other little babes—Procyon, you and Muriel—"

"Crap!" El says, grabbing the hiking sticks and the

sleeve of Mitch's coat, "I told Shannon I'd be right back with you."

"But I don't want to go," he whines. "I want to be with you and Gabe."

"We're staying in the spaceship, too, tonight, goof," she says.

His face lights up again. "Will you tell me one of your stories with a flashlight under the covers?"

She nods and pulls him along. "I have one about a vampiric monkey that I think you'll like."

"*Yes!*" he says. "Then will you tell me about the Indians in your blood?" And they disappear onto the now-dark porch and are gone.

"So, what else needs to happen tonight?" I ask Sean, and I try to stifle a yawn.

"Nothing. We're all packed and ready," he says. "You wanted to stargaze, right?"

"I did, but I'm too tired," I say, letting myself down onto the floor in front of the fire. I stretch alongside Sirius, stroke his long back.

"We can imagine the stars," Sean says, flipping off the lights in the room and getting down next to me, lying on his side at my back. "I don't think Sirius is rising yet."

As if to prove him wrong, the dog gets up and creeps over to where the other dogs are on the far end of the room. He has taken to doing this, Sirius, giving me and Sean space.

"Too bad about Shannon losing the RV," I say.

"She'll land on her feet. There's a lot of confidence in that one. She'd have done better in Iraq than I ever did."

It is strange to hear him bring up the subject. He heeds his therapist's advice to keep his eyes forward, regardless of where his mind might be.

A log in the fire pops loudly, giving us both a start. The firewood out on the waning pile is so seasoned now that it rarely sparks like that, isn't nearly as volatile as it used to be.

"Sean?" I ask.

"Yes?"

"You ever see those headless soldiers anymore?"

I am glad to find no hesitation on his part. It's as if he has been waiting for me to ask. "They're not all headless. Some are missing arms, some legs, some have raggedy torsos. IEDs got them."

"You witnessed that?"

"Everyone witnessed that. IEDs were everywhere, in everything—a soda can, a bush along a path. One was packed into a bear, on the side of the road. We stopped to look at it because we hadn't yet figured out that you can't do that. You can't just pick up a drink, or take a casual step, or stop and look at a dead bear. They're lighter colored in the Middle East. Sort of golden."

"It blew up?"

"Completely."

"Did you get hurt?"

"The phone had rung back in the Humvee, and I'd gone to get it. That's pretty much what happened every time. I was just twenty steps off, or over behind a wall, or slid under a vehicle. The blast would ring in my ears for days—deafening, sometimes—but not a speck of a bomb would touch me. It was never my turn."

I tip my head to see his face, the flames from the sooty firebox reflected in his pupils, orange and blue.

"I'd just scuff around in the red dust, leading a parade of hurts," he adds.

That phrase was in the last sentence we'd read last night

in the book, that *parade of hurts*. I had wanted to keep reading, to finish the chapter, but he'd said he needed to spend some time with those words.

"Like Ma Joad said, it rots you out with crazy mad," he goes on.

"She was talking about prison." But I know he knows that.

"She would've thought the same about the Gulf War," he says. "I haven't one scar, Leda. Not one."

"On the outside." I tug on my shawl, try to enclose him in it again. "They still chase you, the memories?"

"Just in my sleep, really."

This I know. His nightmares wake me up. He'll be breathing so hard, moving his legs, yelling out almost-words in a strangled way. I stroke his back till it passes, don't mention it in the morning.

"*You* still being chased?" he asks me.

We usually leave that subject alone, too.

"Awake, asleep, I still see him, feel him," I say. "But he's fading out. Not tinged in red anymore."

And we lie there, holding each other inside the crocheted lace I made from looking at summer flowers, until, in a lame attempt at changing the karma in the room, I say, "Speaking of headlessness, Orion should be out."

"I know that's how you see that constellation, Leda, but it's really all in how you connect the dots. Think of it this way: Betelgeuse marks one shoulder, Bellatrix the other, right? And Meissa is just above those, there," and he draws the stars against the backdrop of the ceiling with his index finger. "You think of Meissa as marking the neck, but I look at it as an ear. Which means there's a head."

"Well, thanks," I say. "Next time I see that hunter, I'll try to look at him that way."

"You can see him in the desert. We can lie out on our backs for hours and look at the sky."

I point to the window, to the white orb that's just peeking over the ledge. "Look—the Cold Moon."

"But doesn't the full moon on the solstice have a different name?" he asks, in that way that means a person knows the answer but is just being polite.

I'm not surprised, somehow, that I have forgotten it is the solstice. I've been able to work things out right where I am lately. Haven't needed to always be moving toward the horizon to find light to see by.

"I've heard that these things destroy brain cells." He gingerly taps my abdomen. He is so afraid of what's in there, makes love like I'm a sand sculpture and could crumble away with a touch too strong. "What would you say you have here? Waxing crescent moon?"

"Maybe getting to be a gibbous."

"Thought of any names yet?"

I shake my head. Sometimes I like one or another that comes to mind, but it seems tempting fate to be so sure of who will be here tomorrow.

Sean kneels next to me and presses his ear ever so lightly against my belly. He stays there for what seems too long, the now roaring fire making his shadow spread strangely around us.

"What are you trying to hear?"

"I don't know. Pulse, gurgle, dream shudder. Anything."

I tug on his shirt, and he leaves off his listening post and lies next to me again.

"Leda?"

"Yeah?"

"I want you to know that you can stop telling me it's okay

to leave." He takes a deep breath, lets it out, takes another. "I'm going to be a father, so I'm staying."

I run a finger over his neck, touch the dark bit of ink I can see. Shrapnel, I've come to think of it as. "Sean?"

"Yes?"

"You do know that if you ever go bald, you're going to have to get that tattoo removed, right?"

He laughs. A relaxed laugh, all his own. One that skips around inside me.

"Sean?"

"Yes?"

"What *is* the name of that moon?" It is rising quickly in the window.

"Long Night Moon."

"Ah, yes, that's it." *Long Night Moon.* I knew it all along.

"Your smile is like Rose of Sharon's right now," he says. "That mysterious one, in the barn, at the very end."

We haven't gotten to that part of the book, of course, but I know the scene. I once found it disquieting, didn't see the beauty.

We lie there and listen to the whispering room—a dog stretching, charred logs shifting in their iron cradle—and I let my hand move behind his head, hold it against me. He pushes my blouse aside, and I close my eyes. Behind the lids I can still see the moon, shining silvery through the pane.

BOOK TWO
Sullivan's Holler

Imbolc

"WHAT THE FUCK IS a linnet?"

"Mitch! Now where'd you pick *that* up?" Shannon has been making a special point to not use cuss words around him since the new teacher sent the note home about his behavior. And Shannon's sure (pretty sure, anyway) that she never used that one within reach of his hearing.

"Dot," he says, flicking the toes of his sneakers, back and forth, through the rungs of the metal utility stool where he's perched on a cherry-red ruffled cushion.

Shannon looks to the window over the sink, to where her partner is gazing out, pupils pinpoints against the white-out of sun on snow. "I thought we were watching our mouths around the kids," Shannon says.

Dot doesn't respond at first, then comes out with "Oh, *I* know—West Virginia!"

"You're changing the subject," Shannon says, thrumming fingertips on the enameled tabletop in front of her—metal, too. Dot likes shiny things and this is her kitchen.

"No, I'm not," Dot says, smiling, to which Shannon rolls her eyes, though she admits to herself the truth in this statement. Dot is pretty much a one-subject woman. "There's a camp up that way, along the Kanawha River. We should go."

"What are you talking about?" Shannon asks.

"Justice Camp. The people fighting the extraction industries come together up there and help each other think up ways to save the mountains. We could go lead a workshop on what we've been doing with the movies. And get some new strategies. We're about out of places within reach of here to do showings."

"Dottie, it's the middle of winter, and Mitch has school. Maybe you go do that by yourself and bring us a report home."

"I don't mean now," she says. "It just came to me, is all. I'll get us signed up for a weekend in spring." She shrinks from the window, rubs playful knuckles into the boy's flyaway hair. "You want to go to camp, right, Mitch?"

"Do they got snakes there?"

"Shit, yeah," she says. "You should see all the brown snakes in the river. And the trails around there will get you a workout, make your muscles strong. Want to take the mountain bikes up?"

"Shit, yeah," he says, eyes round and with a spark that isn't often there these days. He's homesick for the hollow.

"Uh, Dot…" Shannon signs *zip-it* over her mouth.

"Sorry, sorry," she says to Shannon, then to Mitch: "Don't want you in trouble, pal. Keep it clean."

"Okay," he says. "So, Mama, what the hell is a linnet?"

"*Heck*," she says, looking piercingly at Dot because she's just laughed out loud. "Mitch, say *heck*."

"What the heck is a linnet?"

"It's another name for that finch, the one drawn around the hollow," she says. "Granddad called it by the Irish name in the Sullivan stories. They're told from the perspective the linnet."

"What's that mean?"

"He called it his 'point of view,' the linnet bird being able to peer down onto the family of our ancestors—flying in close sometimes, as close as their most private thoughts, but other times flying way up over Ballydonegan. That was the village where they lived before they emigrated."

"What color is the linnet bird?"

"It has greenish feathers, but I've never seen one. It's maybe like a goldfinch, with the same kind of body shape and size, and that sort of beak. You know those goldfinches. They were always swooping around the meadow out back, somehow or another managing to pull out of the nastiest, thorniest stalks the softest damn—I mean, *dang*—bits of thistledown for their nests. I liked watching that."

"Me, too," Mitch says, and he stops the beat he's been keeping with his shoes, sets his feet on the highest bar of the stool, plunks his elbows onto his knees, and rests his chin in his palms. He sighs a grown-up kind of sigh.

Shannon smiles at him apologetically. She finds herself prone to wistful reminiscing ever since they got off the road and settled into Dot's house a month back; she has to catch herself so she doesn't add to her son's melancholy. "So, the linnet bird, it's got green feathers, Granddad said. And some brown feathers, too. Soft colors," she says, forcing some chirpiness into her voice.

"I saw one at home," he says.

"No, they're Irish birds," Shannon tells him. "Though Granddad used to insist he saw one there, too, sitting on the window ledge, peeking in at us sometimes. But whenever I looked to where he pointed, there was nothing there at all. He tried to make me believe the bird was one of those sí folk and could make itself invisible to one person and not another."

"She folk? You mean girls?" he asks.

"Not that kind of 'she,'" Shannon says. "*Sí*, spelled s-i, with a mark over the i. That's an Irish word for the fairies. In one of the Sullivan stories, there's a little girl brings a linnet bird with her onto the ship when the family leaves Ireland, and the way Granddad tells it, that bird swallowed a fairy somewhere along the crossing, so it lived forever."

"Was Granddaddy on that boat?"

"Oh, no, he's not *that* old. Let me see…" and Shannon squints at the tin ceiling tiles—star-shaped, most of them—trying to work out the generations. "Granddad is actually your *great*-granddad, so *his* granddad was on the boat. Daniel. Came over as a little boy, about your age, Mitchy. He had a sister, Mary, a few years older than he was. She was the girl with the linnet bird."

"I have a question," Dot says. She is sitting on the counter now, having made room for herself by shifting some of her many spice jars (she collects glass jars of interesting shapes and colors—a peacock filled with thyme is at her left hip, at her right is a clear blue kitten half full of cinnamon). She has her hand up like she's in a classroom. "Mitch calls his great-granddad 'Granddad.' What does he call his *real* granddad, then? Your dad?"

"Nothing," Shannon says. "My grandparents raised me. My father was, uh," and she pauses there.

"Drug added," Mitch says.

"Now, where did you hear that?" Shannon asks him, surprised.

"Granddaddy. When I was crying about my papa being gone, he told me the story of your daddy and how he got drug added."

"The word is 'addict,'" she says. "And I'm sure Granddad made it clear that it wasn't all that simple. He had some physical problems, my father, got in a mining accident and hurt his leg real bad. Had to go on disability."

"And he took the drugs, and then your mama took the drugs," Mitch says, as if he were saying any normal thing. He's heard this narrative a lot in the mountains. "And then they left."

"I'm sorry," Dot says. "Are they still alive?"

Shannon shrugs. "Maybe my father is. He used to write sometimes, say he was coming back one day 'to set things right.' But it's been a while since I got one of those letters."

"There could be one there in the hollow," Mitch says.

"We get our mail forwarded here now," Shannon tells him.

"It coulda got stuck in a corner of the mailbox," he says. "We should go check."

Dot lifts a bag of pretzel logs from the counter, holds it out to Mitch. "These are fun to eat. You can pretend they're cigars. Want one?"

"Okay," he says. He takes a pretzel out and acts like he's smoking.

Shannon sighs. "How about we don't pack any of those in his school lunches?"

"Okay," Dot says, taking an imaginary puff from her own pretzel, which makes the boy giggle.

"Mitchy," Shannon says to him now. "You do know that what happened with your father is not what happened with mine, right?"

"How do you know?" he asks back.

"Your daddy didn't have a drug problem. He had a *pride* problem. Whenever he couldn't get work he didn't want to face you and me and Muriel. I guess he thought trying to forget us would be preferential to feeling worthless around us."

"Maybe he's got a job now, Mama, maybe he's at home. How would we know, us not being there?"

"You know he could call me," Shannon says.

"If he did, would we go back and be a family again, in our old house?"

Dot tries to let herself quietly off the counter now, but accidentally topples a purple fish that holds her cumin. She rights it, says, "Is that Muriel I hear, waking from her nap?

I think I'll just go check on her." Then she puts a hand on Shannon's shoulder and gives it a squeeze before she pads out of the room and up a flight of stairs sun-splashed from the skylight overtop.

"I didn't hear anything," Mitch says.

Shannon gets up from the table. "Come on now, why don't we settle onto the couch and I'll start into that story for you."

"About how the Sullivans got to the hollow?" he asks, hopping off the stool and following her, taking loud bites of pretzel and leaving behind a trail of crumbs on the polished wood slats of the floor.

"Yep. And I'm going to tell it in Granddad's way."

"In the voice of the green linnet?"

She nods. "Also in pieces. So you have to be patient. One story on each cross quarter."

"What's that?"

"Well, think of the year as a circle—like that tire on the bike Dottie bought you, only say that there aren't so many spokes, just enough to make four parts. And those represent the four seasons: winter, spring—"

"I *know* what the seasons are, Mama. I'm in kindergarten, remember?" He climbs up onto the couch and sifts through the pillows there. All different, all old, all from flea markets and yard sales, Dot not capable of driving by one without stopping. Mitch especially likes the pillow with the silky tassels around it and the washed out print of the Natural Bridge of Virginia on the front. He leans against it and watches his mother stoke the fire, wakening orange flames that dance off the walls and the plate glass window that makes Dot's dormant garden seem a still picture but for when a car passes along the roadway beyond the fence, or when a neighboring sparrow lands on the roof of one of her many bird boxes.

Shannon sits on the couch now, too, pushes her shoes off and pulls her feet up under her; Mitch nestles into the crook of her arm. She goes on explaining. "Seasons start and end at solstices and equinoxes—those times that Leda is always paying attention to—but it was the midseason marks, the cross quarters, that were most important to our ancestors every year, going back all the way to the ancient days. They had fire festivals then, meant to give them good luck with planting and harvesting and things. That's why Granddad told the stories to us only during those times."

"So I have to wait a million days between parts of the story?"

"Three months. It's February now, and the next will be in May. At first I thought that was long, too, and I was older than you when Granddad got to telling me." She thinks, in fact, that Mitch is too young for the story. But he wants her to tell it so badly, won't leave her alone about it ever since Sean brought it up on their trip out west.

"Will they get to the hollow today?" He has pushed in about as close as he can to his mother now, and his thumb finds its way into his mouth. Lately, he's been reverting back to these ways—holding a raggedy bear a lot, pulling one of his old baby blankets from Muriel's drawer and sleeping with it draped over his pillow.

"No, not today," she says.

•

ON THIS DAY, IMBOLC, or Brigid's Day, they're on their way back from a holy well up on a mountain that stands between their village and the rest of Ireland. From way up high, the linnet birds see them, tiny blots moving along a path through open pastures: one leading the way, a boy; two in the middle, connected by a handclasp; and one trailing behind, a girl, sometimes near to the rest and sometimes far off. She is known for getting lost. At times, from up here, you can't tell her from the sheep in the fields. Closer in now, though, you can see what is what, see the lamb leaping in the grass, now nursing from the ewe who gave birth to her this week. The lamb was the sign, it was, that told the family, and all the other families, that it was time to honor Brigid, to ask the warrior saint to bless home and hearth, bless the plots they'd soon be seeding. This is why the girl, Mary, and all of them are in their best clothes. Though she holds a blanket about her to stay warm, you can see the hem of her favorite skirt flapping in a wind gust, faded now to something close to lavender; but the fabric was the shade of a bluebird when her ma first gave it its color, from a dye made of brambleberries and an ink from a rare ocean mollusk that her ma won't speak the name of—*It's bad luck*, she says, *gets the fairies upset.*

Mary has been tugging at the waistband of the skirt all morning. It is tight, which annoys her, but it shows she's had a fine winter of eating. The pits in the ground where they store their lumpers—what they call the potatoes they grow—had been so full from the fall's final harvest that they hadn't been rationing so much, not worried about running out like usual before the picking of the first tender new potatoes that don't ripen till summer. Never had they seen such a lumper crop, said the old women who stood in doorways and puffed on clay pipes. The ones believing in signs looked upon the abundance nervously but never said, not aloud, what concerned them. They merely exchanged glances behind curls of smoke.

This feast day, then, will end with a real feast, even a pig roast because a couple of the villagers feel confident enough in the future earnings at the mine to give theirs up. The pigs are raised each year—one in each yard, fed off a family's food scraps—to sell at market to pay the annual rents. The pig is just about the only sort of livestock they can manage to have. There'd been laws set up, back when the British first took over Ireland with their armies, saying people of their kind couldn't own cows or other large animals. Couldn't do a lot of things, like go to school—which they had done anyway, secretly, in caves and behind hedgerows—or own any land, not any at all, but instead pay rent to live on the farms and fields that had been in their families from time eternal, now on tiny parcels just big enough to hold a pig and a potato garden.

But none of this was in Mary's thoughts as she waved a slender stick in the air now, walking there behind the rest. This was her prize of the morning, what she'd devoted herself to while the grown-ups prayed at the well, dropping smooth stones to count the rounds. She'd found the tree herself, going off alone, as was often her way, and pulled the branch down, then rubbed it against a rock till it was almost white. It was much better than the one she'd made last year, she thought, and she'd lay it out on the ground outside the hut before going to bed, sure that Brigid would come down and pick it up to do her blessing of their family, of all of Ballydonegan. What Mary didn't know—what one of the older girls might well have told her if she hadn't gone off alone—is that the tree she found was not the right one for the making of any wand. The blackthorn, just now showing its buds to say that, yes, spring would come again this year and push away the dark and cold, was a complicated tree. There were some rules to follow, such as never break a limb off, never.

Daniel, the youngest of the family (if you don't count the speck inside his ma that is too small for any of them to know about yet, too small to start her worrying about losing to a bad hunger year, as had happened with the last one when it stopped growing inside her), had been busy up on the mountain that morning, too, but running with a pack, gathering the grasses and rushes that fill his arms now as he heads toward the village, toward the beehive roofs made of the same stuff he carries. They would be thatching the roofs anew soon enough, the men and women of the village, as they did every year, climbing up on one hut then the next. But the armloads that Daniel and the others are carrying down this midday are not for that task, no. They are for making the thing that Daniel has been itching to start since morning light, this being the first year he will take part and not be sent off by the older kids to help his ma in the kitchen. Now the oldest children of the village, their own arms filled with kindling, would be in charge of making the bonfire, and Daniel would have a real part in the making of Brigid herself. This is what takes up his thoughts as he pushes forward on the path, his pace quickening with each step now, until he is as far ahead of his ma and da as Mary is behind.

They all looked on Brigid in different ways, the four in the family. It was on account of her history, all mixed up as it was in the old Celtic stories that had her as goddess, and the newer Christian stories that had her as saint. Instead of one replacing another, the tales had wound around and through her, building her up until she was bigger than life itself. She was the inspirer of poets (which is how the mother saw Brigid, poetry and song being deep in Julia's blood, her family lines going back to the bards and the harps of Ireland); the protector of blacksmiths (the role the father, Cornelius, though too practical to believe in the stories, was thinking of on this day, as he has been harboring a hope that those in charge of the copper mine will let him work the forge instead of going into the tunnels that are spooking him more and more, the close and deep doing dark things to his mind that he doesn't dare talk about to wife and children); the inventor of the whistle (Daniel's favorite feature of Brigid's, because it had to do with her being a soldier, the whistle a tool to call on the armies and alert the villagers to defend the land); and the grantor of wishes (an aspect that kept Mary in thrall and had since she first learned of Brigid, that she was part of the Tuatha Dé Danann, Ireland's oldest people, part human, part fairy). So, each to his or her own, they honor Brigid as they arrive back in the village now and set to the tasks of preparing the fires, the food, and creating her likeness out of the rushes.

This latter task is a work of art, no mistake, something kept in the village, passed around amongst the children, staying in turn in their homes until it is no more, maybe carried off by small animals, bit by bit, or left out carelessly in a gale and sent all as one over the cliff and into the sea that marks the western boundary of Ballydonegan. On this day, though, this effigy's birthday, it would be new and sturdy and whole. The oldest crafters, experienced in stacking up the long stems and tying them with twine, make her torso, her legs, her arms, her neck and head. She is the size, in the end, of the biggest of the children there, which impresses them all and makes them forget the little bickers they've been having over who does what and how. Eagerly, they set off in groups to beg for needle and thread and trinkets. Brigid will need a belt, a necklace, maybe even a crown.

Mary takes Daniel's hand—she has promised her ma she will keep him with her—and pulls him to the pass between the rocks, where they shimmy down the incline, holding to pieces of sod and roots so they don't topple. (No, her ma may not have approved of this part, but she didn't specify where Mary might or might not take him, now, did she?) Their task is to gather limpets. Not the ones stuck fast to slippery rocks—those aren't touched but in the hungriest times, when the cravings sharpen so that even the danger of collecting them is worth the small bit of meat to be found in each—but the empty shells, ones left by other sea creatures even smaller than the limpets, creatures that drill in to get to the flesh, leaving a hole just right for a thread to go through. These washed up and were strewn at low tide, easy to find. But it is high tide now, water lashing against the cliff face. The two know of a spot, though, where they can always find a bit of sand, even when the sea is at its highest mark. And so they begin weaving their way between black rocks taller than the both of them even if one were standing on the shoulders of another.

As he steps along carefully, Daniel looks into the tide pools that dot the flats. He is fascinated by the contents— brightly colored bulbs and beads of lichens and dulse that an older boy, teasing him, had said were bowls of soup, filled fresh daily by the waves, for the roan that gather there. Daniel still believes this, and loving those seals, he never disturbs the pools, never splashes through them as so many of the other children like to do. He is glad that Mary, just behind him now, isn't either, though it is likely she is just trying to keep herself from slipping, from ending up in the frigid water. The children, all of them, know how quickly a person can go cold from the winter sea; they've seen the worst of it, the fishermen from the harbor town that wash ashore, blue and bloated, their fishing boats pushed by unruly winds to this end of the peninsula, a jagged seascape where the harvest from the ocean, even in warm seasons, is limited to the shoreline and what chooses to wash up. Mostly not things to eat, unfortunately, but the stuff of the many shipwrecks are often finds to celebrate, riches in the raic—what they call the ruined cargo and wreckage that land on the shore. Before Copper John, the mine owner, learned his lesson (one his workers had tried to warn him of, but he looked down on them as ignorant and superstitious) he lost a ship full of ore bound for Wales. The villagers found a beach made of the stuff one morning when out gathering seaweed, and instead filled their baskets and aprons with the sparkling bits, blue-green tinged from the tarnish of the sea water, and then returned with carts to haul up the splintered wood planks that had been the hull of the transport ship. With it all, they built sheds onto their huts, linnies, the mud of the walls still flecked with those colors of the ores, ever irritating the mine captains when they find need to come through "pig-town," what those who look down on Ballydonegan call the village.

You could find at least a bit of the sea raic in every single cottage, no question. The rule they went by: If you haul it up yourself it is yours. So you might see, when having a visit in the starkest hut, a candelabra in the center of a table, or an ivory figurine of an eastern dancer on the floor next to a family's cookpot. A silver ornament might hang from a window, catching the light, or an old crone in rags might have around her neck a red stone set in gold. Maybe a garnet, maybe a ruby. But most of the raic was not so valuable, and it was this sort that the children knocking on their neighbors' doors this day might be hoping to get donated to decorate their Brigid—a bauble to string around her. With some limpets, that would look so nice, was Mary's thought, why she has brought her brother down here with her.

There are pieces of wood on their little strand, the two

can see, and when they reach the boards, shifting to and fro in a frothy current, they can tell right off that, though splintered, these are surely fine enough for their da and ma to make some improvements around the hut. The ladder to the loft has long been missing some steps. And a storm ripped free and blew to who-knows-where one of their shutters just the week before. From a look at the sky now, though, the sun squinting an eye their way through the clouds, they can tell it is too late in the day to bring their parents down in enough light to take up these loads. So the children decide to pull the boards away from the tide line, set them off behind a rock, hidden and waiting for their return in the morning. They work swiftly, not dropping a one until they get to the very last piece, when at the same moment they see what's under it and shove the board aside.

"Is it a whistle?" Daniel asks, bent in half and looking closely at the thing on the sand. He reaches for it, but Mary has it in her hand before he can even touch it. She shakes it gently to let the water out, pulls at the strands of seagrass caught where delicate, shapely pieces of metal press into reddish wood. "No, not a whistle, Danny-boy," she says. (This is what his family calls him.) "It's a fairy pipe." And she looks out over the sea, to the horizon where, just beyond, she is sure—oh, so sure—lies the underwater home of the sí. "It's come from the Tir Na Nog," she says.

Daniel, like his da, is not a big believer in all the fairy talk. Or so he wants others to think, this making him feel grown-up. Sure, it's true that at first glance he did think the raic to be Brigid's whistle. But she is more hero than fairy, and this being her day it's only natural his mind might take him there. Now that he's had a moment, well, it is clear as can be to him that the instrument has come from the ship, the one that was made of the wood they've been hauling. But he knows better than to say this to Mary—not when she has that distant look in her eyes.

She holds the pipe up to her lips, sends some breath into it. The sound that comes out is surprisingly sweet. She carries in her that gift of song from the bards. Tucking it under an arm now, she wends her way back as they came, though not so careful this time, stepping into the seals' soup bowls. "Mary!" Daniel calls after her, "we've not gotten the limpets!" but she doesn't answer. Doesn't even hear him over the fairy music that's in her head.

The board the two had dropped bangs against the boy's ankle now. Shaking off the smarting, he watches as the piece of wood is pulled free of the shore by a strong wave that soon enough pushes it back in his direction. The wood stays buoyant, though doesn't find land. He watches it float, as his feet, cold as ice, are pulled into the sand by the next wave. An ocean's deep breath. This is the moment, the very one, that the tide is shifting from flow to ebb. Two steps, Daniel thinks, that might be all it would take to quickly grab the board and drag it over to where they've leaned the others. It was the best one, they'd both said that. It would be a shame to let it go.

He glances Mary's way, to where she is just now beginning the climb up the cliffside. Holding her treasure with one hand, she is moving very slowly; he can catch up, he knows this. So he takes the first stride seaward, only to be hobbled when something pokes through the thin skin of his shoe bottom. When the wave pulls back out, he spies the culprit: a limpet. A beauty. The color of buttermilk, with fine black stripes radiating down from the point. He snatches it up before the wave steals it back. It fills his palm, or nearly, bigger than any limpet he's ever seen before in his life. The inside is smooth and gleaming like a pearl, the hole in the tip of the cone perfectly centered. This will be the prize piece for Brigid, better than anything the others find today. He looks out at the plank, now more than two steps' reach, and gives it up. Slipping the shell into his pocket, he tiptoes around the tide pools and catches up with his sister. A waft of smoke from the bonfire, now going strong, pushes down around the two of them, and though it makes them cough, they smile and hasten their pace, enjoying the anticipation and warmth it brings. They seem to be already at a run before they pop up over the top, Daniel off to find Brigid, Mary off to find her ma.

Julia is so delighted to see what Mary is holding in her hands—the girl so happy herself that she is dancing on the earthen floor, doing that small stepping they all know to keep from stomping on another's toes when enjoying music of an evening in a friend's hut—that she forgets to scold the child for taking her little brother down to the strand at high tide. Julia wipes the butter from her hands (the whole room smells of this warm butter, melting as it is into the mash) and takes the instrument from her daughter and looks it over carefully. She knows what it is, but hasn't seen one for some time. It was at a festival, maybe Lughnasa—yes, the August fair—and two women had come. It had seemed strange to have just women playing like that. They were from the Continent, from France. She couldn't make sense of their words, but their chords, well, those where voices she understood. One had played this, the flute, as someone eventually told her it was called. She holds it up to her mouth as her daughter had down on the shore. Julia notices the salty taste before she makes the same sweet sound come out of it.

After eating, after darkness has fallen, they are all around the bonfire. Many have their fiddles and tin whistles, some have been keeping a beat on cookpots. A few of the villagers have tried the flute but have quickly given up. It would take some practice, they all could see. It is on Mary's lap now, and Mary is on Julia's lap. They have tired of dancing, all of them except three children—cousins of the family—who won the lottery to have Brigid spend the night with them. They have her in a circle dance, are spinning slower now, and slower. The fire is waning, and though the older kids keep trying to sneak more fuel into it—a peat brick or two has already been put to use since the kindling ran out—the parents stop them, reminding them over and over that it can't burn all night, not on this night when all flames, even those in the huts, must be doused completely for Brigid's blessing to come. They are starting to get cold, those around the dying fire, and so some have begun to migrate home, a few at a time, under the moonlight.

Daniel is not pouting anymore about his cousins getting the first night with Brigid. He leans his head against his da as they stand and soak up the last of the fire's warmth, rubbing their hands together at the circle's edge. Daniel can't help but feel proud as he looks across the fire at Brigid. It was decided that his limpet (they all were impressed with how big it was, how fine) would be used to hold together, at the neck, her cape, which one of the girls had made from sewing a few old cloths together. It surely stands out there, at her neck, looking special, he is thinking as he watches her image warble strangely in that wavy air that hangs above a fire.

"Come on, Danny-boy," Cornelius says, steering his son now toward their hut. "We've got a few things to do yet."

"But the fire, don't we need to put it out?" he asks.

"We'll leave that to those who made it," he says.

"So what will you be setting outside tonight, Da?" Daniel asks, lengthening his strides to stay in step, even while

Cornelius is shortening his own so his son can keep up.

"Hm," Cornelius says, like he's thinking on this, but he always puts out the same thing, "the spade, I guess it'll be." He may not believe that Brigid blesses anything, that she's even real, but his family needs to believe that he will do all he can to feed them, and there's nothing more important than the spade when it's time to set the potatoes in these coming weeks. "What are *you* putting out?"

His ma had always helped him decide, and it was always clothing, as that was customary. But he has a better idea. "Can I put out a sack of seed potatoes?" he asks. It was his job last planting to carry a sack around his waist and help by dropping one in the dirt each time his da pulled up the spade. He knew he'd get even farther up the ridges this year; he was one year bigger, after all.

"Sure, we can rustle up a few from the pit," he says. "That's a brilliant idea." And he pulls the boy close, is heartened by how his son likes the land as he does. In Cornelius's dreams—it is a recurring dream, really, always the same—he has a fine farm, a place big enough to grow more than the one cheap food he can grow here. A pasture with goats, sheep, cows. A chicken coop. Nothing too special; not the luxury had by his landlord, the Earl of Bantry—those wasted acres the man doesn't dirty his boots on but once in a blue moon, gated off so the riffraff don't steal the food he doesn't need. In this dream, Cornelius stands and looks at his crops. The mountains beyond are covered with trees. This is how he knows he is dreaming of a different place.

From higher above, now, you can see the people of Ballydonegan moving into their huts. You can see the smoke dissipating, no longer rising up from the holes in the thatched roofs as fires are quelled on this night of renewal. For a little while yet, you'll see people setting out their things for Brigid to bless—pans and aprons and shoes, a fishing net, a harvest basket, a baby's dress. No one will set out a blanket or a coat, as these they will have piled up on them to keep from shivering this midwinter night with no fires to warm them. You can't see them huddling close, no, not from way up here. Maybe you can see, though, glinting there in the moonlight outside our family's door, the white wand made by the little girl, Mary.

.

THE PAUSE IS LONG enough that Mitch knows this is the stopping point, and he pulls his thumb from his mouth and opens his lips, but someone else's words seem to flow out before he finds his own voice.

"What did Julia leave outside?" It's Dot.

Shannon and Mitch both turn their heads to see her leaning against the doorframe, the hall and stairs behind her. "Have you been there the whole time?" Shannon asks.

"Just about," she says, strolling into the room and picking up the poker from the hearth. What's left of the logs is black and barely smoking, but she prods at a clump until it shatters and a flame breaks free.

"Where's Muriel?" Mitch asks.

"I guess I was hearing things," Dot says, leaning up against warm brick now. "She's still asleep. So, Shannon, what did Julia leave outside?"

"Don't know," Shannon says. "I don't remember that part."

"I think," says Mitch, "that she left the flute out there."

"But that's Mary's flute," Dot argues. "Don't you have to leave something of your own?"

"Don't know," Shannon says.

"Well, you're no help," Dot tells her. "Who does know the answer? Sean?"

"He might have an answer, but Granddad would be the most reliable source." Then, frowning, she adds, "In theory, I mean."

"Field trip!" Dot cries. "Let's go see Granddad."

"That's about a whole day's trip, where he's at," Shannon says.

"Don't you miss him?" Dot asks.

"I think I miss him more when I *see* him. He doesn't remember us so well. I don't know that he'd remember the story, either. He gets so confused. Sometimes he thinks Mitch is Sean, and I'm my mother or granny or someone else."

"But sometimes he thinks you're you, right?" Dot asks. "My grandma was like that, when I was a kid. She was in this nursing home right near here. Not a bad place, but I really thought it was terrible when I was growing up, because people were so old and decrepit, and I guess I just didn't realize that my grandma was old and decrepit, too, because she'd lived with us since I was a baby, and she always seemed the same to me. I had this whole scheme to capture her and take her away from that place. My plan was that when I turned sixteen I would get a minivan instead a regular car. And I'd fit it out with curtains and a ramp and a cooler and other stuff. I was going to park it in a strategic spot one day at the retirement home and then say I was taking my grandma for a walk, but instead I would roll her wheelchair into the van and rescue her! I had maps of that, and a timetable, and I'd cased the place whenever I went to see her. I had a whole notebook about it, like in *Harriet the Spy*. Probably still have it somewhere."

"Bet you do," Shannon says, looking around the room at

shelf after shelf bulging with books and movies and games and nicknacks. It seems unlikely to her that Dot has ever gotten rid of anything.

"So, what happened, Dot?" Mitch asks. "With your granny?"

"Well, she died before I could get my driver's license. Not that I had anywhere near enough money to buy a car. My fundraising mainly involved selling bracelets and necklaces I made from gum wrappers, a business venture that turned out to have a pretty small profit margin. I also never figured out how I was going to effectively hide her from my mom, who would've driven her right back to the home, no discussion about it. She's a practical woman, my mother. Kind of like yours, Mitch."

Shannon suspects that's not exactly a compliment, but thanks her just the same. Then she says, "You probably won't like Granddad's home so much, then, Dot. We didn't have money for anything special, so he had to go where the state put him. He's been complaining a lot, Sean says. He gets over there pretty regular-like."

"When is Seanie coming here again?" Mitch asks.

"Yeah, Mitch, good idea, he'll tell us the rest of the Sullivan story," Dot says, collusively. "You're on the ball."

"I doubt it seriously," Shannon says. "He respects Granddad too much. You'd hear the next part of the story from him at the beginning of May, same as you'll hear it from me."

"But he'll read us *The Grapes of Wrath*," Mitch says.

Dot gives him a look as if she's trying to peer inside his head. "Are you really sure you're a kid, Mitch? You seem to have a whole lot more going on upstairs than any other little person I've ever met. My nieces and nephews spend all day on the Internet watching streaming videos and you're reading

The Grapes of Wrath."

"I can't *read* it," he says, but he has a look of satisfaction on his face, nevertheless. "When Seanie was here he got to the part where the machines come, the Cats. They rolled in like big robots, knocking stuff down, ruining the people's everythings and making them go to the roads."

"Hm, sounds familiar," Dot says, wandering to the window. She sets dark eyes on the garden and its bird boxes sticking up out of the snow, like a little town on stilts. She's been planning to get out and brighten up the boxes with some new paint. Maybe even today, she's thinking, maybe she'll just pull on some boots and get it done before the birds are all vying for their spring nesting spots. The tree swallows are on their way, will arrive in a matter of weeks. She watches a wren fly in and out of one of the boxes, a year-rounder, that species. She makes a mental note to not disturb them when she's out painting, to leave their house alone. It's plenty nice as is, with daisies painted on its sides.

"Mama," Mitch says now, "I was wondering something. Was it flat-footin'?"

"Was what flat-footin'?"

"The dance that Mary was doing, when she was showing her mama the flute."

"Oh, that, yeah. Probably something like flat-footin', sure, something close and tight like that. They were big into dancing and would've had the same issues as they did once they got over here—small spaces with a lot of people crowded in. And they needed quiet feet to hear the music over it all."

Dot turns away from the window, looks at Mitch. "Oh! About dancing—I forgot to tell you. I found a studio. They teach all kinds. You can try that flat-footin' if you want. Or even some Irish dance. They got it all. Not too far from here, either. You could ride your bike."

"I don't know about *that*," Shannon says, grimacing.

"I'll ride along with him," Dot says. "I need to get more exercise. Winter's wearing on me. I think I'll try some dancing myself. What do you think of that, Mitch?"

"I'm not dancing anymore."

"*What*?" Shannon says. "That's all you talk about." Though she's thinking that he hadn't actually brought it up in the last couple of weeks. But he hadn't been talking much about anything, really.

"Reynold says it's gay." He has his thumb resting on his lip now. "Told me so at recess one day when I was showing Luke a new step I made up. He got some other kids laughing at me and—" he stops, his voice choked.

Dot's cheeks have turned scarlet. "That is *fucked up*."

"Lang-uage," Shannon sing-songs to her.

"What is gay, Mama?" Mitch asks. "What does it mean?"

"It just means a woman being with a woman or a man being with a man," she says. "Like me and Dottie. Like lots of people."

"Then how can a dance be gay?" he asks.

"It can't," Shannon says, kissing his cheek.

"What is this *Reynold's* last name?" Dot asks.

"Wilford," Mitch says.

"Oh, I know that family," she says. "His dad was in my class all the way up through school. He was racist, sexist, you name it. What a prick." She turns to the window again, not wanting to meet the look she knows Shannon is giving her.

"What about this idea, Mitch," Shannon says. "Go ahead and stop dancing at recess, but still take a class at the dance school. I assure you that Reynold will not be anywhere near that place. It'll be our little secret."

"Oh, *that's* progress," Dot mutters. "Dancing in a closet."

"Just for now, I mean," Shannon sighs. "Just so things aren't *harder,* you know?"

Dot doesn't answer. She watches a purple finch land on the head of an angel poking through the snow, the tallest of her garden statues and the only one at all visible today. She looks at shapes in the white, tries to discern exactly where each of her other statues is hiding—the horse, yeah, that's easy to tell, the fawn, maybe there. The turtle…well, she can't even guess where that one is.

Shannon gets up and takes a turn with the poker, busting up another charred log to get to the pink glow inside it. She leans against the brick where Dot had been, takes a stab at changing the subject. "There was another name for Brigid's Day," she says. "An old Irish name—Imbolc. Meant 'in the belly,' Granddad said, because of it being that time when the animals were growing their babies inside them."

"Like Leda?" Mitch asks.

"That's right, like Leda. And Seanie."

Dot hears the sound first, but tuned into the garden as she is, she thinks for a moment that it is coming from the purple finch, still perched on that angel's head. It's not until the now familiar "Da-da-da-da"—Muriel's ironic attempt at her name—reaches her ears that she realizes it's a human call.

"Muriel's forgotten who I am," Shannon says, feigning jealousy. Truth is she is real pleased that her little girl has taken so to her partner.

"*Hardly,*" Dot says, hiding a smile as she makes a beeline to the stairs. Though the toddler's affinity had put her off at first, now she is equally enamored.

"Let's go up, too, Mitchy," Shannon says. She pulls on his hand till he jumps off the couch to follow her. "It'll be fun. Muriel will like the audience."

And they are up the stairs and gone, leaving the room empty but for a wisp of smoke from the fire caught in the draft of their exit.

Beltane

"MAYDAY! MAYDAY!" BLARES AGAIN from the speakers. "Mayday! For your own safety, evacuate *immediately*!"

On the first morning, there had been more than a few people scurrying around in response to this, and then a couple of newcomers on the second day who hadn't been forewarned. But on this, the third day in camp, no one is fooled by the trickster in charge of the announcements. No bodies, save for a few dogs sniffing at scent trails, fill the piney spaces between the domes and points of the encampment.

Dot reaches up and unhooks the flap above their heads. "What I want to know is how they get up so early. I mean, they outlast us at the campfire every night."

Shannon is sitting up now, and glances toward the other sleeping bags, to the lumps that are her children within. "Probably not by much," she says. Then adds, in a whisper, "I think they just wait on us to take the kids away so they can light up."

"Their cigarettes smell like skunk." It is Mitch, who pops up like a groundhog from his burrow of green down.

"Mayday!" the announcer shouts out again, but he's soon cut off when there is a rustling over the speakers, a lot of giggling, and a few choice words that cause Shannon to put her hands over Mitch's ears. "We've taken him down!" a female voice booms, and some hoots and applause erupt from tents now opening up and giving birth to morning in camp.

Muriel's arms poke out of her tousled nest, and she joins the applause. She likes to clap her hands.

"Why don't his friends want him saying that?" Mitch asks.

"They're just having fun," Dot tells him. "They're college students. That's what they do."

"Is that what I'll do when I'm in college?" he asks.

"Probably," Dot says.

"And will I smoke skunky cigarettes?" he asks.

Dot says again, "Probably."

"*Not*," Shannon adds, giving Dot one of her *How about trying to act like a parent?* looks.

Dot gives Shannon one of her *Just watch me* faces, and says, "Hey, Mitch, you want to know what 'Mayday' means?"

"I already know. It means the first day of May," he says. "Which was yesterday, which was when Mama promised to tell us a Sullivan story but didn't."

"We never had enough undistracted time together," Shannon says, rolling up her sleeping bag and tucking it up against the side of the tent. "Didn't help that you and Dot went off and biked up a mountain."

The whole camp had gone to see a mountaintop removal site the day before, in groups, some biking (as Dot and Mitch had), some hiking, some going in cars with local guides. The latter involved tours of affected communities, and Shannon and Muriel had gone along with one of those. Their driver had taken them to his homeplace, a house now abandoned in a hollow now abandoned, everything soot-covered and sad. It had made Shannon think better of her vociferous protestations of an hour earlier regarding the cycling trip Dot had in mind for her son. Standing in the weeds of a man's lost ground, she was glad Mitch wasn't there with her. No matter how hard the cycling might turn out to be for him, this, she knew, would have caused him more pain. In the end—just as she had predicted—the trek was too much of a challenge for Mitch, and they'd left their bikes along the path while Dot carried him on her back the final stretch to the plateau where all the campers were converging to view the mining site. Shannon had hugged them both when they arrived, turning Dot's spent and sheepish expression into one of relief, and then they'd stood together and looked out over the wreckage: mountain ridges flattened into miles of looping tracks peppered with machines. All idle on a Sunday.

"It's a distress signal," Dot says to Mitch. "A universal symbol of a major emergency: *Mayday!* You have to say it three times. That's the rule. Only it's against the law to yell it in public if there's no emergency. So I guess that guy with the microphone could get arrested if there were some police around."

"What if he was just happy about the first day of May, and was yelling about that?" Mitch asks. "You can't prove what he was meaning."

Dot, impressed, waggles a finger in his direction. "You, buddy, should become a lawyer."

"What do they do?" he asks.

"They argue in court. The guerrilla environmentalists around here need lawyers all the time because they make the coal companies so mad. They're always getting arrested and thrown into jail."

"Okay," he says. "But can I wear armor?"

"Why would you need armor?" she asks.

"I seen gorillas on the Nature Channel," he says. "They're really big and scary."

"Different kind of guerrilla altogether," she tells him, keeping a straight a face, because it has started embarrassing him when he gets words mixed up. "This kind is a human being who carries out surprise attacks to fight an enemy that's too powerful to go up against in the regular way. In the case of these here, they set up roadblocks and such."

"Oh," he says, disappointment clear in his voice.

"Hey! Let's start up a law school fund when we get home," Dot says. "We can sell stuff to make money for it. We'll brainstorm together."

"Can we have a notebook to keep track of things?" he asks.

"Sure."

"If we save up enough, can I go to the law school next year instead of first grade?"

Shannon and Dot exchange glances. He is still left out of things, has few friends at school. Shannon looks for reasons to give him days off, letting Dot take him to work with her now and then. Dot'll tell him she needs his sharp eye to catch tadpoles for the nature center's educational displays, or that she could use an assistant for a snake talk. Sometimes they conjure long weekends as a family, like this one at Justice Camp, which they've made even longer by adding a stopover on the way home to see Sean and Leda and the new baby who has burst into the world this past week.

"Come on, Mitchy—roll up your sleeping bag. Help Muriel with hers," Shannon says. She's got the door-flap open now, is peeking out, sniffing the air to see if the morning campfire has been started yet.

"But I'm all achy," he whines, not moving an inch. "And Muriel doesn't want to get up either." The little girl has crawled out of her sleeping spot, but is now in a ball next to Dot, who is petting her like a cat. "We're really tired, Mama. Can we just stay in here? You can tell us the story."

"I've got an idea of a good place to do it, just need to figure out the best time," she says, rolling Muriel's bag now and pushing it up onto hers. "Once we go to morning circle, we'll have a schedule for the day."

"*Nooo*, then you and Dot will get all busy giving shots."

"*Shots?*" Shannon and Dot ask at the same moment.

"Work shots," he answers.

"Oh, those," Shannon says, nodding. "We're done with that part of things, Mitchy." She and Dot had led a workshop they called "Fight With Film," the preparation and program having taken up just about all of their time and energy the first day of camp. But there had been a lot of people who attended and asked questions and then said they would start doing what Dot and Shannon had with the movies, showing them on campuses, or in churches or parks. "But Dottie and I are trying to find at least one workshop to go to today, to get new ideas. That's a big reason for us being here at camp; you know that."

"Shan," Dot says, "why don't you start the story now, and finish up later, when we get the time. I don't think that fire is ready yet."

"That's not how Granddad did it," Shannon says.

"How about you just tell us what they did first thing on May Day, after they woke up? Sort of setting up the scene," Dot suggests, winking at Mitch. A pain shoots through her neck, and she rolls her head, rolls her shoulders. While she is physically fit for any kind of biking, carrying a boy on her back uphill is not something her muscles are used to, and they are vexing her this morning. She straightens her back now, pushes her legs into a yoga pose. The lotus.

"First thing?" Shannon is leaning against the two tidy bedrolls now, her eyes on the tent's skylight. She can't see the sun but knows it's out, just above the horizon and warming the morning mist, making it rise up off the hills, hover around scaly trunks of trees. She can feel it settling in the tent, that air. "The girls, they'd be out gathering morning dew, wiping it off leaves and rocks, rubbing it into their faces."

"Why would they do that?" Mitch asks.

"It was considered restorative—it could make a person beautiful, more youthful. That's what they believed."

"Why only the girls?" Mitch asks. "That's not fair. Boys should be allowed to get beauty and youthness, too."

"That's how Granddad said it was."

"Let's change it," Dot says. She has her hands up by her shoulders now, palms up. Her head is as still as a statue's, eyes closed. "We need to recognize evolving societal standards. I put forth an amendment to eliminate all gender bias in the story."

"*Yeah.*" Mitch doesn't know what she's just said, but he can tell Dot's on his side.

"If things were a certain way, then they were a certain way," Shannon sighs. "I can't just change the truth of their lives like that."

"Come on, really?" Dot says. "I mean, isn't a lot of it imagined, after all?"

Shannon crosses her arms and looks up to the tent roof. It's jiggling from something unseen that is hopping across the flat of it. "Who's telling the story, here, anyway?"

"No one," Mitch mutters.

"All right, all right," Shannon says.

•

THE GIRLS OF BALLYDONEGAN—and *maybe* sometimes the boys, too—are gathering morning dew, and they're also racing to the creeks and the wells to be the first to draw water. That worked, too, like the dewdrops, to make them beautiful. Their attractiveness was something people came to see, in fact. It was not uncommon to have visitors from across the channel rolling over the narrow roads on the way to townlands, stopping now and again so the people inside the carriages, in their fine clothes and hats and shoes, could take a break and draw the peasants at work or at play. They'd set up easels and paints sometimes, or write about them in careful cursive in their journals. Sometimes these would be published as books or magazine pages in London or Paris, because more than just the sightseers on the roads were intrigued by how a race of such poor people, living on such a poor diet—the *potato*, of all things—could be so full of life.

Beltane—the "bright fire"festival at this, the beginning of May—was a favorite of the onlookers, the heavens having finally pushed off the chill and the cold squalls of winter. The villages and villagers would be decked out in garlands woven of green leaves and yellow blossoms picked in the hills and boreens: primrose, rowan, hawthorn, gorse, hazel, marsh marigold. It was so popular a time that even our tiny townland on its windswept perch along the far western coast might have seen a carriage by midday, its wheels spinning and stumbling over rocky cart paths. Perhaps the horse would be halted near a low stone wall, close enough for hearing the fiddles and the odd tongue, the Irish language these visitors knew not a word of. The songs, some of those might be in English and might then be recognized, like the words of the one sung by the woman who has just been playing the flute but has now handed it off to a girl who accompanies her, but nervously, missing a note here then there. She knows the tune, has practiced it often, but not in front of so many people at once. Not in front of strangers on the road.

It's a poem by Speranza that Julia has set to music. This poet in Dublin is her idol, though Cornelius writes her off as just a member of the plantation class, those once given Irish lands by English kings who handed out farms and fields like party favors. Speranza was born of such a family, sure, but

Julia knew better. "Look at what she writes," she always tells her husband, after she's struggled mightily to read from the page in the *Nation* newspaper saved for her by the wife of the Cornish miner who lives up the road and has the paper delivered by post. Cornelius says he can't read a word, doesn't want to read a word of a language forced upon them, so she translates for him. (In truth he can read quite a bit from examining the advertisements strewn all over Berehaven, their market town, where the ships take away the grains and animals grown on the plantations, take away their kin for far-flung jobs. He'd rather his wife not know he spends so much time studying those handbills.) *If thy mighty heart has stirred / With one pulse-throb at my word / Then not in vain my woman's hand / Has struck thy gold harp while I stand / Waiting thy rise Loved Ireland!'* is a stanza of what Julia has put to music this day, Speranza's latest clarion call to the people to take back what is rightly theirs, a movement swelling from east to west, calling itself Young Ireland. Julia sings with a passion that would stir Speranza (a dream of Julia's, that, a visit from the poet herself) and she hopes to inspire her neighbors—despite their inherited memories of crushing defeats and horrors—to battle once more for Ireland, to win it back for their sons and daughters born and yet to be born.

She holds a hand to her belly, just barely rounded, as the dancers stop and clap for the mother-daughter duo. A fiddler starts up and the dance turns to a jig. Julia sits a bit, watches; she's overly careful with this one growing inside her, doesn't even join the dances, or not the fast ones. She imagines the baby plump already, skin soft with fat, because that last lumper crop is still holding up, a supply in the pit and the loft, enough to barter for milk each week. And it being full spring, foraging has begun—wood sorrel, wild garlic, nettles—and the sea has even been calm enough for shellfish and dulse gathering. Cornelius, though, says it's the game he has been showing up with that has been helping this new baby to thrive in the womb. Julia doesn't know where he gets the meat, nor the blood she made into a pudding for all of them just this morning. It worries her to think on that, so she puts her mind on other things, the fiddlers, the dancers. She claps as the jig comes to an end.

•

MURIEL IS CLAPPING, TOO, but it's hard to say if it's in response to the story. The call for morning circle has just boomed across camp, and the little one knows this means breakfast. She loved the bacon her mother cooked on the fire yesterday, couldn't get enough of it.

"We've got a fresh supply of milk in camp this morning," crackly speakers squawk, the voice that of the original announcer, apparently freed and so far behaving himself, "and the market in town has just delivered fruit and bread for those of us who are morally responsible. For the rest of you, another pile of sliced pig flesh has been rounded up from a local farm—er, swine prison. *Mayday! Mayday! Mayday!*" To this there is a mix of boos and cheering in camp, and then a rising riposte of *Bacon! Bacon! Bacon!*

Muriel is through the tent opening in a flash, her hands coming together over her head with each chant, and Shannon shoots after her.

Mitch stands up, arms raised and touching the tent's ceiling. He feels large in this place, safe. "Dot?"

She comes out of her lotus position now, opens her eyes. "Yes?"

"Did you already know my ant-setters were vampires?"

"I don't remember knowing that, no."

"They drank blood. Or ate it with spoons. I'm not sure."

"Oh, that. I don't think they were vampires, Mitch. Blood pudding is sort of a normal food in those places. It's like a sausage patty, with oats and herbs and other things mixed with animal blood. Good source of iron, so seeing as Julia was pregnant, that would have been real healthful for her."

"That's gross," he says, nose crinkled. "I would never eat blood."

"I hate to tell you this, buddy, but you do every time you eat meat. It's in it. That pudding is just more honest about it, blood being on the actual ingredient list."

"You ever ate it?" he asks.

"Yes, actually. My grandmother used to make it, and her mother used to make it, and her mother used to make it. My mother wouldn't touch it with a ten-foot pole, so she stopped that tradition passing down once my grandmother moved out. It was a Scots-Irish thing, those ancestors having come from not too awfully far from yours. My family's been in Kentucky since the 1700s."

"Is that a long time?"

"Sure is. That was before this was even a country of its own. My other line is Italian. They came over later, to work in the mines. There were lots of Italians in coal camps, for some reason. Long-ass trip to live poor in towns run by despots."

"What are despots?"

"Tyrants."

"What are tyrants?"

"Oppressors." And anticipating his next question, explains, "People who take advantage of those with no power, crushing their spirits, stealing hope from them so they can't live decent lives." A familiar anger is warming her insides now.

She thinks of it as fuel. "Hey, let's head to morning circle, see what's on the agenda for today."

"Mama says I need to take care of my sleeping bag first." He tries to pull it out flat and roll it the way she's shown him, but it's more like a wrestling match that he's having. "How do you do this?"

"Beats me," Dot says, pushing hers into a clump against the wall opposite Shannon's neat bedrolls.

Mitch pushes his up next to Dot's, and they both look at what they've made, a miniature mountain range, slate blue and green.

"I like it better our way," Dot says. "More natural."

He smiles a big one at her, and then she zips up the overhead flap and they both emerge into the camp, grab their mess kits from the tree limbs where they hung them to dry last night, and then wind through the tent village in the direction of the wood smoke.

There's a crowd at the circle by the time they arrive, more than had gathered either of the last two mornings. Seems no one has left camp, it just accrues more bodies. The weather has cooperated, which surely helps, but today's programming seems to be what many have been anticipating, judging by all the animated talk going on, mouths full of breakfast.

"First thing this morning, then," a woman is yelling, holding up a clipboard, "we've got us the river trips!"

Mitch looks up at Dot and mouths, "She's *old*."

"She's a legend," Dot whispers back. "Used to lie right down on the ridges with a big-ass sign that said 'Kill my mountains, kill me!'. Needed a lot of lawyers in her time, you can be sure."

"Clipboard's circulating! If you're going, mark your first, second and third choices—canoeing, kayaking or tubing."

Voices rustle more loudly now, but the woman raises her own above it. "Remember! The focus of these trips ain't just fun, but for ways to create and market *ecotourism*. Keep that in mind and jot down ideas or make mental notes for the afternoon follow-up sessions!"

A young person gets up to do the next announcement, but, not nearly as experienced at crowd control, he's bombarded with *Louder!*s and *Repeat that!*s. He is organizing interpretive walks in the national forest, focused on geology, biology, and ecology. He extolls participants to take notebooks in their backpacks, and reminds them, too, that there will be afternoon sessions to share thoughts on how to draw more people to the area for hiking and camping.

Mitch squeezes in next to his mother now, she and Muriel with a plate of bacon ready in front of them and a pan set over the fire with another few strips. He pulls a piece off the plate and inspects it carefully.

"What's the matter?" Shannon asks him.

"I'm seeing if there's any blood," he says. While he looks at it, Muriel leans over and takes a bite of it, right out of his hand, giggling. He hands her the rest of the strip.

"Up for canoeing, Mitch? Or kayaking?" Dot asks, reaching for one of the many coffee pots at the fire's edge and filling her tin mug. It's not until she offers the pot to Shannon that she notices the *Tell me you're not serious* look on her face.

"Ha! Just a joke, there, Mitch," Dot says. "My back is way too cranky for any paddling today."

"Darn," he says, but a relieved look comes over him, and he leans against his mother's shoulder. She kisses the top of his head and then pours him some hot chocolate.

"Be a silicon holler pioneer!" the next person with a

clipboard cries out. "We IT students at State have teamed up with some MBA candidates," she sweeps a hand toward a clutch of others who are standing now, some nodding, some fist pumping, "and we're leading a workshop on getting high-speed internet into remote places so entrepreneurs can set up businesses. We think that'll be a great opportunity for Millennials like us who think mountain sports are the *best*, and who want low costs of living so we can get student loans paid off. There are lots of abandoned Main Streets waiting to be claimed in these mountains. And if you have any experience writing grant applications, *we need you badly*."

"Maybe we should work with them, Dottie," Shannon says. "There are some beat-up and lonely little towns near to us. We could learn to write grant applications."

"Too much paperwork, and too tech-y," she says, pulling an apple from a basket of fruit that's going around and taking a loud bite from it.

"That'll be it for the morning workshops!" the woman who started things calls out. "The folk leading the afternoon workshops will give you details at lunch, but I'll paint you some broad strokes: (1) Small scale farming; (2) Water and soil cleanup; and (3) Cultural tourism—expanding or creating artisan and music trails.

"Like the Crooked Road, Mama," Mitch says, looking up from his orange, which he's peeled himself and has been sharing with his sister. "Can we stop along the Crooked Road on the way home?"

"I don't think so, Mitchy," she says. "You're already missing a lot of days of school as it is. There's a jamboree here tonight. That'll be fun, right? I've seen a few other kids in camp; maybe they'll come out for it."

He looks at his feet pushed up onto the rocks that outline

the fire circle. Sniffing, he realizes he's gotten his sneakers a little too close and pulls them away. "Why doesn't Kentucky have a Crooked Road?"

"We've got music trails," Dot says.

"Well, why don't I know that?" he asks. "I been there a long time."

"I know—four whole months," she says.

"Yeah," he agrees, not catching the sarcasm in her voice. "That's a long-ass time."

Shannon raises an eyebrow, first at Mitch, then at Dot, who coughs and then points off through the grid of hickory boughs and conifer branches overhead. "Clouds pushing in," she says.

The end of announcements has seemed to signal a dismissal, sending one after another into their scraping and cleaning routines at the wash station. The signs all over about black bears have worked to turn most of the campers into fastidious dishwashers. Those in charge of the big tasks—composting, food storage, trash disposal—head off to take care of business, and the fire-dousers set to making sure the flames are quelled. It isn't long at all before just about everyone has scurried to the river, to the trailheads, to the workshop pavilions, in diverging lines, like ants.

"So, what'll it be?" Shannon asks Dot.

"What happened to those radicals, anyway? I didn't see any of the guerrillas at breakfast."

"Someone said they went off to the MTR site before dawn," Shannon says.

"Crud. I wanted to do one of *their* workshops. They had that mechanic the other day, the one who'd defected from MES. Did you hear about that? He was demonstrating how to jam up the gears of those draglines. Went on at the same time as our workshop. I was hoping he'd be back."

"You do know that the theme is restoration today, right?" Shannon says. "And haven't we been talking about sticking to projects that won't get us in trouble?"

"*You* have," Dot mutters.

"No mo' bacon?" Muriel asks, looking sadly at the now spotless pan in her mother's hand.

"All gone," Shannon says, sliding their clean dishes and utensils into her cinch sack while Muriel, lip out in a pout, swipes at the smoky air, leaping and landing a little closer to what's left of the fire than her mother is comfortable with. Shannon slings the sack onto her back and then picks up her daughter and sets her on a hip.

"Dottie," Shannon says, "I'm more interested in the afternoon workshops than the morning offerings. What about the one on art and music trails? That's work we can take back home, something the kids can be a part of. If you want to raise up activists, as you say you do, you need to be realistic. I mean, they can't be crawling up into the bellies of machines and jamming up gears."

"Why not?" Mitch asks, looking earnestly from his mother to Dot.

Shannon just shakes her head, spotting now over her son's shoulder, and through a sparse windbreak of cedars, a hillside lit up. It's the one she discovered yesterday out on a walk alone, the perfect place. Tall stalks of thistle push out of rocky outcrops on the field, and one side rises up and meets the sky, its craggy ridge-line made of limestone, black boulders with white striations. She makes a motion in that direction with her chin. "Lookee there, Mitch."

He turns his head and grins—he likes to climb rocks—and then runs full-speed ahead, his weariness apparently forgotten.

"Slow down!" Shannon calls after him, realizing she hasn't

any idea if there is a drop-off beyond the ridge. She runs after him, tin pans clanging against her back, Muriel struggling against her to get free now, her eyes set on those rocks, too.

Mitch is to the top before anyone else even reaches the base. "Cows!" he calls out. "Lots of 'em! Come on up!"

"I'll take Mermaid," Dot says, using the nickname she's been calling Muriel by since she started taking her to swim lessons at the YMCA. She holds the squirming child firmly around the middle, guides her up the rocks to a good ledge for sitting, and sets her on her lap. "Look at *that*," she whispers in her ear, pointing to the panorama: white rays pushing through spaces between clouds—spotlights on smoky blue mountains and sloping pastures.

"Moo," Muriel says, calming now, reaching a hand out to the ambling black hyphens on green hills. Then again: "Moooo," a note now, sweet and musical. A pair of swallows pass over her head, their white breasts flashing, and the little girl reaches in their direction.

Shannon has found her resting place, too, not an arm's length from Mitch, who is still on his feet. There's no sheer drop from these rocks, she's glad to see, but she still worries he could trip and get hurt. "How about you sit?" she asks him, patting a smooth spot on the rock next to her. "You can see the cows fine from here."

He sits, but enjoying his feeling of freedom, of being in the sky, he chooses a different rock to settle on. One just a little bit more—just teasingly more—than an arm's length away from his mother.

"Was it cow's blood, Mama?" he asks her.

"Was what cow's blood?"

"The blood Julia mixed into her pudding."

"It was, yes," she says.

"Did Cornelius kill the cow to get it out?" he asks now.

"No, he wouldn't have done that. Drawing blood from animals can be done same as with people. Doesn't have to harm them," she says.

"Good," Mitch says. "I like cows. I don't want to eat them anymore. Will you tell me when something's made of a cow so I don't eat it?"

"Okay." *We'll see how long that lasts,* she thinks. Her son's favorite food is hamburgers.

Dot's eyes are on the cows, too, moving along with them as they graze, heads down, south to north. "You know what's coming back to me that I haven't thought of for a long time? My grandmother had stories about cows, in old picture books—Celtic myths where the cows were as big as giants and lived on islands shaped like whales. They could fly, too, and they would come inland and feed people with milk when there were famines. She'd always add details that weren't on the pages. I didn't realize that until I was old enough to start reading on my own. There'd be maybe two sentences on the page, but she'd be going on and on, describing a whole world inside a picture." Dot absentmindedly pats Muriel's head, which is against her shoulder. The girl's eyes are still set on the swallows, more of them having amassed now, swooping from tree to rock to meadow and back, a bird ballet.

"I wonder if any of those books were about Beltane, because that was originally a cattle-worshipping holiday," Shannon says. "According to Granddad, the cow was their symbol of subsistence." She has articulated this last word for her son. "Which means that as long as a family had a cow, it could survive. With the wheat and vegetables they also grew on their farms, and the hunting they could do before the laws made that near impossible, they had a real healthy diet.

They hadn't even heard of the potato, which wasn't brought to Ireland until those British planters came to see that they wouldn't get much labor out of a hungry person. And the Irish, tired of watching their children starve, were relieved to have something so filling to grow on their small bits of land. They planted all they could. Dropped a little wish in the ground with each root, because they knew that depending on one plant like that was a risk."

"They wished for a cow, right?" Mitch asks. "One of those kinds with wings, to fly over them and rain milk down everywhere, so they could just open their mouths to the sky to get full up?"

Shannon smiles, stretches her fingers toward him, though she knows she can't reach. "You, Mitchy, are going to be a good teller of the Sullivan stories one day, I can see that."

"Maybe one of those books *was* about May Day," Dot says. She's been thinking on this, has called up a buried memory. "Did they walk cows around the bonfire?"

"Yeah, that's right," Shannon says, "some kind of purification ritual. And then the people would take the whole community's herd up to summer pastures. Probably looked a lot like that," and she sweeps a hand toward the view of the cattle. The sunbeams have turned to one blinding eye in a thickening cloud cover.

•

ON THIS MAY DAY, the only animals that seem part of the festivities are dogs—herders and hounds, all of them, wandered off Bantry's estate over the years. You could say these dogs are worshipped, in a way, welcomed by those who can ill afford to feed them. It is thought by some in Ballydonegan that the spirits of Irish rebels live in these mutts, choosing as they do to be hungry in the company of the poor rather than fat from the hands of the landlord. Skinny as they are, they don't lack energy. They nip at dancing heels, race around the fire, leap at the garlands of yellow flowers. Some sit sentry next to the old men who pull chairs out of their huts on this day and prop their feet onto upturned buckets or three-legged stools.

Cornelius is sitting with these elders. Most younger men have chosen to dance, but he's enjoying the talk and drink— good "craic" they say of this social time as they watch the revelers. Ever since his brothers went across the sea, he's gravitated to his uncles, especially Jeremiah, who's got the best poteen, makes it up in the bog. It is a scourge among the miners, their drinking, but Cornelius has learned to sidestep the worst of it. He knows to never take drink when he's just come up from a shift, though it's offered to them all, a shot of whiskey from the casks the company brings in on ships, Berehaven's largest import by far. "It's part of the pay," they say, "take it!" But the shattered nerves crave another shot, and that must be bought at the company's shebeen, as does the next and the next. When Cornelius pointed out to the captain that he should get extra coin if he's not taking that "part of the pay," they begrudgingly added a bit to his wages. He's determined to save more than will be due next gale day, no matter how high Bantry chooses to spike the rents. Not a ha'penny will he waste, not on anything, not on drink. No need, thanks to Jeremiah's generosity and the potatoes that keep feeding the hidden stills this spring. Cornelius has probably had too much today, he's thinking now, because he can't say just how long McCarthy-Moor has been standing in front of him, staring at his boots.

"What happened there?" the landlord's agent asks, running a finger over a gouge in the side of Cornelius's shoe. The hole in the leather exposes the wool of his sock and extends on down to the sole, which looks as if someone has taken a bite from it.

"What business is it of yours?" Cornelius answers, pulling his feet away and setting them on the hard earth.

"Maybe none, you're right, but at the next assizes it might be the judge's business."

"Ah," Jeremiah chimes in, "a new law on the books, eh? What's the punishment for damaging your own boots? Drawing and quartering?"

"*No*," McCarthy-Moor says, "but you can still hang for stealing from a rabbit warren."

Cornelius sets his eyes on Julia. She has just started in singing a sad air with the fiddler. Her voice calms the rumbling within him, always does.

"I may be sauced," Jeremiah goes on, "but I'm not following your line of reason. What does a boot have to do with a rabbit warren?"

"Think about it," McCarthy-Moor mutters. He follows Cornelius's gaze, and then says to him, "Fine color, there, in your wife's cheeks. The kind that comes from a thick steak or, say, some roasted game? What could account for that, I wonder?"

Cornelius is up in a flash, one hand on the agent's throat, the other in his own pocket. Jeremiah has shot up, too, and gets his own hand on his nephew's wrist. He knows what Cornelius is reaching for, knows it is, in fact, what they were making at the forge when, due to their inexperience and rushing so as not to be discovered trespassing, they'd dropped the red-hot tongs on his boot. "Don't take his bait, Con," he whispers.

"Get out *now*, you traitor," another of the men is saying, ominous despite his long beard and shaky stance. A dog, scruffy and ginger-haired, with piercing eyes, is by his side, teeth bared.

"Just doing a job," McCarthy-Moor says to him. "I'm Irish, same flock as you."

"Your *job* is to pull every penny from us for that land-thieving Bantry," the shaky man says, teeth clenched. "No real Irishman would do that."

Cornelius spits, "But if it's a flock you're looking for, maybe the buzzards will take you in."

"Better not be testing me come gale day, Sullivan," the agent says to Cornelius. "There's talk of turning all this here to pasture."

"*Pasture*, hmm," Jeremiah says, scratching his head. "So, we're to eat grass, now, is it?"

"Oh, *quite* the funny man, Jeremiah. When cattle have taken your place here, maybe you can find a job as a performer in Cork City," McCarthy-Moor sneers. "And Bantry's ready with the battering ram, you better believe it. All's I have to do is say the word 'arrears.'"

By now a gaggle of others have gotten out of their chairs and are glaring at the agent, pointing to the road. More dogs have gotten in on the act, and, not one to get along so well with the canines, McCarthy-Moor takes a tug on his vest (which doesn't nearly cover his portly belly) and struts to the post where he's tied up his horse. He steers the animal out of the village to a barrage of applause and curses.

"Let's get that boot repaired," Jeremiah says to Cornelius as they settle back into their chairs, pass the jug again. "We've got a little time before the assizes. If there's no evidence, they can't bother you. And steer clear of there from now on."

"He must've set a trap," Cornelius says, "some ash or lime laid for a print on the walk outside the gate, maybe. It was dry as a bone, not a bit of mud, every night I've gone in there. I've been careful."

"You weren't being careful today when you reached for that tool of yours. Though I know you have good reason to want to skin or bleed *that* animal."

Cornelius watches as Julia makes her way to him now, her song finished. She is smiling serenely. It appears she hadn't noticed the agent there at all, and Cornelius has no intention of telling her of the encounter. Nor has he ever told her how desperately he begged McCarthy-Moor for milk, for meat, for *anything* that summer she was carrying their last one. Such a hungry time, summer, and just around the corner. He takes a swig from the jug, gives it back to Jeremiah and stands to greet his wife.

"You look tired, Connie," she says to him, taking the garland off her neck and putting it around his. She smirks, then says, "Might you be wanting a nap?"

"Where are the kids?" He looks over her shoulder to a clump of children dancing. Others are off in a field, tossing a hoop around. A game of nine-pin is underway in a raked yard, a pig looking over a makeshift pen at the competitors.

"Mary's practicing the flute somewhere. And Danny's gone with the big boys to learn how to high jump for the games tonight. He may leap right up to the heavens, he's so excited to be included." She smiles again. "They'll be busy a while."

Cornelius looks down at Jeremiah in his chair, who motions impatiently that he should go. So he takes ahold of his wife's hand and they walk the short distance to the edge of the village and their hut.

From the stoop, they can see their rows of potato plants, white blossoms dotting deep green leaves. Cornelius blinks his eyes a few times, because he can swear he is seeing cows trampling his beds. It's the poteen, he knows, working on his imagination, too keen these days as it is. Sometimes, when he's on his belly in the mines, he is sure he is looking down on himself, and what he sees is a ferret tunneling through the dark.

"We need to bless the plants at the end of the day," he says to his wife, ducking in through the door and taking a few clumsy strides to their mattress tick of rushes. He drops heavily, fatigue like a veil falling over him. "Let's don't forget. We'll do it all together, the four of us."

"Of course," she says. But she's surprised he's raised it. He usually tries to bow out, lets her carry out that Beltane rite with other believers, that walking the perimeter of the garden, praying at cardinal points. She drops to her knees beside him, peers into hazy eyes.

"Sorry," he whispers, "I meant the five of us." And he reaches a hand out to her, but sleep takes him off before even a fingertip's touch.

She sighs deeply and gets back up, makes her way to their little window that looks out over the sea. A songbird has been there, shoots off now with a *chichichit*. She leans her elbows on the deep ledge, notices now the swift movement of steely clouds toward land, blackening the sea below like a curtain being drawn. Soon there is a crack of lightning. *How rare*, she thinks, not recalling a thunderstorm on a May Day, not ever in her life. She pulls her skirt up into an arm, darts out the door to find the children.

On the road, the travelers are noticing that sky, too, and are fearful. They hurriedly pack up their picnic baskets and sketch pads, and soon they are on their way, their carriage shrouded in a salty mist that follows them eastward.

"A fairy blast," an old crone who is watching their retreat from the half-door of her hut says to the air.

•

"Just like us!" Mitch cries, pointing to the blue-black clouds clinging to the zig-zag of mountaintops in the distance. "Lightning!"

Dot looks askance at her partner. "Can't *change* the story, huh?"

"What? You don't think there was a rainstorm in the original story?"

"I don't. I think it was an adaptation. You *imagined* it into the story."

"No, it's all true," she says. "What's say we go find cover?"

"That rain's miles from us," Dot insists. "It won't even track this way. Our storms don't come out of the east like that."

"Yeah, we'll be okay, Mama. Were Mary and Danny-boy okay?"

"Yes," Shannon says. "Julia found Mary playing her flute to the seabirds. Same melody she'd been trying to play with her mother, only she wasn't missing any notes this time. Mary was so carried away by her feathered audience, that she hadn't even noticed the raindrops until her mother arrived. They rolled the flute up into the girl's skirt to keep it dry and then rounded up Daniel, who was not in nearly as good a mood as his sister was. The big boys, it turns out, had just wanted him to hold one side of the stick while they practiced their own high jumps."

"They were mean to him?" Mitch asks.

"Not mean, just leaving him out."

"Same thing," he says, and he moves nearer to his mother now, lets her put an arm around his shoulders. He keeps a weather eye on the sky, counts lightning strikes. There have been three so far. The swallows' paths crisscross, more hectic than before.

She runs her fingers through his hair, but a burst of wind sets the strands free again. "That's out of the east," she informs her partner.

"Well, it's a slow-moving system," Dot says.

Shannon gives her a skeptical look, but goes on. "So Julia took them to a friend's place to ride out the storm. She said it was because their hut was closer, but really it was that she didn't want them to see Cornelius sleeping in the middle of the day."

"Is that stuff—the punchin'—like moonshine?" Mitch asks.

"That's right," Shannon says.

"Like what Uncle Seanie was drinking, before he went to the hospital and got Beetle Juice because he'd gone bat-shit crazy?"

"That one's on *you*, Shan," Dot says. "I didn't even know y'all back then."

"Just say 'crazy,' okay?" she says to Mitch. "And, yes, Seanie was drinking, but not moonshine."

Mitch has gotten up to six now, counting the lightning bolts, and the wind is pushing that blue-black cloud bank nearer, making some of the mountain peaks disappear.

"Did they get out to bless the potato plants?" Dot asks, still acting like there's nothing going on in the sky in front of them.

Shannon goes on with the narrative, but at a markedly more rapid pace: "It rained hard for most of the day, but there was enough light left for the walks after the sky cleared. They stopped at the southern point and got down on their knees, then moved along to the eastern point, then the northern, then lastly to the west, where they'd planted right up to the cliff's edge. Cornelius said an extra prayer at that spot, looking out at the still churning sea, nothing between him and our coast here, nothing but ocean. If his eyes were sharp enough, or if he had some sí magic in him, he might have seen clear across to these very mountains."

Mitch is up to eight lightning strikes, and the last one has come with a startling crack of thunder.

"That's it!" Shannon yells, scrambling down the incline.

"Say 'bye to the cows, Mermaid!" Dot cries, scooting down the slope, the rain coming by the time they hit the ground and break into a run.

"Moo-moo-moo!" Muriel chants, bouncing along on Dot's shoulder.

Mitch is last one down. "Mama," he says, "maybe it's a flying cow going over us."

"Let's hold out our tongues, then," she says, and they run, side by side, both with heads tipped and mouths open, weaving drunkenly through the thistle and around the blackened fire circle and down to the encampment and into their makeshift home.

From on high, you can see others flitting around to find shelter here and there, stumbling into their own tents. Move a little farther up, and you can see the river, a few watercraft steering toward shore, many paddling on as if there were no threat. Over there, through the canopy of oaks and poplars, if you try, you can glimpse hikers, some tromping on in ponchos, some huddling together and waiting.

And coming from the direction of the mining site is an especially satisfied-looking bunch, all with green bandanas around their necks. They have spent the last few hours in trees, watching workers paint and scrub to remove messages left before the first horn sounded of the day, before the first blast of dynamite took off a ridge. Messages like this one covering the front of the office trailer: *Over 1,200 miles of streams buried or destroyed by coal mining.* Or this on its roof: *The Appalachian Mountains are the birthplace of the east coast's water supply.* Or this on the parking lot pavement: *The rate of children born with birth defects is 42% higher in mountaintop removal mining areas.* Or this on a dumpster: *The public health cost of pollution from coal mining is $75 billion each year.* Or this on the side of every one of those machines built to destroy the mountains: *Mayday! Mayday! Mayday!*

Lughnasa

"'FIDDLER'S TRACE,'" DOT READS from the sign as she steers the car into the parking lot. "*Right.* It's like those housing developments named for the trees they clear off for the construction—'Maple Grove' or 'Orchard Hill.' I'll give you a hundred bucks if we see *one damn* person with a fiddle while we're here."

"*Dot,*" Shannon says, exasperated. "Could we give Mitch one tiny little chance of keeping his mouth out of trouble this school year?"

"Oh, he'll be fine," Dot says. "Mitch, you won't be getting your teacher upset, will you?"

"How do I know if she'll get upset or not?" He answers from the backseat. "I never met her yet."

"Well, you do know better than to repeat cuss words by now, right?" Dot asks him.

"Yup," he says. "But I heard Muriel use the f-word the other day."

"*Dot!*" Shannon hisses.

"Could've gotten it from a movie," she says, slowing down and scanning one side of the lane, then the other.

"*Why* are you passing all these empty spaces?" Shannon asks her.

"I'm looking for shade. It's hot as hell." Then feeling, perhaps, the burning of Shannon's glare from the passenger seat, she adds, "*Fire.* Hell*fire.* That word is okay with people for some reason, which just goes to show that the rules of polite society make no sense whatsoever." She pulls the little car into a spot under a pear tree and shuts off the engine.

Shannon looks over at the entrance now, at a small collection of white-haired women on benches and in wheelchairs. "I'm sorry I'm in such a bad mood," she says. "It's just that Granddad and I had a whole life together, and it's mostly just, *poof*, gone from his head. It agitates me so much to be here. That's why I don't come, and then I just feel guilty on top of it all."

"I know," Dot says, leaning over and kissing her cheek. "That's the only reason I haven't poured my water bottle over your head."

Mitch giggles from the backseat, then pulls the door handle in and out, in and out, in and out.

"*Stop* it, Mitch," Shannon says, getting out and opening his door. "You know there's a child safety latch, so why do you *do* that?"

"For fun," he says, holding up his own water bottle and unscrewing the top, an impish grin on his face.

"Don't even *think* about it."

"It's weird not having Mermaid with us." Dot is looking through the window at the empty carseat. "I miss her."

"We only left her two hours ago," Shannon says. "And given that fit she pitched, *I* sure don't miss her."

"I'm still thinking about that move of hers," Dot says. "How'd she know that we wouldn't be able to fit her in the door if she threw her arms and legs out like that? Impressive spacial reasoning going on there, if you ask me. She looked like a sky-diver." She gazes up at the low white ceiling of the muggy day. "Hm. I wonder how old you need to be to take sky-diving lessons."

"*Salvation*," Shannon mutters, looking up, too.

"I know how we can get her into the car," Mitch says, taking the hand his mother has offered him. "Put one of Leda's new lambies in the backseat with us. There's room."

Dot casts an arm toward the car, theatrically, "'Enough space for your entire family, plus livestock!' We could be in a commercial for electric cars."

"How about we let Leda keep her lambs for her yarn-making," Shannon says.

"Do *you* have a plan for getting Muriel away from those baby animals?" Dot asks, following them onto the sidewalk.

"Wait till she's asleep, and grab her and run," she says.

"See, that's why you're the mother. I'll drive the getaway car. Always been wanting to do that." Dot's eyes wander to the women by the door. One is grinning, can't keep her feet still as the three of them approach.

"I feel bad about leaving Leda to take care of Muriel all day," Shannon says. "What with the baby and all."

"Remember, she was the one who insisted," Dot says. "She wants Muriel to be close to her cousin Luna. And, anyhow, Sean is the one who's always holding that baby, except for feeding time. I bet he'd grow breasts if he could."

Mitch pulls away from his mother now, darts toward the entrance. He likes how the glass doors open when he stands in front, then close when he steps back.

Shannon runs after him, taking his hand again. "It wastes energy, Mitch, don't do that."

"It's okay, honey," the foot-tapping woman whispers to Mitch. "We think it's fun too, but we get in trouble when we do it." The whole bunch starts cackling now.

"You look so much like my grandmother," Dot tells one of them, a woman hunched over in a wheelchair.

The woman pushes her eyes up in an unnatural way, an adaptation for not being able to move her neck. She whispers mischievously, "Maybe I am."

"Why can't she move?" Mitch asks as they step through the doors, a rush of cold air coming at them from above.

"Old bones," Shannon says as the doors slide closed and

a tune fills the air—an electronic version of something from an old TV show, *Gilligan's Island*.

"Fiddlers, my ass," Dot mutters.

"There he is." Shannon is looking off toward a sofa set under a corner window of the lobby.

"He looks like Rip Van Winkle," Mitch says. "You can hear his snoring all the way over here. And his beard is *so long*."

"Good for him," Dot says. "There's got to come a point in life when you just say no to shaving."

Shannon takes a deep breath and sets off in his direction. Dot goes to take her hand, but Shannon slides it away and whispers, "Let's not say anything about *us*. Too confusing for him."

A man in scrubs has arrived at the sofa a couple of steps ahead of them. A plastic ID tag tick-tocks back and forth on his lanyard as he leans over. "Mr. Sullivan," he says, loudly enough to make him startle. "No sleeping in the lobby."

"Since when?" Shannon asks, loudly enough to make the man in scrubs startle. She sees now that the fabric is covered with smiling teddy bears.

"Months ago," he says to her, not making eye contact. "It makes a bad impression."

"Well, you go and tell your members of parliament," Granddad says, sitting up straight now and smoothing a hand over his silky beard, "that I have no plan to follow any penal code."

"Just stay awake or go to your room," the employee says tiredly, and he turns on squeaky heels and disappears down a hallway, poorly lit.

"Persecutors," the old man mutters, then seems suddenly aware of the three of them standing over him.

"Nice to meet you, Mr. Sullivan," Dot says, first to the draw. "I'm your granddaughter's lover. We live together."

Shannon kicks Dot's foot before taking into consideration that Dot is in heavy-soled hiking sandals and she is in flip-flops. "*Ow*," Shannon moans, letting herself down onto the sofa and squeezing her big toe.

"I don't believe in that there nonsense," he says to Dot.

"You mean same-sex relationships?" she asks.

"No, I mean couples living together in sin. People should get married, for God's sake."

Dot looks down at her partner, who remains focused on her foot. "Shannon, will you marry me?"

"*Dot....*"

"I mean it."

Shannon looks up at her now. "You can't be serious," she says, even while she can see the earnestness in her partner's expression.

"When did you get *this*, Granddaddy?" Mitch asks, noticing the walker parked next to the sofa. It's red as a tanager, with shiny black wheels.

"Just woke up one day, and there it was, I had me a brand spanking new vehicle. Fairies left it," he says.

"No, Papaw," Shannon says, patting his knee. "Seanie and I got you that. He brought it over for you himself. It's nice, isn't it? Sleek. I'd only seen a picture."

"Thanks, darlin'," he says to her. "And thanks, Sean," he says to Mitch.

"I'm not Sean," he says. "Sean's at Way Out Farm with his baby, wanting to grow some breasts."

"Glad he's doing well," Granddad says, nodding.

"Yeah, he read me a chapter of *The Grapes of Wrath* yesterday. The Joadses are at the Weedpatch Camp now."

"I always liked that book," Granddad says. "Steinbeck."

Shannon sighs. "Now, how do you remember a *book*, and not, well, more important things? How long ago did you even *read* that?"

"I read it with Sean, there, when he was in high school." His eyes are on Mitch, and he looks the small boy up and down, then his face squinches with confusion. He twirls a lock of his beard around a knobby finger. "So who's your favorite character?" he asks.

"Mulie," Mitch says, without hesitation. "He won't leave, you see. He stays even when the Cats come. He watches out. He takes care of what's left after everyone else runs away from the dust."

"That reminds me," Dot says, settling down in a wing chair next to the sofa. "I happened to notice when Sean was reading to him that there is a fair amount of cussing in that book." She tilts her head at Shannon. "Just saying."

"So, how's things at the holler, Julia?" Granddad says to Shannon now.

"Papaw, I'm not Julia. I'm your granddaughter you raised up. You drove me to school in the tractor that first day of second grade when I wouldn't get on the bus. You taught me how to use the bush hog. You took me up to minor league baseball games on those Saturdays when they gave out little souvenir bats, remember? There's a collection of them still in the house in the hollow."

"I want to get those," Mitch says. He's rolling the walker back and forth on the linoleum. "There's other things I been wanting, too, like the turtle shells I found in the woods. And my fairy stones. No one is watching out, Mama. Our stuff could get stole." He pushes the walker harder now, and it hits the wall and bounces back.

Shannon looks over at the reception desk, where a woman—in scrubs, too, hers an unnatural shade of bright pink—is shaking her head disapprovingly in their direction. "Mitchy, sit down," Shannon says to him. "See? That walker has a little seat. Climb up on it."

He tries, but the wheels keep rolling and swiveling this way and that.

"Here," Granddad says, reaching with a groan and grabbing onto a handle with a curled, arthritic hand. He pulls the walker as close as he can and takes a few clumsy swipes at the brake lever until it locks. He pats the seat, and the boy hops up, starts a drumbeat with his shoe tips against the leg of the coffee table the furniture is set around.

"Deer camp," Shannon says now. "You *do* remember deer camp, right Papaw? Mamaw was always telling you to stop treating me like a boy, but you didn't listen."

"Oh, I never listened to Mamaw," he says with puff.

"Oh, so true," Shannon says.

"You were a good shot," he tells her, patting her leg.

"Yeah, I was." She smiles now, a little.

"When did you learn hunting, Mama?" Mitch asks.

"When I was ten."

"I don't want to learn hunting," he says.

Granddad pipes up, "I know, I know, Sean. It's not for everyone, killing animals. That's why I stopped taking you hunting by the time you were a teenager. Wasn't doing you no good." A touch of bafflement returns to his face as he scrutinizes the little boy again. He shakes it off. "Life's too short."

"I'll live long 'cause I'm a vegetarier," he says.

"Ain't that some kinda dog?" Granddad asks.

"No, it's a person who eats veggie burgers instead of cow

burgers," Mitch tells him. "Did you have cows in the hollow, Granddaddy?"

"Not me, personally, no," he says. "Had a brother in the holler who had him better pasture ground, so his property was where the milch cows were. But *you* know that, Sean. That was the house you were raised up in. Why you asking me *that?*"

"Because I'm not, uh," Mitch starts, but then pauses, seems to shift gears, "remembering things so well." He sets his eyes on his still-swinging legs, avoiding eye-contact with his mother, who has, in the past, reprimanded him for playing along with the old man's slips of memory. She said it was not honest, that you had to tell him what was real and true. But if Mitch looked up at her now, he wouldn't see disapproval there on her face. He'd see resignation.

"Now that I think on it," Granddad says, twirling his beard again, "there was a cow on our land when I was a youngun, back when my granddad was still living. He said he would have a cow his whole life, need it or not, on general principle."

"You mean Daniel?" Shannon asks.

"No, not my son. My *granddad*," he says.

"Your granddad was a Daniel, too, Papaw," she reminds him.

"*Whew*, this is confusing," Dot says, leaning deeply into the chair and putting her feet up on the glass top of the table.

"Huh," Granddad says, a distant look coming into his gray eyes. "Right you are—Danny-boy. We called him Papaw Danny-boy."

Shannon, noticing now the hot pink receptionist heading their way, a stony look on her face, whispers to Mitch, "Stop banging your shoes against the table," and to Dot, "Maybe you should take your feet down."

"Their feet ain't harming nothin'," Granddad says.

"Could you please take your shoes off the furniture?" the woman, now within earshot, says blandly to Dot.

"No she will not," Granddad says.

"Mr. Sullivan," the woman says, drawing out the syllables of his name, as if she's speaking to a child. "You know the expectations."

"I ain't never seen a law about that," he says. "Take me to court."

"I'm going to be a lawyer," Mitch says, intending to punctuate the statement with another tap of the table leg, but his mother puts her arm out to stop the motion.

"Good, I need one around here," Granddad says.

The woman crosses her arms over her chest and clears her throat, but she doesn't get any closer. "If you want to live here, Mr. Sullivan—"

"I don't!" he barks at her. "Evict me, go ahead. I'll find me a place to live where the citizens ain't oppressed by the government."

She turns on her heels, settles back behind the desk and picks up the phone, her eyes set on them sitting there.

"We kinda don't have anywhere else for him to *live*," Shannon says softly to Dot from behind her hand, to which Dot gives her a *Well, what can I do?* look, nodding toward Granddad's self-satisfied expression. "You could get up and stretch your legs," Shannon whispers.

"Hey, Granddad," Dot says, popping up from the chair. "Where can a person pee around here?"

He points to the dimly lit hall, and when she's left, he says, "I like that girl. She uses plain language."

"She does," Shannon agrees.

"Granddaddy, do you know how Danny-boy got to the hollow?" Mitch asks.

"Of course."

"How?"

"His daddy bought that scrap of land from a Cherokee Indian," Granddad says. "But why am I telling *you* this? You know the Sullivan story, Sean. I told it to you myself."

"Mitch, I said I'd tell it on the road, on the way back home," Shannon reminds him.

"I know, but you'll end it without anyone getting to the hollow. You always do."

"They'll get there eventually," she says.

"I don't want them to get there ventually. I want them to get there now."

"What month is it?" Granddad asks.

"August," Mitch says.

"Tough luck," he says. "It's only Lughnasa. He's still in Ireland. But you know that chapter."

"No, I *don't*," Mitch says, impatience creeping into his voice now.

"It was the harvest festival," Shannon says to him. "Started back when the Celts would pray to the god Lugh to make sure the crops came in good."

"You mean the potatoes?" Mitch asks.

"Our ancestors in the story would've had the potatoes in mind, yeah," she says.

"Is that all that grew in Ireland?"

"Oh, no," Granddad says, gruffly. "The plantations grew a lot of wheat. And they grew barley, and oats, and who knows what else. All for sending off to England, so it might as well have grown on Jupiter for the good it did our people. Papaw Danny-Boy railed about that till his dying day."

"Will you tell me about the day of the festival, Granddaddy?" Mitch asks.

"The festival?" he repeats, and then he pauses, twirls a bit of beard and takes a tug, as if on a lever. "Do you smell that?"

"You mean that really strong antiseptic-mixed-with-baby-powder smell?" Dot says, settling back into the chair. She knocks off her sandals and tucks her feet under her. "It's overpowering in this place."

"Not that smell, Dottie," Shannon says. She leans now against her grandfather's shoulder, nearing its century mark but still ample. The food is something he doesn't complain about here. He was taught from a young age not to scoff at a meal, never.

"Not that one, no," he says.

•

MARY NOTICED IT FIRST, early in the morning. It woke her up, it did, so strong was it, though the others would soon tell her they didn't smell anything at all. It was there, nonetheless. Mary could actually see the particles of it. Not against the dim sky, but against the full moon framed in the window that Lughnasa morning. Sí horses, silhouetted against the white disk, drew carriages full of it, the pieces of smell flying from the windows like dry leaves. The highest race of fairies, the ones full of hubris, were hootin' and hollerin' as they kicked the smell around, dragged it, pulled it apart till it was a black miasma. The lesser fairies had it piled on their backs in willow creels. It was so heavy, that smell, that they were staggering under it; some had to stop right there on the moon and take a rest, panting, their wings trembling by their sides. That was the halfway point between the Tir Na Nog and Ballydonegan, Mary surmised, as she watched from her bed, Daniel's arm curled around her, her nightdress bunched into his fist like a security blanket. He thought of her like that, as a protector, she knew this, and it was all the more why she wanted to get up, to see if her flute could change the course of things. It had often made the fairies dance, hadn't it? But doing that would mean waking up her brother, waking up her ma and da. And everyone knows it's disrespectful to pull a body from sleep like that!

•

GRANDDAD'S SHOUTED THIS LAST part, in the direction of the man in the teddy bear scrubs, who has reappeared and is now setting up a few rows of chairs in the center of the lobby. He acts as if he didn't hear, but everyone heard: the women now gathered around a table putting together a jigsaw puzzle, who give him a collective giggle, one a fist pump, and the receptionist, who sighs in his direction.

"I like the Appalachian style you bring to the story, Granddad," Dot says.

"What do you mean?" he asks, tucking the wavy tips of his beard under his belt.

"You know, the exaggeration, the mountain tall-tale. You do it well, sir."

He wags his head from side to side. "Oh, no, it's all true."

"Keep going, Papaw," Shannon says.

"I forgot where I am."

"At a nursing home," Mitch tells him.

"I know *that*," he says, but there's a tinge of terror in his expression as he takes in the room.

"If it were me," Shannon says, "I'd move on to Cornelius now."

Granddad pats his beard, in that way you might pat a crying baby's back. He lets his eyes settle on the window next to the sofa. A tree has grown so close that it is touching the glass. "There's a nest there in that branch," he says, pointing a crooked finger, remembering a messy collection of twigs and feathers. But maybe it's not that tree. Maybe not even that window. He sees a lot of trees, after all, spends his days in pursuit of windows.

·

"It's the fever," Cornelius says to Julia, after Mary tells them of the smell, after she goes outside with the flute to sit atop the raised rock the ancients put out in the field, what they call the stone table. Her parents can hear from the hut the melody she plays out there, one she has been perfecting for weeks. *Conversing*, she tells her parents it's called when they ask her the name of the song. *Pleading* is what she might call it this day, but they don't ask.

"Nonsense," Julia says. "I felt her head. She's fine."

But he is not convinced. He is certain he can see the children shrinking. He puts fingers around his wife's wrists in the night when she sleeps, measuring the loss since the end of the lumper supply. They hadn't exactly run out, but there's a limit to how long you can store the crop before the rot sets in, no matter how big the harvest of that last fall. They knew it would be coming, were in better shape than usual, Julia reminds him often, but still he watches them all carefully as they sleep each night. Still he curls around her warm body, an arm over her growing middle, waiting for kicks, elbow jabs, and cursing silently the guards Bantry posts as soon as he knows they've no food left in their stores.

Not many lumpers had gone to waste, really, what with feeding all but the very nastiest ones to the pigs. They were fattened to the point of being round as barrels, each and every on. Their stubby legs would give out now and again, and they'd roll down the hills, some right over the cliff. "Mine rolled all the way to Ameriky," a woman said in front of the chapel last Sunday, standing with her children by the ditch where they'd built a scalp from the remains of their toppled home. Those passersby who still had their pigs were suspect, thought that the family had given in and eaten theirs—"the man who pays the rent," as they call it—and that's why the woman and her children were on the roads now.

This is the reason Cornelius doesn't go to the festival today. Not because of the woman or the rolling pigs, exactly, but because of his own mounting fear. Every Lughnasa, it was true, he suggested they stay in their townland, not go to the big fair in Berehaven. He didn't like how the miles-long walk, while not a great burden when they were hardy, drained them fast during this time before the harvest could begin, before they could dig up those first tender orbs, the ones just below the surface, so easy to pull from the dark, supple soil that even a small child could scoop them up in cupped hands.

"Connie, relax, the new potatoes will be ripe in a matter of weeks," Julia reminds him, looking into hollow eyes getting hollower from little sleep, from little food (he claimed to be full on half an oatcake this morning so the children could take his share). "The pilgrimage is an important part of the day, you know that. The bilberries will be out on the ridges, so we'll pick and eat as we go—no worries. And Mary has been aching to hear the harpists, Danny to see the games, the vendors. Someone always gives in to his sweet face, lets him have a bun or a candy. And you know what *I'm* looking forward to." He does, and realizing he has no sway, tells her he will get there later, that he has errands.

It's Young Ireland, of course, that Julia's thinking of. She's sure that Speranza will be there, and even more sure of it— for some moments, anyway—when she hears a woman at the fair reciting a poem with a rise-and-fall cadence of a bard.

She rushes to the performance, pulling the children with her, and stands at the back of a crowd that has gathered.

> *Mine eye is dull, my hair is white,*
> *This arm is powerless for the fight,*
> *Alas! alas! the battle's van*
> *Suits not a weak and aged man.*
> *Thine eye is bright, thine arm is strong—*
> *'Tis Youth must right our country's wrong.*

These are, for sure, Speranza's words, from "The Old Man's Blessing," but it takes only a verse for Julia to realize it is not her Dublin poetess in the flesh. These lines are spoken in Irish, a translation, and Julia has learned enough about Speranza to know that she does not have the Gaelic language among her talents. So it is with a measure of disappointment that she listens to the rest of the poem.

> *Arise! arise! my patriot son,*
> *By hearts like thine is Freedom won!*

There is rousing applause at this last line, led by the Young Irelanders, who, Julia can see now, have a strong presence at the fair, men and women with placards and handbills encouraging rebellion. These written, too, in the language of the West Cork peasants.

"I want to be a rebel," Daniel announces, loudly enough to be heard by some members of the constabulary, whose heads tip disapprovingly in his direction. There are many of them at the fringes of the crowd, standing tall with hands behind their backs, sticks at the ready. Tipping her own head disapprovingly at their ranks, Julia tugs on the children's hands, leads them away.

"You're not old enough to be a rebel," she says to Daniel as they stroll the harbor. A schooner is anchored just off shore, its name, *The Circassian*, painted into its hull. She recognizes it as one of the emigrant ships, one of the many from this port during the crossing season, now winding down for the year. "But others will fight for you and take back Ireland, so you'll have no need to be a rebel yourself. You can be a farmer, grow what you want, on land you own."

"Will I have a cow?"

"Always."

Daniel sniffs the air now, smells the baked goods, and says, "You want a roll, Mary? I can get you one."

"No stealing," Julia reminds him. "No getting in trouble."

"But they're all over *there*, ma," he says, pointing to the police still gathered around the poet. "They're not near the food."

Which was precisely Cornelius's thought that morning, and why he planned the detour. Bantry—who himself would be in London, as always—would surely not, on this day, have a full contingent of guards around the game preserve. The planter's highest priority would be the granary and the cattle, for the exports were of the most value to him. He'd have all the redcoats posted around those, and the Irish police he normally contracted would be attending the fair, reveling or guarding, one or the other. McCarthy-Moor himself went to the fair, Cornelius knew from the years, for it was a place of business transactions, land deals that Bantry would surely want his agent to get a part of. Maybe Cornelius would have to face a local boy or two, he figured, hired to keep out poachers, but he wasn't worried. On a day such as this, with no supervision, any young man would be into the whiskey by now. It was human nature. That's the kind of confidence Cornelius carried with him as he sidled through the gate.

Mary was listening to the harp when she saw some of it skating along the bay, bouncing off the mast of that tall ship and doing a loop-de-loop. When it hit the pier just next to where they sat, she gasped and pulled her feet up under her, so sure it was going to reach them, touch land. But instead it shattered into the air, rained down on the waves like sparks from a volcano. It was awfully close, and she wished she had her flute to push it back to sea. It had seemed to work this morning. "I want to go home," she says to her mother.

Julia looks at her, surprised that her daughter would ask to go before the music was over. But the girl had not been right all day, had seemed in a trance going from one thing to the next, her hand never letting loose of her mother's. Julia touches Mary's forehead for the umpteenth time, but it is not the fever. She is sure of that, at least. "Don't you want to wait on your da?" she asks, but it's half-hearted, her eyes on the sun, its journey to the west begun.

"What does this say?" Daniel asks, picking up a piece of paper that has blown their way, almost blown off the pier.

Julia studies it there in his hand, and says, "It's an advertisement for laborers to work on a railroad."

"In the Blue Ridge Mountains," an old woman sitting near them says.

"The mountains are *blue?*" Daniel asks, wide-eyed.

"So they say," the woman continues. "My grandson's going to find out. He's leaving on that boat this week." She nods toward the ship. "He'll be working in the Virginia colony—*commonwealth*, I mean. That's what he says it's called. States or commonwealths over there, not colonies. They have their freedom."

Julia looks to the square where the Young Irelanders had been, gone now. Back to Dublin, maybe. "The Yanks have proved you can win a rebellion against the British, haven't they?" she says.

The old woman shakes her head. "Never here. We're too close. All they have to do is reach a boot over and stomp us down. So I send my son off, never to see him again, send my grandson now—" Her voice catches, and she turns back to the music, the plucking of harp strings.

"I want to go home," Mary says again. It has been gathering more fiercely now, has filled the air around the port. The ship is as if in a fog, the figurehead on the bow the only thing she can make out—is it an angel? A selkie? She can't tell, and now it's too late.

Julia, with a sigh, gets up and leads them off the pier, through the main street of Berehaven, and up the hill behind to the path on the ridge, the old road of their own ancestors— past the stone circle where they worshipped their gods; past the burial mound with the chamber that saw light only on the solstice; past the grassy fields where they grazed their cattle in summer; past the derry once their hunting ground but now a peat bog; past the feasting site where they cooked their meats in the fulacht fiadh, lost under centuries of windblown soil, under gorse and bramble. The last thing they pass before descending is the holy well. Julia stops here, thinks it might be wise to pray a round, to pray for Mary. But the girl, who can see now over the crest to Ballydonegan below, makes a strange sound like a bird in pain, and pulls on her mother's arm. Though all that meets Julia's eyes is the village in half-light and a calm sea beyond, she rushes down the mountainside, nevertheless, and through the boreen and onto the low road. From the bridge over the Ballydonegan River they can see their hut, and a man standing in the doorway.

"Look, it's Da," she says, and the children run ahead, Daniel to see his father and Mary to find her flute. Four, five steps more, though, she finds it is not Cornelius on the stoop.

"Jeremiah," she says, stopping in the path. "So Con was with *you* today."

"Part of it," he says, motioning her to come into the hut with him.

She stands firmly where she is on the dirt. "The poteen?"

Mary shoots out of the door now, flute in hand, nearly knocking over her great uncle, then races out of sight.

"Let me explain inside, Julia," Jeremiah says, looking up and down the road.

"Ma!" It is Daniel from in the hut. "Da's hurt!"

Jeremiah ducks in now, shushing Daniel and closing the door behind Julia, who has rushed in after him.

"Connie!" she cries, getting on her knees on the tick, where he is curled onto his side, cradling an arm wrapped in rags. Tears drip from his eyes—not from his pain, which the poteen has relieved, but from his failure.

"It was a bullet," Jeremiah says. "McCarthy-Moor didn't go to the fair today."

"What are you talking about?" Julia asks, but she knows, she can piece it together. "His arm?"

"Went clean through. A rifle shot from enough of a distance that maybe he didn't see it was Con. But we need to get him out of here. I could take him to my place, but McCarthy-Moor will have that second-most on the garda's list. There's a souterrain up by the stills. I'm thinking to take him there to hole up in one of the tunnels."

"But what then?" she asks. "He'll be found out sooner or later, with a wound like that."

"I have enough coin, you know, from selling the poteen. It was such a good year for the making of it." He knows she is looking straight at him now, but he keeps his own eyes on his nephew. "So."

"Jeremiah, you're *not* meaning emigration?"

"Con talks about it, Julia." He is whispering now. "About going on his own and sending money back for you, so you can get the children out of this place. He sees doom here, all around."

"What's that smell, Ma?" Daniel asks.

He's been sitting so quietly that she's forgotten he's there. And she hears now Mary's flute (she hadn't been noticing that, either) which is playing furiously, the tune turned terrible and beautiful all at once.

Julia sniffs the air, then she gets up and goes out the door, Daniel on her heels. She walks to the plants in their rows pointing to the cliff, and she scoops into the earth until she pulls up a potato. It is black, slimy, and she digs some more, and then Daniel digs, and as far as they can reach, all the potatoes are black. They run from row to row, but it is the same. Soon their neighbors are out of their huts and following their noses, too.

"*No*, not *this*." It is Jeremiah, come up next to her now, where she sits in the middle of the potato plot. He looks at her fingers, stained with the ruin. A low moan begins to rise off all the fields.

"Take Con," Julia says. "Take him now while he doesn't realize, while he doesn't see us as skeletons. There's a ship in harbor."

"I know," he says.

"Get him on that. Do what you need to do. *Lie*. Tell him our crop is fine, no matter what he hears people saying."

"I'll help you, you know it," he says. "And Con'll send money, so you'll have passage on the first boat when the sailing starts up again."

"*Go now*," she says, turning away from him. She pulls Daniel up into her lap and holds him so tightly he cries out.

Mary, still on the stone table, stops playing the flute because it's no use. Because she can't hear it over the howling that's filling the world. She can't see the downy notes curling out of the end, can't even see her fingertips pressing and lifting. She lets herself down off the flat stone, and runs against that thick air, against the wormy beings that cling to her hair, climb up her legs, crawl into her ears and her nostrils, all their tiny wings like razors. Each swat she takes turns them to billowing, heaving waves that pull away, then crash around her, circling, circling as she presses against the fairy blast.

Julia sees her, though she is too far away to do anything. She puts her hands over Daniel's eyes, and she opens her mouth to yell, but no sound comes out. Her lips frozen in the shape of *Mary!* she looks on as her daughter races to the cliff's edge, then stops abruptly and throws the flute into the sea.

•

DOT EXHALES LOUDLY, A hand over her heart. "You had me there, Granddad! Was she just sending the flute back to the Tir Na Nog?"

"She never said," Granddad tells her. "Never spoke a word after that. Would whistle, sing to the birds. But not in any human way."

"What happens to them next?" Dot asks. "You can't leave them there, just when the blight comes."

"I have to," he says, "until Samhain. November Eve. That's how the story works."

"But what about the hollow?" It's Mitch. "Will Cornelius get there?"

"Of *course*," Granddad says. "If he didn't, you wouldn't be sitting here today."

Two sounds fill the air around them, suddenly, simultaneously. The first is a droning, outside the window, and they look out to see a gardener lopping off the branch that touches the window, then another branch.

Granddad staggers to his feet and maneuvers around the sofa. He puts his face up to the window and bangs with his atrophied fists. "That's someone's *home*, damn you to *hell*!" And the gardener, stunned, backs up and moves on, the buzzing receding like a swarm of bees flying off to their hive.

"Well, well," Shannon says now, getting up and standing in front of Dot's chair. "Looks like you owe me a hundred bucks." Because the second sound is a fiddler warming up in the center of the lobby. A parade of the elderly is filing into the rows of folding chairs.

"Hey, Mitch, look," Dot says, pointing to the floor left empty between the fiddler and the first row. "Let's show 'em what we got."

"But this is 'public'," Mitch says.

"How about you, then, Granddad?" Dot says. "You up for some dancing?"

"If I could I would," he says, tapping at his hip. "Got me a bum axel. I miss flat-footin' something awful."

Shannon slings an arm around Mitch's shoulders. "Well, *he's* some kind of good at it, Papaw. He won a medal at his dance studio."

"Didn't mean nothin'. Everyone won a medal," Mitch says, but his cheeks are bursting with the smile he is trying to hide.

"I *know* that Sean's a good dancer," Granddad says impatiently. "I taught him myself. Go on, boy, the dance floor is filling up."

There's one couple, in truth, the two of them having

dressed for the occasion—the woman in a checkered red and white skirt and pointed boots, the man with what's left of his hair combed nice, a bright blue bowtie on his neck. They've started a careful buck dance to "Foggy Mountain Top," holding each other's hands for balance.

Mitch looks at their feet, then at his own, then at Dot, who's been studying him.

"I'll take that as a *yes!*" she says, and jumps up from the wing chair and pulls the boy to the dance floor, where they flat-foot for the rest of the tune, then bow at the end, along with the couple.

Granddad and Shannon, standing at the edge of the dance floor, whoop and clap.

"He's got him some happy feet, that boy!" Granddad says. Then he swipes the air next to Shannon. "You go now. You're a good dancer, too."

"This one's a slow song, Papaw."

"Well, anyone with ears can tell you that," he says. "'*Few More Years*'—you'd think they'd pick a tune more uplifting for folk getting ready to fall into their graves. *Shee-it*. Least you could do is entertain us with some youthful dancing."

"Okay, Mr. *Grumpy*," she says, and joins Mitch and Dot, who are trying mightily to flat-foot to the sluggish tempo. Mitch looks gratefully at his mother for showing up, and goes off to stand with Granddad.

At the end of the song, the old man in the bow tie gives his wife a little kiss on the lips, which livens up the room again with clapping and shouts of "Encore!" Caught up in the spirit, Dot plants a kiss on Shannon's lips, too, which quiets things down a bit, someone even gasping. "Great," Shannon mouths to her, "now you've killed someone." But then the hunched-over woman, her wheelchair pulled up to the back row next to the rest of her clutch of friends, screeches at the top of her lungs, "You go girls!" Another one calls out, "Encore!" Dot puckers her lips and sends a dramatic air-kiss in her partner's direction. Shannon rolls her eyes, but then pulls Dot close and gives her a full-on kiss, long and hard, there in front of everyone. "It's like on *Ellen*!" another of the old women cries.

When it's time for them to go—the look on the receptionist's face palpably relieved—Granddad pushes his walker out the glass doors with them and down to the car to see them off.

"I want to go back to the holler," he says, not to anyone in particular. "See how things are going there."

It would be the end of you, Shannon thinks.

"I want to go, too," Mitch says, pulling the car door open.

"What the hell kind of vehicle is this, a tin can?" Granddad asks.

"It's the hell an electric car," Mitch says, climbing into the back seat.

Shannon reaches for the handle on the passenger side. "I'll be back soon, Papaw."

He clumsily wraps his arms around her. "You weren't last time," he whispers in her ear, "Shannon."

She remembers how he held her this way when her parents would breeze through the house in the hollow and then be gone. *I'll be back soon,* her mother would say.

"I promise it'll be sooner next time," Shannon says to him, patting his beard, giving it a tug before pulling away. "Anything you want me to bring you?"

The gardener who was lopping off that branch earlier appears from around the side of the building and gets to work pruning a crabapple tree.

"How 'bout my pokestock?" he says, and he grabs onto the handles of the walker with a death grip and totters back to the home.

Samhain

"COME ON, COME ON, come on, come on," Mitch is saying under his breath, nonstop, has been for several miles. He's making a point to keep it low so his sister, in her carseat next to him, stays asleep. She's in *a bugging phase,* to his mind, always poking at him. "Come on, come on, come on." It's as if a train's chugging around the floorboards of the car.

"I will, I will, I will," Shannon says, steering onto the highway, the final stretch, pointing east. "I'm thinking how to start."

She's remembering how Granddad told it at deer camp. Considering how bleak this part of the story is, it should've given her nightmares, but what she recalls feeling at the time was a fascination with Mary and Julia, their relationship. Shannon hadn't seen her own mother in a long while by then, so that likely accounted for it, she thinks now. She'd asked her Granddad a lot of questions about Julia, and he'd given her detailed answers, told her, too, that she looked like Julia. She liked that idea, at least until they got home after the hunting trip, when he dug out the one photograph he had of her, an old sepia print of a haggard woman with sunken eyes. "Suffering turned her old on the outside while she was still young," he'd said. "But if you'd seen her in real life, you'd understand what I'm saying about the resemblance." At some point, Shannon came to the realization that Granddad could not have ever laid eyes on Julia. She'd died before he was even born. When she called him out on this, he just shook his head and said, "*Oh,* I see her in my dreams. She strokes my forehead and I look right up at her face."

"Come on, come on, come on."

She hits the blinker, looks in the side view mirror, and goes to pass a truck. A line of semis on this route can stretch for miles, and she hates getting stuck between any two of them, not able to see the road ahead or behind. She guns the engine until she's passed it, then returns to the right lane, gets back to cruising speed, gets back to thinking.

By this time in Ballydonegan, the weaker ones, the ones with fewer reserves and connections, would be dying already from fever, and that would ratchet up the panic in the rest of them. They caught the typhoid easily when they were malnourished, so they'd avoid others, keep to their families. The laborers showed up at the mine less and less, until it closed altogether. And it was already getting hard to bury the dead, to do the digging, to find pine boxes. The word was that the workhouse in Berehaven had begun using the coffin with a trap door at the bottom, set up over a pit. No one wanted to end up there. They'd rather their homes be knocked down around them, die in the ruins, arms around their children. So they lay, more and more, in dark huts, waiting for gale day and the battering ram. It was eerily quiet in the townland, few crunching over paths or scaling the cliffside to forage on the rocks. Not one pig grunted—all long eaten by now— and the few dogs that remained were seemingly mute. Up on the road, no carriages rolled by, no one drew pictures of pretty scenes. *How do you find something to tell to a child in that?* Shannon wonders.

"Come on, come on, come on."

"It's not easy to describe. It was a very desperate time for our ancestors. But the Quakers made soup," she says, with some forced cheeriness.

"Yes, they did," Dot says from the passenger seat. "The Quakers shamed the British leaders. I've been reading about this. Instead of giving out food, the government created work projects, like breaking and carrying rocks, building walls with no purpose. And then the few pennies they gave the Irish at the end of a day of hard labor wouldn't even pay for a loaf of bread, the prices going up by the hour because of the food shortage. If the British parliament had just stopped the exports from Ireland for a while, everyone would've been fed. Instead the *assholes* blamed free market forces and a microbe for the starvation of millions of their own citizens, for turning *whole* families into piles of *corpses* that—"

"*That* kind of detail isn't necessary," Shannon says.

"If you're sugarcoating a gentlemen's genocide, it isn't."

"Come on, come on, come on."

Shannon sighs loudly. "I don't know where to start."

"How about the road?" Dot says, her voice a warble from a passing truck that makes the little car shake. "Describe a scene."

"Okay. Well, the last of the season's harvest would have been rolling along to the port, to Berehaven, from Bantry's plantation, Redcoats walking alongside the carts. Probably pointing muskets at the people who stood along the roadsides."

"The *glassy-eyed* people, you should say, if you're not mincing words," Dot interjects. "The people who can manage to stand and aren't on their hands and knees, their lips grass-stained."

Shannon glances over her shoulder at Mitch, to catch his expression. But it hasn't changed, it's the same exasperated one he's had on the whole time.

"Come on, come on, come on."

"Some people in the government tried to help," Shannon says. "There was corn imported from America."

Dot snorts. "It was livestock feed. Too rough for a human

gut. So the people who tried to eat it got sicker, throwing up and having—"

Shannon stops her again. "*Not* that kind of detail."

"*What* then, *what* then, *what* then?" Mitch starts up with now, Dot joining the chorus, too: "*What* then, *what* then, *what* then?"

"If everyone would just be *quiet*," Shannon says, "I'll figure it out."

And for a minute or two it's only highway sounds—tires rolling, air pushing through cracked-open windows, semis whooshing by. And now a train whistle, and clattering tracks, close by but out of sight.

•

MARY HAD BEEN FEEDING the grains to the birds, something that had irked her ma until it became clear that eating the stuff was not possible. As with the pigs and dogs, there weren't many birds around, little song to be heard from the bushes or the roofs of the huts, where they tended to make their nests in the thatch. No, the children of Ballydonegan had devised ways to root the birds out, kill them in flight with slingshots, eat the eggs in their nests. Mary had tried, always, to chase off the raiders, but they made fun of her, flapped their arms, calling her "Birdie" because of the avian-like sounds she made now, the squawking and chirruping. But they aren't prowling much anymore, so Mary can sit right on the stoop and feed the few songbirds who gather round. She's come to recognize them, calls one, in her mind, "Briste." This one is her favorite, a green linnet bird fallen from the eave of their hut in the summer, its nest mates having met the fate of the hungry marauders. It had landed on a stone and toppled behind it, unnoticed. Its wing had never healed, so Mary had built a small cage for it from twigs and vines, a pyramid of sorts, with a cross for a perch. She's woven in new vines today and star-shaped mosses; she likes to pretty up the bird's world. Now she sets the linnet back inside and carries the cage into the hut, puts it up on the ledge of the window.

Julia is on her back on the tick, her eyes set on the cold hearth. There's only the one peat brick, what's left from Jeremiah's last visit. She'll get the fire going after her trip to shore, her one outing today, to gather down on the rocks. It's why she's lying still now, collecting her energy. "It's Samhain," she says aloud, again, reminding herself. It's important to remember. No, not to dance with friends in the square or build bonfires on the hills—not this year, not ever again—but to stay safe. It is, feast or no feast, the time when the veil between the sí world and the human is at its thinnest. A night of fairy high-jinx that a mother must keep her children safe from else the morning find them as changelings. "It's Samhain," Julia whispers again.

Mary lies flat next to her now, rests her head, too. She'll be helping her ma at the shore, always does, and low tide is near.

"We'll just invite a few in," Julia says to the girl. It's the dead she speaks of. Souls fly with the sí on this night, revisiting their homes and people. They find their way in by the fire, these grandparents and lost sisters. Angels will glide through the window, Julia knows, curl up with them for the night. The littlest ones will crawl into her palms.

But maybe they look just like fairies, the girl thinks, the panic rising in her. *How do you tell the difference?*

·

"Boo!" It's MURIEL, POKING a finger in the side of Mitch's face.

"Come *on,*" Mitch says, rolling his eyes.

"Boo!" Muriel says again.

"What are you, a ghost?" he asks her.

"No, Mitsy, *boo!*" she repeats, poking him again.

"Boo yourself," he says, scooting closer to the door, out of her reach. He asks his mother, "Where's Danny-boy?"

"He's feeding the birds, like his sister," Shannon tells him. "Only in a different place."

•

"NOT THE BARLEY, DANNY," Jeremiah says. "Go ahead and give them some of the maize, but the barley is precious. We'll need every bit of that." A lucky stroke, he'd told the boy, being able to get the stills fired up again. With a little barley, he'd said, those rough grains of maize would make some fine poteen. But the trip to Berehaven to stock up had shown them that, for most, the inedible grain was no lucky stroke, had not changed their fate. The scenes on the roads were dire. It had frightened the boy, who had thought, at first, that the visiting souls of Samhain had forgotten to wait for the dark.

"Why were they naked?" Daniel asks now, tossing a handful of the golden grains to the birds.

Jeremiah knows who he's referring to, a family they'd passed, five of them crouching together. They had been only inches away, staring at Daniel and Jeremiah from sunken eyes. "They must've sold what they were wearing," he says.

"But it's cold out," the boy says. "And who would buy their clothes?"

"The paper mills," Jeremiah says. "They make pulp from it, for pages of the newspaper." He thinks of the cartoons that are always aimed at denigrating the Irish, and the anger rises in him as he imagines those insults printed on pages made of that family's last vestiges of dignity.

"Why was their hair so short?" Daniel asks now.

"Must've sold that, too," Jeremiah says. He'd seen someone at port shaving heads and handing out coins.

"What happens to it?"

"God knows," Jeremiah says. "It's a new one on me." He hands the boy the long wooden spoon. "I've got the water boiling now. Time for the stirring—your turn."

Daniel reaches the spoon into the pot and begins moving it in circles. "Why were the dogs on the road so fat?"

"God knows." Jeremiah says again, but not with any curiosity in his tone this time, because he does know the answer. He doesn't want the boy asking more questions like these, so he says, "You're good at that stirring, Danny."

"Is it done?"

"No, no," Jeremiah says. "It takes a few days. Luckily, I have some friends to help so we don't need to sit here the whole of the time. You need friends if you're a distiller, Danny, because it takes tending. You need someone to talk to. That's the good craic of it. And you need someone always guarding. Not exactly legal, the poteen-making. You have to pick a good spot, hidden away, like here under this rock ledge. Used to be a mass rock before the still was here, my da told me, back when he showed me how to brew."

"What's a mass rock?" Daniel asks.

"Ah, well, those are from the days when the laws didn't let us go to the church. The priests would say mass up here in the mountains, and everyone would come." He decides to leave out the part about the decapitating of the priests when they were found out, their heads put on pikes and displayed for all to see. The boy's had enough to spook him for one day, out there on the roads. "This here is also a good spot because it's at the edge of the plantation lands, technically *inside* the bounds." He laughs now. "So if the stills are ever discovered, the garda can take our dear Lord Bantry before the judge."

"My da would like that," Daniel says. He switches hands with the spoon, the one getting tired.

"Aye, I bet he'd like it if you learned how to make him poteen, too. Important thing is to stay sensible, not let it take you over. Reliable income, the stilling. Make it, sell it, feed your family. These batches we'll be brewing now will guarantee you get through the winter, so the three of you board that ship." He wishes now he hadn't worded it just like that, hadn't given a count. So he keeps talking, changes course again. "From what your da said in his letter, there will be plenty of good spots for poteen-making in those mountains over there."

"What else did Da say?"

"He's building tracks for a railroad that's going west through the mountains."

"Like these mountains?"

"Kind of."

"Can you see the ocean from the tops, like you can here?"

"No, you can't. They're not nearly as close to the sea. And, anyway, there are lots of trees, big forests, so you can't see very far at all, I imagine."

"I don't think I'll like that."

"It used to be that way here, right at this very spot, on all these mountains. But the trees were cleared a long time back, real long. First thing stolen from the Irish, to build boats and castles. Then when the trees were all gone, they started taking everything else that grows. England's breadbasket, we're called. They leave the crumbs for all of us to fight over." He stops himself, again, before saying what he had in mind to say next, that soon enough there would be a lot fewer to fight over those crumbs. He's thinking of the scenes on the road, of the bodies off in fields and rotting in toppled huts. Even if they couldn't see all of them, they could tell they were there, from the stench. From the fat dogs. "Here—let me take over with the stirring. I told your ma I wouldn't tire you."

Daniel passes the spoon to Jeremiah, then sits on the ground and tosses more grains out. A linnet lands, pecks at them, then flies off. It brings Mary to mind. He hasn't seen her in a week, worries about her between visits. And his ma.

Reading the boy's mind—or the swipe he makes at his eyes with the back of his hand—Jeremiah says, "Next chore for us is to stack the peat for taking to your ma. You know where the peat comes from, Danny?"

"Of course," he says, picking up a rock and scratching at the dirt. "The bog."

"No, I mean how it came to be. It was from those trees that were cut down. The people must've thought that was the end—no place to hide or hunt, no wood to burn. But you know what was happening all the while? The tree trunks and branches that were left behind on the ground were changing into the peat that we now dig up and dry for our fires. So, you see, even the things we lose can come back to us somehow. In time."

The boy keeps his eyes on the ground, keeps scraping. He's made a bird, standing on scrawny legs, wings out and ready to fly. "It's Mary's linnet."

"You're quite the artist, Danny," Jeremiah says, peering over his shoulder.

"Do you think my da's seen any linnet birds over there?" he asks.

"I don't know," Jeremiah says.

"What do you think he's doing right now?"

"My bet is that he's looking for someone with a piece of land to sell."

Jeremiah knows a good bet, *and* his nephew, who is, yes,

at this very moment tromping through leaf litter, on his way to the Cherokee.

Cornelius has never met an Indian. One of the other Irish on the railroad told him they'd lived all through the hills, not so long ago, but that they'd all been forced west by law. *Indian Removal Act*, he'd said it was, *left a trail of tears.* The Cherokee, though, he'd just been married to the daughter of a homesteader when the decree came down, and their stake was hidden enough in the mountains that the government troops missed him altogether. It was difficult land, much of it steep, but the Cherokee had cleared the flattest ground— with fire—for a pasture and a corn crop, just enough for eating and trading. He'd left wild the sheerest mountainside, the deepest ravine, and this is what Cornelius has set out to talk to him about.

Ever since steadying his sea legs, he'd been asking around about land. "Even if you weren't Irish, you'd need money, Con!" Shea had said to him, a fellow he knew from Berehaven who had come to work on the railroad, too. Cornelius had seen the "No Irish Need Apply" signs in the city when he'd arrived, and he'd overheard the "Fool Irish" jokes told behind their backs in camp, but this didn't dampen his determination. Nor did the fact that money was scarce, what with sending the remittances, trying to get his family over. Jeremiah had insisted, even in the last post, that Julia was fine, but with the stories he heard when others got letters—*a famine like no other*, they'd say; *the entire crop wiped out*, they'd say— well, he suspected his uncle was skipping some details. So, no, he couldn't risk keeping a savings, a land fund, out of his paycheck, as he'd long figured on doing. But he had a new plan: he'd find a landowner and offer work in exchange for a piece of ground to call his own at some set point in the future. Shea had laughed at the notion, but Cornelius had only to look around to see all the untamed acreage in these mountains, to imagine tracts too rugged to be valued by their owners. He'd build a place for them all—for Julia and the children—so they wouldn't have to live in a shanty town that moved along with the tracks.

Not that the railroad work was all bad. His arm ached after an hour or so of lifting and pounding, it was true, that bullet having gone through muscle that was not especially forgiving. And the blasting, no, he didn't like that part of it, making passages through the limestone, but there were enough of the others to volunteer for those jobs. He could hang back, work with the men and women, the African slaves, brought in from the plantations on barges. The planters were paid for the conscription, but with the understanding that their "chattel" would stay whole, not detonate explosives. Until his English improved, Cornelius had thought they were saying "cattle," which had seemed insulting enough. He couldn't communicate with the slaves, so much daylight was there between their languages, but he often worked in tandem with them. Sometimes he'd glimpse them being put back in shackles, being led to the barge, but a shot of whiskey with his mates would blur the image, his disillusionment.

Suppertime in the rail camp was good craic, always, listening to stories, hearing the boasting about the day's perils. Many of the workers had long been on the job. They knew their way around, knew people. That's how he'd learned of the Cherokee. It was Murphy, from Cork—a boisterous sort with sights set on a management job at the railroad—who'd taken Cornelius up onto a trestle, to where the river looked like a snake below. "See," Murphy had said, pointing off to a pair of mountains, "right there in the middle." Cornelius could just make out the Indian's clearing through treetops ablaze in orange, red, yellow. "Isn't it something, that turning of the leaves?" Murphy had said, bragging on his new homeland, as he was known to do. "Nothing like *that* in the west of Ireland," he'd added, then coughed to hide the crack in his voice before retreating to the rail camp for another tin cup of spirits. Cornelius stayed and looked out at the view, at the soft shapes of the summits, going on and on. The Blue Ridge. And, yes, especially in the morning, when a flaxen sky turned to white mist, the mountains really were blue.

•

"Boo!" MURIEL BURSTS OUT with again. "*Boo!*" She reaches hard in the direction of her brother.

"*Stop* it," he says, pushing his back against his door as best he can with the seatbelt holding him. His eyes rest on a truck out the opposite window. It's crammed full of chickens. He looks from one little head to another, all protruding from tiny steel windows, their white feathers blown back or blown off. "Where are they taking those chickens, Mama?" he asks.

"I'm not sure," she says. *Not specifically,* she adds in her mind so she doesn't feel like a liar. She's been aware of their black stares, has tried to outpace the truck, but the traffic has kept them in lockstep.

"Boo!" Muriel says again, and has started kicking the air in frustration.

"What a scissor kick, Mer!" Dot says, turned now to the backseat. "You are a *natural*. I'm finding a swimming coach who can get you to the Olympics, girl. Let's see, which year would that be…."

"Boo!" She moves side-to-side now, until one arm is freed of its shoulder strap, and then she wriggles out of the seat altogether and gets up on her knees next to her brother. She wipes a hand behind his ear and then holds it up for Dot to see. "Boo!"

"Oh, *blue*," Dot says. "She's saying 'blue,' Mitch. Looks like you didn't get all your make-up off." He'd dressed as one of the Blue Man Group for the Halloween party at the dance studio. Two of his friends there had done the same, after he'd shown them videos of the performance they'd gone to see in Louisville the weekend of the wedding.

"What color is *this*?" Dot is saying to Muriel now, holding up her left hand and pointing to the malachite inlay on the silver band she wears every day now. Same one Shannon wears.

"Gleen," the little girl says.

"You are one brilliant kid!" Dot claps, starting Muriel clapping.

"Uh, *Dot*?" Shannon says. "Is she out of her carseat?"

"Umm, kinda." Dot shoots Muriel an *oops* face, which makes the girl laugh. "I'll climb back and fix her."

"No, that's not safe," Shannon says, putting on a turn signal. "There's a pull-off just ahead. An overlook." She's glad to have a reason to lose the chicken truck, which she knows from her sidewise glances that Mitch hasn't taken his eyes off.

"Look, Mama, the Crooked Road!" Mitch cries, running to a signpost after they've parked and stretched. "We're near, we're near!"

She stands in front of the sign, too, feeling the same nostalgia he is, looking at the banjo in the middle of it. There's a map of the music trail at the bottom, too. They've just hit the western edge of the 333-mile loop.

"We're almost at the hollow!"

"Little ways to go yet," she tells him.

"You need a sign for *your* heritage trail, buddy," Dot says, standing behind them, Muriel on her hip. She's been working with the dance school and some local music teachers, getting the kids involved, to start a music trail, one just for youth performers. "But you should have a flat-footer on your sign. Draw up some ideas. You're creative."

"I'll make him blue," Mitch says.

"Lellow," Muriel says.

"No, *blue*," Mitch insists.

But it's a sugar maple Muriel is talking about, one with a great limb casting a shadow over the parking area. It drops yellow leaves around them, and the little girl reaches out her hand to try to catch them in the air.

"And red, and orange...." Dot points out other trees to her in the view beyond. It's a profusion of color, such a clear day, most of the smog from the coal refineries that usually gets trapped in the valleys having been pushed off by the breeze.

"I've never noticed those windmills, there," Shannon says, peering deep into the mountains at a far peak.

"Did Uncle Seanie put those up?" Mitch asks, a hand over his eyes, trying to make out the blades glinting white in the near-noon sun.

"I don't know," his mother says. "You can ask him."

"Will he be there when we get there?" he asks.

"Around the same time," she says. "He's picking up the trailer for the furniture, so it's hard to say just when he'll roll in."

"And Leda and Luna will be there?" he asks.

"Yeah, but they're coming separately so she can go home in the evening," she says. "Seanie'll be following us back to Kentucky, to help us get all the things moved to Dot's house."

"*Our* house," Dot says, correcting her. She sets Muriel on the ground now so the little girl can pick up the leaves that have fallen. She holds tightly to the other tiny hand.

"But Dot might like the house in the hollow better than the one in Kentucky," Mitch says to his mother. "You don't know. She's never seen it before."

"Can't live there, Mitchy," Shannon says.

"So it won't ever be ours anymore?" Mitch asks.

"It'll always be ours."

"What if some Cats come and knock it down some day?" he asks.

"You'll sue their asses, Mitch," Dot tells him.

"We'd still own the land, in any case," Shannon says, guiding him back to the car. "Come on, we better get a move on."

"Hey, Mitch," Dot says, picking up Muriel now, her arms loaded with the maple leaves. "Did you know that our ancestors were the ones who brought Halloween here?"

"Really?" he asks, opening the car door and sliding past Muriel's carseat into his own spot.

Dot settles the little girl in, giving the straps a vexed look. They always seem more complicated to her than they need to be. "That's right. On November Eve, when they went outside, they'd put on masks or costumes to trick the bad fairies that were out. Or they'd scare them away with lanterns they made out of turnips. They'd carve goblin faces into the sides."

"Like Jack-o-lanterns," Mitch says.

She snaps the last latch over Muriel, and gives the contraption a pull to make sure all is tight. The little girl yawns now, slides her thumb into her mouth. "Exactly," she says. "Mischief Night—that's what my grandmother called it."

"Did they go to doors and get candy?" Mitch asks, picking up one of the leaves that litter the seat and holding it up. It looks like a bird claw to him. On fire.

"They recited verses, or sang songs, and then someone

would give them a treat. Apples, I think my grandmother said." She shuts the kids in now, goes around to her own seat.

"But way back in the earliest times," Shannon says, switching the car on and rolling back toward the highway, "it was really about the end of harvest, putting up the stores for the winter coming. They'd bring the cows in from the summer pastures and slaughter a few of them, because it was cold enough by that time of the year that the meat would keep. And they'd use the hides to make warm clothes. The old Celts wore a lot of animal skins. But not our Sullivans. By the time of the story, it was just wool and linen they wore. No animals were killed for that, you'll be glad to know, Mitchy." She's been waiting for some eighteen-wheelers to careen by and now merges into the lane of traffic.

•

I'M SO SHAMEFUL, JULIA is thinking, looking at the dirty blanket around her daughter's shoulders as they begin down the cliffside. She vows to clean the thing. She'd do it today, with the little burst of strength she'll get from the seaweed and limpets, but then there'd be no time for it to dry before bed. No, first thing tomorrow it is. She has to start taking better care of her. It had been she who had insisted Jeremiah leave Mary. He'd wanted to take the two of them, to give Julia time to rest, recover. "I can feed them both," he'd assured her. "No," she'd told him. "I want her here." But it was just that she was afraid of that cavern inside her, needed someone there to keep her from falling in. *Selfish,* she thinks now, as she watches the child let herself down onto the shore, the gray rags of her skirt—that one that used to be the color of a bluebird—wrapping like so many eels around her calves.

They aren't the first there on the strand. Seems each day there are a few more of their neighbors desperate enough to risk getting out on the rocks before the sea calms. Julia slides the creel off her back and begins picking what she can of the rubbery ribbons and dropping them into the basket. Mary walks lightly around the tidal pools until she notices they are picked clean. If Danny-boy were here, she thinks, she'd want him to think the roans had done it, eaten the good stuff in their soup. She wants to believe that, too, she realizes, so she tells herself it's true as she splashes through them. Stopping at each tall black rock, she squats on her haunches and digs a thumbnail into the sides of shells hidden in the ledges, prying them off and dropping them in the basket, too. The bottom is but barely covered when they've worked their way to the far reach of the sea's edge, all done with this day's foraging.

"I was saving a cup of oats for the morning, but I'll cook them up tonight," Julia says to her daughter, making as she speaks a bench of sorts for them to sit on from wood that has been gathering at the shore. No one can manage to pull it up to the village anymore. "Maybe Jeremiah will be back tomorrow. If he's found a buyer for the spade, he'll have some flour and milk for us." He had wanted to sell the thing since the start of the hunger, before everyone else had got to selling theirs and it would be hard, as it's been for him, to find a buyer. But she had held him off. He'd reminded her that she'd be clear across the sea by next planting, that Con would have one there. "What need do you have for this?" he'd asked, impatiently. It wasn't until after the little grave had been dug by the chapel that he understood. She'd known all along, since Lughnasa, sitting there on that fetid earth. She'd felt the baby going. It was only a matter of waiting for the emptiness.

"We've nothing to spare for the fairies," Julia says, resigned to the fact that they won't be doing as they've done every Samhain—leave an offering, a plate for the sí so they don't bring their misdeeds into the hut. Mary starts trembling noticeably, and thinking it's the cold that's gotten to her, Julia tightens her own dirty blanket around her daughter's. She reaches a bare hand under the wool layers and rubs the child's arms. The feel of them is startling to her, the boniness. Sure, she sees her every day, sees them all, but maybe the eye, taking it in so gradually, can't really see the truth.

Julia notices the woman in front of her now, though she could swear there was no one standing there a moment ago. The tide laps at the woman's legs, each ebb revealing bare feet sinking into the sand. "I lost her" is what she's saying to Julia. She's said it several times already. "She slipped right off the rock and was gone. My Isola."

"I'm sorry," Julia says.

"No!" the woman says, glaring now. "I'm grateful. She was spared." And she tips her chin up, her features flatten like a bard's.

Dying, dying wearily, with a torture sure and slow.
Dying as a dog would die, by the wayside as we go.

She points now a thin arm, straight as an arrow, to a ship with such crisp lines that Julia thinks it must be conjured. The cross of the Union Jack is so bright it appears painted against the white wisps of evening sky. The woman roars out to sea at it:

We are wretches, famished, scorned, human tools to build your pride
But God will yet take vengeance for the souls for whom Christ died.

Now is your hour of pleasure—bask ye in the world's caress;
But our whitening bones against ye will arise as witnesses,
From the cabins and the ditches, in their charred, uncoffin'd masses,

For the Angel of the Trumpet will know them as he passes.
A ghastly, spectral army, before the great God we'll stand,
And arraign ye as our murderers, the spoilers of our land.

When the woman turns back to the shore, Julia sees that she is no longer wearing the tatters of Ballydonegan. She is not gaunt but with ample curves and a dark dress, dark hair, crimson lips, a circlet on her head. *Speranza*, Julia thinks, *come finally*, but she no sooner has this idea that she casts it off, calls it a fever taking hold. It will be years yet before she stumbles upon the book, on a trip to the city with Cornelius. She will not have thought of the poet for a long time, but there it will be in a shop, *Poems by Speranza*, the book will be titled. And in it will be the very lines the woman has spoken this day, there on the pages of "The Famine Year."

Mary stops shivering and flaps an arm toward the sea now, then flies from her mother's lap and alights onto the surf. Before Julia can even get her legs under her, the girl is back with an apple in her hand, red as the cross on the Union Jack, red as the woman's lips. A red so perfect that Julia calls the apple, too, hallucination. But soon the others on the shore are loping into the waves, picking them up one by one, taking large bites with their eyes closed, filling their aprons, racing back and forth to drop the apples into their creels. And Julia and Mary do the same till the sun begins to melt like blood into the sea.

"Let me do all the work tonight," Julia says when they arrive back at the hut, but Mary grabs the pail and skips to the river. When she returns, before setting it next to the hearth where her ma is bent over and starting the fire, Mary fills a tin mug with water and sets it behind the linnet's cage on the ledge while Julia isn't looking. It will be much later— after their boiled sea scraps, after they've set out an apple for the fairies, after Julia has closed her fingers around her palms in her sleep—that Mary will return to the ledge. Through the twigs of the cage, she'll admire the bird's breast, hardy from the maize. She'll reach around and take the mug in hand, let a few droplets fill the bird's dish (that limpet shell, all that's left of Brigid, turned up like a teacup, its hole plugged with clay), and then Mary will tiptoe to the hearth and douse the fire. And then, only then, will she close her eyes.

•

"WAS THAT PART TRUE, about the apples?" Dot asks.

"I told you, it's all true," Shannon says.

"You didn't just take that idea from me and—" Dot starts, but then is shoved against the door when the car swerves sharply, Shannon trying to avoid a direct hit by a fragment of a tire that has exploded in the lane over, not two car lengths in front of them. A tanker truck's.

"*Fuck*," Shannon says, steadying the wheel now. She puts a hand on her head and lets out a long breath.

Mitch giggles at his mother's cussing, but in fact he's shaken, too, from the flying debris smacking against the car.

"She meant *fudge*," Dot says, surveying the back seat, making sure the kids are okay. Muriel's eyes have popped open, but the lids slide shut again.

Shannon eases into the right lane now. "This next exit'll get us there. Not my favorite route, but it sure beats getting pelted by self-destructing semis."

"How can it still be driving without all its wheels?" Mitch asks, looking at the back of the truck as it races ahead.

"They have two on each axle, Mitchy, so there's an extra there," Shannon says.

"What happens if they both break?" he asks.

"Worse things," Shannon says, rising up the exit ramp

now, and turning onto the back road that will take them up and around and then into the hollow.

"That's better," Dot says, looking out at the trees up close to the pavement on one side, a meadow on another. "Nothing wrong with the slow road."

"Just wait," Shannon says out the side of her mouth.

"Mama?" Mitch says now. "If it's nighttime in the story, how's Cornelius going to find his way to the Cherokee?"

"He has a few hours of light," Shannon says. "It hasn't gotten dark yet in Appalachia."

•

HE WONDERS AS HE approaches if it's part of a Samhain costume the man's wearing, that thing on his head. But that doesn't make sense, Cornelius tells himself. How would he know what the Celts did today, thousands of miles— thousands of years—away? He guesses the headdress on the man's head to be of buffalo. Vast herds, he'd been told, had once turned views of the valleys and balds black, but all Cornelius had ever seen of them were pelts or trophies, decorations like this one with its braided leather and beads. Yellow spots painted on the horns brought to mind the gorse he still looked for on his treks to the worksites. (He just couldn't get used that, no gorse growing here.) Big feathers hung down from the ears—eagle? turkey? He can't say, isn't so good at identifying the avian species of his new home. As he gets closer, he sees that the man in the rocker is otherwise dressed like the other men of these mountains, maybe tidier, his cuffs folded neatly above hands that Cornelius can now see are resting on a single barrel shotgun. He stops there in the grass.

"Sullivan," Cornelius says, giving his chest a thump.

"Is your English that bad?" the Cherokee asks him.

Cornelius pauses. "Near so," he says.

"Are you poor Irish?" the Cherokee asks.

Cornelius nods.

"Where are you from?"

"West Cork," he says.

"I read about the famine in the newspaper last time I was in town. There's a charity ship sailing soon out of Boston. I made a donation. Maybe it's going to Cork, but I can't remember. I saw some drawings in the paper. Awful. You from anywhere near Skibbereen?"

"A little wester."

"You should say 'more westerly,'" the Cherokee says. "Do you have a wife over there?"

Cornelius nods.

"Children?"

Cornelius nods.

"How many?"

He shrugs. It's not that he doesn't know the English words for numbers. But he doesn't know the answer, and Julia would say that too much optimism is a jinx. He's taken up her superstitions. Found a feather a few days ago, sage-colored. He couldn't remember what she claimed that to predict, but he had it in his pocket in any case.

The Cherokee gets up and leans his shotgun against the wall, then lifts the headdress off, sets it on the floorboards next to the gun. He runs a hand over his hair to smooth it. "Tribal dress. I don't know how my father stood it, stomping around in that thing. Good for scaring off trespassers, though." He settles back into his rocker and looks at Cornelius. "Some."

Cornelius clears his throat, gets to what he's practiced. "I'm wondering if you have land to sell. I can offer you work as pay."

The Cherokee pulls two cigars from a box on the rough-hewn table next to his chair. He gestures to the empty rocker on the other side of it, and Cornelius rises onto the porch and sits to his right, takes a light and puffs on the cigar. It's a treat, one he can't afford on his wages. Sometimes he rolls his own, though. The tobacco, he's found, is so much richer, tastier, in these hills than any that had ever come his way in Ireland. The two men rock and smoke.

"I don't own the land," the Cherokee says, finally.

"I heard—"

"It belongs to Unetlanvhi."

"Who is he?" Cornelius asks.

"Not he," the Cherokee says. "Unetlanvhi is the great spirit."

They smoke in silence again, listening to the chirping crickets in the woods on the hill that rises behind the house. A snarl and the sound of a predator wrestling prey emanate from the same woods. Murphy had said these were panthers when they'd heard them around the camp. *Painters*, he said they were called in these parts. There's a final screech, and then just the trill of crickets again. Cornelius stamps his cigar out on the sole of his boot and then gets up to leave.

"Paper I own," the Cherokee says now, getting up, too. "I can sell paper."

He leads the way off the porch and onto a dirt road skirting the pasture. "I guess I could use some help with the livestock. Droving to market. Slaughtering. We'll be putting a steer up to cure soon." He looks Cornelius up and down, his lean frame. "Maybe two this year. When's your family coming?"

"After winter," Cornelius says, gazing over the Cherokee's shoulder to the cattle gnawing on grass, their faces white as ghosts, a breed foreign to him. The eyes, though, those he recognizes, a cow's look of powerlessness, of resignation. Same look he has to shake out of his own eyes when he stumbles across a mirror or a flat of water.

They've reached a creek now and follow it into the woods, the path hugging the bank sometimes, sometimes winding through trees—a hunting trail, something first created by animals, chased or chasing. The elevation drops, steeply at times, causing Cornelius to trip on roots and then steady himself on tree trunks, some as wide as he is tall. The Cherokee never falters, his familiarity with the terrain from generations in the highlands, the same ease Cornelius had known in the boreens and bogs of his homeland, the hillocks and strands. That salt air—he hadn't realized how much it was a part of him, how his heart had kept pace with wave against shore, wave against shore, his blood coursing with the rhythm of the Ballydonegan River as it wound its way from mountain spring to rocky cleft, where it cascaded into the sea. The sound of rushing water fills his ears now, and he thinks at first he's imagining it. But it's the creek, turned waterfall now, spilling into a pool down below. When the two men reach its edge they stop. Frogs leap from the rushes and land with small splashes.

·

"Is that my hopper pond, Mama?" Mitch asks, a catch in his voice.

She nods, smiles at him in the rear view mirror.

·

"If you clear a few trees, you can get a cabin in here. Have you ever built from logs?"

Cornelius shakes his head. "Mud."

"That's what we did until we were shown to use the

timbers. Corners are the hardest part. I'll teach you how to keyhole them. Get that right and it'll last a lifetime, they said. Only we forgot to ask whose." He pats a chestnut trunk. "I'd start with this one, leave a stump for a chopping block."

Cornelius has been taking in the spot. The earth is covered with leaves like strange hands and paws, like stars, some as bright as the sun overhead, some dark as the earth beneath. The steep sides of two mountains rise up from where they stand. "They have names?" he asks, looking up at the peaks.

"You can name them whatever you want," the Cherokee says. "They still won't come when you call."

Cornelius smiles now, lets go a soft laugh. There's something familiar in the Cherokee's sense of humor, he thinks, something settling. "One year of work for the land?" he asks.

"You can have it now. Magistrate's a friend." He tromps back toward the trail, saying over his shoulder, "Not mine to give, though. Just paper."

Cornelius looks up, to the channel of sky over the hollow. A lone, large-bodied bird sails lazily on the wind currents. A hawk, maybe, he thinks. But he's wrong. It's not a bird of prey. It's a vulture, patiently scanning the earth for the no longer living. He might have guessed this if he could have seen it up close, seen the featherless flesh of its head. But he's too far away from it yet. He kneels at the pond, cups his hands and scoops cool water into them. He takes a long drink, and another. Then he follows the Cherokee.

The end.

•

"THAT'S NOT THE END," Mitch says. "Danny-boy hasn't gotten there yet."

"That's where Granddad always ended it," Shannon says.

"Add a chapter," Dot says. "That's what storytellers do."

"I'm not adding a chapter."

"An epilogue, then," Dot suggests.

Shannon sniffs the air. "Okay, an epilogue."

•

A FEW YEARS AFTER the arrival of Julia and Daniel, the Cherokee came to the cabin one morning while it was still dark. He handed Cornelius the deed for his property, the whole of the hollow. The government, he said, was pressuring him to go to the Cherokee Nation, saying an Indian couldn't own U.S. land and that they'd be taking it from him. So he'd transferred the lot to Cornelius, every bit of it. And the Cherokee and his family were gone before the sun peeked over the ridge of Whiskey Mountain. When the troops arrived, they found Cornelius on the Cherokee's porch, a shotgun across his lap and his hand clasping a piece of paper.

That became a regular pose for Cornelius, rocking on that porch with the shotgun in his lap. He was right there when the railroad man came and offered to buy his property because, he said, the mining would be coming soon and the coal man would not offer as much. *It is in your best interest to sell to me, Mr. Sullivan, can't you see that?* Cornelius's answer was to lift the shotgun off his lap and point it at the railroad man. So he went away. Then the coal man came and said Cornelius had to sell to him, that the company would be needing his flat land to set up the coal camp, and his mountainside to blast their tunnels. *Can't you see, Mr. Sullivan, that prosperity will come to all from the coal?* Cornelius's answer was to lift the shotgun off his lap and point it at the coal man. And when the coal man sent his attorney in to discuss the selling of "mineral rights"—*Everything under you, that's all, you can stay right here on top with your family, no disruption to your lives*—Cornelius lifted the shotgun off his lap and pointed it at the attorney. Eventually, they decided to build their mine elsewhere. And all was well in Sullivan's Holler for a good long time.

·

THEY'RE GETTING GLIMPSES NOW of what Shannon had wanted to avoid by keeping to the highway and taking a different way in. Each time they swing out on a switchback, the ashy mountaintop removal site spreads out in front of them. The inhabitants of the car say nothing, their silence all the more palpable in the stuffiness, the fan off and all windows closed tight to keep out the noxious air. It isn't until they are in the pass and descending into the hollow that they crack the windows again, that they speak.

"So this is Elephant Mountain?" Dot asks.

"Yeah, and that's Whiskey Mountain to the right," Shannon says.

"They haven't carved them up, not this side at least," Dot says. "That's good."

Shannon had been worried about what she'd find, in fact, it being so long since she'd gone back.

"You forgot Mary." It's Mitch who says this. "She was on the boat, Mama. That's what Granddad said. She brought the linnet bird."

"That's right, she was on the boat. But it was very, uh, crowded. There were lots of sick people."

"Oh," he says, and after a pause: "She was the fairy the linnet bird swallowed?"

"Granddad tells it that way. But I think this is how it goes: The ship got half across the ocean, to where the Tir Na Nog is, and only Mary could see that place—because she had the sight—and she took a beautiful dive off the deck and swam like a fish to where the sí were, and she found a family of fairies to live with. Not bad fairies, but good ones. They live side by side, the bad and the good, just like people."

"Did she get her flute back?" Mitch asks.

"You bet," Shannon says. "She would swim around all day in her new watery home, playing that thing for the seahorses, the starfish floating overhead."

"You think that's how Muriel got her talent in the water, Mitch?" Dot asks.

But Mitch doesn't answer. He's looking out at the boarded-up houses, at one with a roof collapsed into it. He remembers when people still lived in some of them, a cousin, a friend from Head Start. "So that was the Cherokee's house, Mama, the one Uncle Seanie grew up in?" he asks as they pass the log house beside the pasture—no grass, anymore, just bull thistle.

"That's right," she says, slowing down and looking over at it herself, at the sagging porch roof, the broken wooden steps.

"Hey, is that Leda's pickup in front of us?" Dot leans over now, honks the horn at the truck, which seems to have slowed down as it passed the house, too. Someone in the passenger seat ahead turns and waves excitedly.

"It's *El*," Mitch says, his mood perking. "I haven't seen her in a hundred million days."

They follow the pickup down the road and into the driveway of their destination, and before they come to a stop Mitch is banging at the car door, locked in by the child safety latch. El races from the truck and rescues him before anyone else can.

"You're strangling my neck," she croaks as he squeezes her.

"Whoa, girl," Dot says, lifting up one of her arms, looking it up and down. "You've got some tats going."

"Keeps me sane," she says. "They're threatened and endangered species. Just got the California condor." She points to one on her bicep.

"Beautiful," Dot says. Then she touches the smallest of the tattoos, one on the inside of her wrist, drawn amidst scars. "I didn't know goats were endangered."

"That's the only one that isn't. First tattoo I got. It's Violet," she says.

"What's this one, and this one, and this one?" Mitch asks, bouncing his index finger along her arm. He's liking this game.

"Jaguar, black-footed ferret, grizzly bear."

Muriel is getting in on it, too, reaching from her carseat and poking El's arm.

"That's the Arizona trout," she tells the little girl. "Jeez—look how big you are, Muriel," El says, lifting her out of the car and setting her on her hip. "You are beast!"

Muriel, laughing, grabs El around the neck the way her brother does.

"You're choking me to death!" she croaks, making Muriel laugh even louder.

"She's going to be in the Olympics, maybe a diver, like her ancestor Mary," Mitch says.

"Oh, there's a Baby Olympics now?" El asks. "If there's a breast-feeding event, I think Luna could be a gold medalist. I've never seen anything like her appetite."

"Is that why Leda is still in the truck?" Dot asks.

"Ye-ah," El says. "That baby was crying the last fifteen minutes. I could *not* help her out, I'm afraid."

"So, do you like it here, El, in my hollow?" Mitch asks.

"Oh, sure," she says, nodding her head and looking around. "Is that a sculpture of some sort over there?" She points to the seesaw and wagon, the mud that covers them baked on in layers, like a crust.

"Used to be my things," Mitch says, looking wistfully at them. "Got a little messed up. Everything can be fixed, though."

The sound of gravel and twigs crunching reaches them before Sean's truck appears around the bend and maneuvers into the driveway with the empty trailer hooked to it.

"Who's that in there with Sean?" El asks. "Rip Van Winkle?"

"Granddaddy!" Mitch cries.

Sean hops out and pulls the walker from the bed of the truck, then races around and folds it out in front of Granddad just as the old man lets himself down onto his feet.

"I'm not using *that*," he says, waving the walker away. "The damn thing doesn't work on grass. Sean will help me get around." He nods in Mitch's direction.

Sirius leaps out of the door now and makes a beeline to the other truck and jumps into its open door.

"Where's Betelgeuse?" Dot asks, kissing Sean's cheek.

"Home babysitting Procyon," he says. "Sirius doesn't like being away from Leda since the baby came. So I didn't want to leave him behind with all his anxiety."

"Thoughtful, as always, my little Seanie," Shannon says, reaching up on tiptoes and kissing his other cheek.

He smiles his shy smile. "Congratulations, you two. How was the wedding?"

"Awesome," Mitch tells him. "The Blue Man Group was there."

"*Sean*—come *on*," Granddad huffs at Mitch. "Let's go catch some frogs in the hopper pond."

"They're all gone, Granddaddy," Mitch says.

The old man looks around the yard, the tufts of long grass growing out of dirt drifts, pokeweed tall and scraggly everywhere, a few brown leaves clinging to each stalk. "Shannon, you need to take better care of this place," he says.

"*Huh*," Shannon says, hands on hips, "you remember my name when there's work to be done." She leans into Sean's ear and whispers, "So, why, exactly, did you bring Granddad?"

"He got in some trouble last night, so I had to go pick him up this morning."

"It was Mischief Night!" Granddad barks. "Ain't they never heard of Mischief Night? You're *supposed* to scare people."

Shannon winces. "What'd you do?"

"I just told some jump tales!"

"Did you tell 'Who ate my toe?'" Mitch asks.

"Of *course* I did," he says.

"And the one about the frog legs?" Mitch asks.

"Well, how could I tell jump tales without including *that* one?"

"What are jump tales?" El asks.

"*What* are *jump tales*?" Granddad repeats. "Where you from?"

"The Reservations."

"You Cherokee?"

"Maybe."

"That a buffalo on your arm?" he asks, looking at a tattoo.

"An American bison, yes," she says. "There used to be a lot here."

"I *know* that," he says, giving her a long look now.

"I don't know what jump tales are, either," Leda says now, joining them. She's passed the baby off to Sean—whose arms were opened out for the little thing from the moment she stepped out of her truck—and gives Granddad a warm hug.

"And where are *you* from, girlie," he says to Leda, "the city?"

"In another life," she says. "So, what's a jump tale?"

"I'll tell one, and then you'll know," he says, and he leans against the truck to steady himself and puts on his "storytelling eyes," as he calls the intent stare that he's known for directing over the heads of his audience to some unknowable scene.

Sean whispers to the baby, "You aren't old enough for this yet, Luna," and he takes her for a walk around the yard.

"On the *dark-dark* mountain," Granddad starts, Mitch joining in with the *dark-dark*s, as is customary.

In the *dark-dark* holler,
Stood a *dark-dark* house,
With a *dark-dark* door,
And a *dark-dark* room,
Th'had a *dark-dark* closet,
With a *dark-dark* floor,
Where a *dark-dark* box,
A-had a *dark-dark* lid,
That hid a *dark-dark*—BUGBEAR!

He has yelled this last word so loudly and with such fervor that everyone has jumped, even those who knew what was coming. All except Sean, of course, who is off a distance, swaying back and forth with the baby cradled against him.

"So *that's* a jump tale," El says, Muriel so tightly wrapped around her now that the words come out as a squeak, no melodrama involved.

"That there's the one that caused the hubbub," Granddad says. "But the old bat didn't have a *stroke*! She just fainted, 'twas plain as day. Happens sometimes with jump tales, is all. No one needed to be calling an *ambulance* and making such a *fuss*."

"Maybe it'd be best if you didn't tell anymore there," Shannon says. "They keep saying they're going to kick you out, Granddad. This might be your last chance, when you go back this time."

"In that case," he says, standing tall as he's able and taking a step toward the house, "I'm *definitely* gonna need my pokestock. Lead the way, Sean." He sets his hands on Mitch's shoulders from behind.

Mitch walks slowly, grinning. He likes this game. "Was your pokestock Cornelius's shotgun?" he asks.

"Of course it was," Granddad says.

"So, newlyweds, let me see those rings." Leda takes hold of Shannon's and Dot's hands. "How was the wedding?"

"The Blue Man Group was there!" Mitch yells over his shoulder.

Leda looks askance at the couple. "So…the wedding was too small for *me* to be invited, but the Blue Man Group got to go?"

Shannon smiles, takes her hand back and twirls her ring around her finger with her thumb, something that's a habit already. She likes how smooth the ring is, how cool to the touch. "We went to the show after, to celebrate. Mitch is obsessed with them now."

"So, Leda," Dot says, "when are you going to make an honest man of Sean?"

Leda looks over at him, still swaying, still with that blissful look about him. She shakes her head. "I'm not jinxing this." She scratches Sirius behind the ears and then on the front of his neck when he looks up at her with his caramel-colored eyes.

"So, *that's* the compost pig," El says now, striding to the thing, still in the yard, but set right and cleaned up, not a smidgeon of dirt on it.

"Weird," Shannon says, walking over to it, too, taking a

tug at the tail, still firmly in place. "Who in the world—" but she's interrupted by a call from inside the house.

"Mama! Come quick!"

She races to the door, expecting from his tone that a wild animal is in there, but that's not what she finds at all.

"Whoa. Who's been cleaning in *here*?" She runs a hand over her table and the backs of chairs, barely a speck of dust coming up on her fingers.

"And digging roots, Mama," Mitch says, pointing to the bowls out on the counter. One is filled with sassafras, another burdock, another Jerusalem artichoke.

"And nuts," says Sean, who—like everyone else now—has come in to see what's going on. He scoops a handful of acorns and hickory nuts from an upturned turtle shell on the table, shows them to the baby, tells her what they are.

Granddad picks up a pignut from a cutting board. "A fairy potato," he says. "Dirt's still fresh on this. I know where these grow—up by your old house, Sean," he says, looking at Mitch, then at Sean, then back at Mitch. "Why don't you get me some lard from the pantry and I'll cook this up," he says, "whoever you are."

"Granddad, there's no lard in there," Shannon says. "There's no food in there at all. I cleared it out back when Aunt Sue moved out. Didn't want bears moving in."

"Maybe that's who's cleaned up," Dot says. "The three bears."

"*Mulie?*" It's Mitch who's said this. He's looking into the pantry, the old quilt that serves as a door pulled back.

"*Steinbeck's* Mulie?" Granddad hobbles over and peers in. "No, no, no. That's not Mulie. It's *Daniel*."

"*Danny-boy?*" Mitch says, looking up at Granddad, mouth agape.

"What are you *talking* about?" Shannon says, looking in, too. But then she jumps back, pulling Mitch by the arm. A man steps out of the pantry, frail and saucer-eyed, his bald head red from sunburn.

"I told you," Granddad says. "It's Daniel."

Shannon releases the grip on her son. "What are you *doing* here, Dad?" she asks.

"Watching out," he says.

"See?" Mitch whispers, looking up at Sean. "It *is* Mulie."

"How long have you been here?" Shannon asks.

"Don't know." He looks puzzled. "Since the morels, maybe."

"That's spring," she says. "You've been here since *spring*? There's no electricity."

"There's fire," he says.

"And no *water*," she says.

"Oh, there's water," he tells her, and he tramps out the back door with a noticeable limp, leading the whole procession of them, the oldest man in the rear, holding onto the youngest boy.

The creek, as Shannon can see, is as low and turbid as it was when she left, the pond just a hole with orange scum clinging to its sides.

Granddad, suddenly tired to the bone, sits heavily on a stump, the one Cornelius left as a chopping block when he felled the tree for the one-room cabin he and Julia and his son would live in. A rusted ax lies on the earth next to it, the handle worm-holed. He clears his throat and begins singing in that way of the hills, a song he's sung on this very stump before. Many times before.

I'm just a wayfarin' stranger,
While travelin' through this world below.

There ain't no sickness, toil, nor danger,
In that bright world to which I go.
I'm a-goin' there to see my daddy
I'm a-goin there no more to roam
I'm just goin' over Jordan.
I'm just goin' over home.

Leda high harmonizes now. She knows this one from the Crooked Road.

I know dark clouds will gather o'er me,
I know my pathway's rough and steep.
But golden fields lie out afore me,
Where weary eyes no more shall weep.
I'm a-goin' there to see my mama.
She said she'd meet me when I come.
I'm just goin' over Jordan.
I'm just goin' over home.

Leaves swirl around the yard, the steep slopes dropping their colors into a wind gone capricious. A solitary bird makes rounds over them, as if caught in an eddy. Mitch points up to it, says, "The linnet bird."

"Sure is," Granddad agrees. "See it there, Julia?"

Shannon nods, because she knows he means her, and because she *can* see the bird. It's too high up to pick out the green pinion feathers, but she knows it is the linnet. And she watches as it widens its arc and disappears behind the mountains.

What she can't see, not yet, is that everything it's passing is turning back to its best time. The particles of the chestnut trees are pulling themselves from the soil and sprouting out of Elephant Mountain. Rising out of the coal-wasted lands beyond are the spines and crests, the summits that once were. Headwaters begin to trickle from the mountainsides. And as the green linnet completes its circle and passes over Whiskey Mountain to return to the hollow, to the people with heads tipped to the sky, the sound of water flowing down the rocks toward them fills the world.

ABOUT THE AUTHOR

JANE HARRINGTON teaches at Washington & Lee University and is a fellow at the Virginia Center for the Creative Arts (VCCA). Her wordcraft has appeared in a range of publications, including *Chautauqua, Anthology of Appalachian Writers, New Square, Feminine Collective, Big Fiction, Irish America,* and *Mountains Piled Upon Mountains: Appalachian Nature Writing in the Anthropocene* (West Virginia UP 2019). Jane has also authored bestselling books for children and young adults (Scholastic, Lerner). Her fiction has been nominated for a Pushcart Prize and has been shortlisted or named a finalist for the Dana Award, Sean O'Faolain International Short Story Prize, Fish Publishing Short Story Prize, Leapfrog Press Fiction Contest, Portable Stories Contest, and the Colm Tóibín International Short Story Award. She credits the Carlow University MFA program and her mentors on both sides of the Atlantic for their invaluable part in the creation of *In Circling Flight,* the 2019 winner of The Brighthorse Prize in the Novel.